T0128257

THE SNATCHERS

KATE
CABRAL-MCKEAND

authorHOUSE®

AuthorHouse™
1663 Liberty Drive
Bloomington, IN 47403
www.authorhouse.com
Phone: 833-262-8899

© 2020 Kate Cabral-McKeand. All rights reserved.

No part of this book may be reproduced, stored in a retrieval system, or transmitted by any means without the written permission of the author.

Published by AuthorHouse 02/28/2023

ISBN: 978-1-7283-7784-1 (sc)
ISBN: 978-1-7283-7782-7 (hc)
ISBN: 978-1-7283-7783-4 (e)

Library of Congress Control Number: 2023901098

Print information available on the last page.

Any people depicted in stock imagery provided by Getty Images are models, and such images are being used for illustrative purposes only. Certain stock imagery © Getty Images.

This book is printed on acid-free paper.

Because of the dynamic nature of the Internet, any web addresses or links contained in this book may have changed since publication and may no longer be valid. The views expressed in this work are solely those of the author and do not necessarily reflect the views of the publisher, and the publisher hereby disclaims any responsibility for them.

DEDICATION

In my canopy, I am very grateful to have my wonderful friend Carol Ann Belanger, whose insight gave me direction and a clear path on my travels. Along with my patient and kind cousin, John R Postma who gave those travels a destination. Without you both my efforts would be futile. Thank you for allowing me to keep my head near the clouds.

PROLOGUE

In the first book of the Tree Dwellers trilogy - The Clan, Brill, and his young couriers have returned home from a successful grain-gathering mission at Memmcaro's grain facility. Their community, known as The Clan, resides high in the hidden canopy of the tallwoods. The couriers stole their way into the corrupt seed conglomerate Memmcaro's compound, but in doing so, it cost them the lives of their friends.

Captain Mullins and his ruthless Rooks run Memmcaro. They control the compound where tainted and rare, untainted grains are stored. Horrific experiments on innocent children snatched from their homes also occur at the complex. Through these experiments, Mullins hopes to develop a serum that can cure the toxic effects of the diseases that affect virtually everyone on the ground. At a different location, Mullins' nemesis, Civantes, is also conducting cruel experiments on the children. These endeavors have been unsuccessful due to the lack of healthy specimens - until now.

Mullins wants to capture the tree dwellers whom he has seen. He wants them for their healthy compositions but also because they blew up his Farm, where battles to the death between men and mutated monsters took place.

With the help of friends they have met, the companions must find and destroy Mullins, Civantes, and his deadly mutant men - The Snatchers - before being discovered. With the invaluable help of Mama Kilee's knowledge, SheShe's loyalty, and the antics of their pets, Cat and Dog, they must avoid the relentless Demonis, the silent Shivers, and the terrifying Humonsters if they want to live. Their mission is no longer about food. It's about friendship, hope, and survival; time is running out.

CHAPTER 1

Double Life

For days after the events at The Farm, the elders and Mama held meetings with everyone in the canopy to discuss the recent food mission and to inform them about what was happening outside of their world. The crowd was on edge as Gotl, Brill's father, explained the letter from Dr. Hamm to Dr. Swallow detailing the imminent arrival of Civantes' Snatchers, who were searching for them and their home in the canopy. Paralyzed with fear, the atmosphere above the tallwoods was ripe with rumors and misunderstandings about their future.

The elders held nightly discussions in the center square, allowing anyone to voice their concerns but also to help them understand the urgency of their current situation. Several debates got so heated that they were quickly adjourned to avoid physical confrontations. While this occurred, the couriers; and the pets who assumed residence in Mama's nest were shielded from the discussions. The kids had enough to worry about, so they were isolated to focus on regaining their health, planning for the upcoming mission, and grieving the loss of their friends before heading out again.

When Ilse's involvement behind the scenes at The Farm was exposed, everyone in the canopy was astonished at his clandestine role in the competitions and with Civantes. They were shocked that one of their elders, who had lived with them for as long as anyone could remember, could be so deceitful and scheming while living such a secret life amongst them. As a result of his shocking betrayal of The Clan, neighbors became suspicious of one another and even of their family members. Everyone became suspect except Mama Kileee, whose dealings with Ilse were not seen as a threat to the others but as an example of a victim whose relationship with him was forced and coerced.

As the fearmongering within The Clan settled down, Gotl and Mama turned their attention toward Ilse. They went to his nest for anything they could find to aid Brill and the others on their next mission. Meticulously, they searched his belongings without finding any reference to his double life. Feeling frustrated that he could have concealed his true agenda from them without a physical trace in his nest home, Gotl looked up. High above his nest was a thin rope stretched across the branches and foliage and seemed to end at the tree trunk. Gotl swiftly scaled the tree and retrieved the string and the small black bag attached to the end hidden in a crevice.

"He must have been in a hurry and forgot to conceal the string in the hollow," Gotl said to Mama as he jumped beside her.

The bag was tightly sealed until Gotl cut the knot with his knife. They found maps from other provinces, and routes were highlighted on each map. There was also a list of names and clinical notes detailing various medical treatments and procedures and the results of those treatments. The last piece of paper was a bulletin announcing the time and locations of the upcoming man and beast competitions.

Mama looked around the nest while Gotl continued to investigate the bag. She noticed that the dust on his shelves had been lightly disturbed. Below the shelves, there were fresh markings on the floor. She wondered if someone else had gotten into Ilse's nest before them. Mama thought that even though Ilse was older, like many people in the canopy, he was still quite agile, evidenced by his constant comings and goings from the canopy. She also believed that he would find it exceedingly unnecessary to climb up the tree to retrieve the small bag to review his messages in his nest. It seemed odd that they hadn't seen a single item of interest among his belongings.

The info in the small bag could help the couriers find Mullins and Civantes and may help them to avoid the many other dangers that lurked in the outside world. As Gotl placed the items back into the sack, Mama continued to investigate Ilse's belongings, sure they were missing something. As she followed Gotl out of the doorway, she looked around Ilse's nest before leaving and wondered how many other secrets he had been keeping from them and who in the canopy now had them.

CHAPTER 2

Time to Go

On the day of their departure, Brill and Mama watched the sunrise together alone on the lookout. She knew she didn't have to tell him about the dangers ahead. He had already experienced many. Instead, they sat silently, watching the sunrise and giving thanks for their peaceful surroundings, until they heard the bird call to assemble in the center square.

Gotl and the elders addressed Brill, Dao, Callow, and Dwell one last time while Mama presented them with their packs. Everyone took a careful inventory of their supplies. Inside their bags were various items, some familiar and others not. Each had rope, small yellow balls, and sweet-smelling plants, amongst other things, including food and water. Everyone continued to search until they found the most desirable items, Mama's antidotes, and her elixirs. Everyone received a vial of red and blue medicine and clear instructions for using all the other things in their packs. The instructions outlined what the items could do to help them and how they could hurt them. After their last mission, everyone understood and trusted Mama's wisdom. They knew it was best to heed her warnings if they wanted to return home.

The couriers said their goodbyes to friends and families and were ready to head to the exit but were waiting for their leader, Brill. Dog and Cat were looking for a free ride and tried to stow away in Callow's pack, but she was having none of that and tossed them aside. Brill stood and looked throughout the center square for his mother, Jith, but she was nowhere to be seen. She couldn't bring herself to say goodbye to her two boys.

Overcome with grief; she stood sobbing on the lookout while her husband sent them off with his blessings and final words of wisdom.

"Take care of and rely on each other; trust each other. Each one of you has tremendous talents and gifts. Use them to destroy Mullins and Civantes and come home. We are all relying on you just as you rely on each other to return to us as soon as possible with good news." He directed his message at all of them while staring intently into his oldest son's eyes.

When Gotl finished talking, only quiet sobs could be heard amongst the canopy until Brill broke the silence and directed the others to leave.

"Let's go," he said. As much as Brill wanted to say goodbye to his mother, he knew she would not show, and there was nothing else to gain by staying and delaying their departure. Everything about the mission had been reviewed and discussed more than once, so he got up to leave, and the others followed.

Dao overcame Brill and ran ahead, leading the group through the canopy towards the portal, high-fiving the children he passed. Brill and Callow followed behind, with Dog and Cat skipping closely behind them on their heels. Dwell lingered behind. Respectfully, they acknowledged the desperate pleas sketched on the faces of everyone that they passed along the way to the portal tree. Brill felt their pain, which drove home the reality that they could not fail as everyone's life depended on their success. At the tree portal, Dao turned to speak to the others, but when he turned, he couldn't see Dwell as Callow and Brill stepped in front of him and crossed over the threshold into the shaft of the tallwood.

"Hey, where's Dwell?" he asked.

"He's right behind us," Callow said as she turned back in time to see Cat riding cowboy-style on Dog's back, flopping from side to side with each forward lunge that Dog took. Laughing, she saw Dwell running along the branches above them. Effortlessly, he dropped down near Dao and, without stopping, stepped in front of him and into the shaft, saying, "What, are you waiting for me to lead?

Okay, let's go."

The pets rode on Brill's shoulders in the shaft until he contacted the ground. Then they launched themselves forward, hitting the ground with a thud, and took off running around in circles after one another while Brill took out his map and confirmed to the group the direction that they would be heading in. The elders had directed him to take the group as far north as possible, where they would come to Basking Falls and then follow the river west. They were told to be incredibly careful at Basking Falls because Ilse's notes mentioned that it was used as a resting point for *all* weary travelers. Dao took over on point from Dwell and led the group through the tallwoods and thick forest for hours and miles until dusk, where they stopped at a grotto built into the ground to rest and eat.

"Stay together; we're in unknown territory now," Dao warned.

Dao crawled into the opening and sat with his back against the rock wall; exhausted, he closed his eyes. Brill and Callow sat in the diminishing light at the entrance on watch for any unwelcome company. The pets remained on top of the small cave darting up the tree trunks to a height of about ten feet, where they would stop, release their hold, and crash to the ground causing disgusting but funny noises to escape from their orifices. They thought this was so hilarious that they continued to do this at a frantic pace, climb up, fall, climb up, fall, until Brill told them to knock it off, at which point they both collapsed onto the ground, exhausted.

Dwell paid them no attention as he sat atop the shallow cavern just above Callow and Brill with his feet dangling over the rim. Brill turned back to watch Dao and wished he could rest, but now was not the time. With night falling, he needed as many eyes open as possible. Facing forward, he watched Callow as she tipped her head back to drink water from her bottle. Tiny slivers of the day's last remaining sunlight danced upon her hair as she closed her eyes, savoring the cool, crisp water on her tongue. He was mesmerized by her beauty until his gaze was broken by Dwell's nearby swinging legs, causing his thoughts to turn to his little brother. He was happy that Dwell was going with him, but he was uncertain of his brother's abilities and whether he would be an asset or an obstacle on this trip; only time would tell.

Dwell continued to swing his legs as he opened his knapsack and removed his water bottle, which he drank from hungrily. Replacing it into his bag, he gently pulled out a small, tattered book with a worn cover and torn pages. As he began to read, he made mental notes.

Half an hour passed in the stillness of the early eve when suddenly a cry came from behind them, breaking the silence as everyone turned their heads towards the direction of the sound.

Callow nudged Dao awake and quickly shuffled to the back of the cave while Brill scanned the area. Only Dwell remained undisturbed, engrossed in his book and oblivious to everything around him, including the sound. When a second cry rang out, Brill grabbed Dwell's legs and pulled him down hard onto the ground below as the pets dove into the cave next to Callow.

Dwell hit the ground with a thud causing the book to fly out of his hands and onto the floor in front of Callow. She stared at the writing but couldn't make out the words. However, she saw a symbol that she had seen once before but couldn't recall where.

Dwell quickly grabbed the book, closed it, and shoved it into his bag as Brill turned towards the three of them and motioned for them to be quiet.

The sound of approaching footprints and breaking twigs froze them in their tracks. Everyone wondered to themselves if the sounds were coming from the Snatchers and how they could have found them so quickly. They held their breath as the sounds came closer and got louder until they came from right above the overhang. It sounded as if something was slowly being dragged across the ground.

Callow felt shivers up her spine, wondering if it was the captured children being dragged about. Dao hoped it wasn't an escaped mutant creature from one of the competitions. No one spoke or moved. The only sounds came from above. The group stayed silent until the noises moved away and the silence of the night returned. Brill ensured that no one, including the pets, left the overhang until he was confident it was safe. He scanned the area by peeking above the cave in the silent night.

He couldn't see anyone or anything moving. Slowly, he crawled up the side of the incline, stood, and listened. He heard nothing but saw wide, deep grooves cut into the dirt before him.

"Come up here," he whispered to the others.

Callow reached him first, followed by Dao and Dwell. Brill pointed to the deep grooves in the front of him.

"What do you think they're from?" Callow asked while Brill and Dao bent down to investigate.

"Don't know, but we need to follow the trail to see where it leads us," Brill said.

CHAPTER 3

Footprints

Everyone agreed with Brill, and he led them forward, following the grooves. They walked for hours in the darkness, staying far enough behind to keep themselves concealed. The last thing they wanted to happen was to be confronted by an adversary in an unfamiliar forest at night.

In the distance, the glow of firelight could be seen in a small clearing, so they stopped. Brill motioned for the others to stay put and low to the ground while he took a closer look. Crawling on his stomach toward the fire, he saw a group of men sitting and lying in a circle on the ground.

As he got closer, he could hear them talking and recognized one of the voices. Carefully, he inched forward, hid behind a nearby tree only yards from the men, and took a good look. He saw the face of the familiar voice. To his relief, it was Jaes Bonder, the guard's son, who was almost beaten to death in the bin.

Brill could barely control his excitement. There were only six men; two must have been injured and were lying on makeshift stretchers made of branches while the other four were tending to them. Brill quickly crawled back to his group.

"Dao," he said, "it's Jaes from the bin."

"That poor kid," Dao exclaimed, "They almost beat him to death!"

Brill nodded, "Ya, it looks like six of them made it through the gunfire in the field. Two are on stretchers, but the others seem okay. I going to speak to them, so I want the three of you to stay put. If I come back, great, and we'll go ahead as planned, but if not, continue heading north until you find Basking Falls, then head west. Here's my bag; it's got everything you need to find your way there," he said as he dropped his knapsack at Callow's feet.

She touched his hand as he released his pack and dropped it at her feet. He felt the warmth of her skin, but before she could protest, he turned and ran back toward the men. He circled them from the right side of the campfire so he could approach from the north and lay in wait, watching the men briefly before he got up enough courage to walk through the trees directly at the group.

Three of the men got up quickly into attack position when they first heard and then saw Brill approaching. Brill stopped.

"Jaes," Brill said just feet away from the men.

Jaes strained to see who had called his name. "Who knows me?" he asked.

Again, Brill said, "Jaes, it's me, Brill, from the bin."

Jaes got up, walked towards Brill with a broad smile, and embraced his life-saving friend in a hearty bear hug, lifting him off the ground.

"Brill, it is you," he said as he released him.

Brill smiled and returned the embrace.

"Hey guys, it's Brill from the bin, the guy who healed and helped us." The men let up a small cheer, circled him, and welcomed him.

"Where are you going?" Brill asked.

"We're heading north. It has been slow going with the injured men, but we'll get there," he said.

"Do you mind if my friends and I join you? We're also heading north up to Basking Falls, and then we'll be heading west. We've received notice that the Snatchers are coming for our families and us, so my friends and I will try our best to stop them before they find us," he said.

"Of course, you can join us, but first, you need to tell us who the Snatchers are," said a young boy not much older than Dwell. He came up to Brill and held out his forearm to him. "I'm Snag, not only the brains of this here group but also the best looking," he said as he laughed while glancing back at his friends.

And he was good-looking with his deep blue eyes, tanned body, and muscular build. The only flaw visible on Snag's physique were the many scars all over his body that he tried to hide under the dark hue of his tan. Brill smiled and shook his arm. Brill told them about the Snatchers and their quest to find his Clan in the canopy. He explained that according to Mullins and Civantes, Brill and their families were the only group of people anywhere in all the provinces unaffected by the 'sicknesses.' He told them how they would be used in experiments to restore the health of those in power who were sick. Brill explained what Dr. Swallow had told him about the levels of sickness. He said everyone on the ground had some level of exposure, so the tree dwellers were the only hope for them to regain their health and stay alive. Brill warned the men that Mullins and his Rooks, Civantes and his Snatchers would do anything to capture, experiment on, and ultimately kill Brill and his family and friends if that would prolong their lives because, in their eyes, everyone was expendable."

"Well, Brill, it looks like you're going to be our leader after all," Jaes said and laughed while patting Brill on the shoulder. Brill negatively shook his head as he moved to the makeshift stretchers where two men lay on their stomachs. They weren't moving, and their skin had become grayish from the massive blood loss. He removed the foliage covering their torsos to investigate their injuries. Large holes from the Rook's guns were in the upper part of their back. The projectiles seemed to have penetrated through the muscles and into their lungs, puncturing their organs. Bloody bubbles appeared at the bullet sites after each exhalation.

Brill looked up at the others and said, "I'll be right back," and ran through the forest until he found the others.

"Come on," he said excitedly, "They're friendly!"

He grabbed his sack and ran back towards the fire so quickly that his group had difficulty keeping up with him. When he reached the men, he opened his pack and pulled out his blue vial. Jaes instantly recognized the liquid and came over to help turn Slas' head to the side while Brill let a fair amount of the precious drops fall into the injured man's mouth. Then they did the same to Sith, the other injured man. Instantly their health improved as their injuries began to heal, and the projectiles that had damaged their vital organs were expelled from their bodies. Once the physical wounds had vanished, both men got off their stretchers and gingerly moved about as the intense pain from the injuries remained. But they were so thankful to be alive that they tore through the pain and quickly readied themselves to lead the group north and out of the clearing. Jaes ran after the excited men and asked them to slow down so that he could extinguish the fire and gather their meager belongings for the long journey. They did so, and soon they were en route to Basking Falls.

During the trek, the men shared their stories with the group. There was Klen, the most muscular of the men and the oldest in the group. He was fair-skinned with long brown hair down to his chest, matched by the length of his unruly beard and large brown eyes that held a lifetime of pain. He mostly kept to himself but was very pleasant and helpful when spoken to. He didn't ask questions or volunteer information unless asked. He looked tired to Brill and spent most of the journey in deep thought.

Snag was the opposite of Klen with his wide beautiful smile. He was young like Jaes, laughed all the time, was brazen, outlandish, and never stopped talking. He exuded confidence, and his antics and jokes kept everyone smiling and relaxed. Despite his situation, he seemed genuinely happy, and the group fed off his contagious cheerful outlook.

His buddy Jup was a big dark-skinned man who constantly scowled and seemed angry at everyone. He had only negative things to say about everyone and everything, so he spent most of his time isolated from the others because they preferred it that way. Cat and Dog enjoyed the company of all the men except Jup, whom they also stayed clear of. Brill also felt this way about Jup and told his friends to do the same. Brill thought that in today's world Jup had many good reasons to be consumed by anger and hatred. He could sense that if Jup ever snapped, neither friend nor foe would be safe. The only person that Jup seemed to tolerate with any warmth or patience was Snag, who seemed to know what to say and when to say it to keep the big man calm. Snag knew the group's survival depended on him staying as close as possible to Jup.

The two injured men, Sith and Slas, were brothers. Immediately, and even during their recovery, they became the protectors of the group and scouted ahead of everyone to ensure safe passage. They only spoke amongst themselves in a tongue that no one else seemed familiar with, except the pets, who seemed to understand what they were saying and took a shine to both. Both Dog and Cat became so comfortable with the men that they rode on their shoulders, messing with their hair as the two men led the group through the forest and fields without complaint. When they finally arrived at Basking Falls two days later, all that fun stopped!

CHAPTER 4

Captain Mullins

Captain Mullins and a crew of his security forces set out for The Farm to inspect the blast and the massive destruction it caused. The Rooks who remained at the site had stockpiled any functional weapons into trucks for return to the compound. Mullin's driver slowly made his way down the driveway dodging left and right to avoid the carcasses of the Howls and Demonis dogs that were still burning and littering their path. Steeling his nerves, he tried desperately to avoid them without angering the Captain. However, the Captain didn't mind the mess, so he commanded his driver to stay in the middle of the road and motor over anything in their way. Much to his chagrin, the driver managed to obey the order, as did the others following behind. The men cringed from the sounds of crushing bone and exploding organs as they drove over them. He wouldn't let a few corpses delay him from getting to the blast site to investigate and find out who destroyed his Farm and why. Then he would think long and hard about how he would exact his revenge.

As the driver parked where the buildings once stood. The trucks following behind Mullins did the same, and the men got out. Nasty smells assaulted their senses. Mullins climbed out of his vehicle with a pistol drawn. His Rooks followed behind.

The Captain was enraged at the level of destruction of his property. He had built this facility and worked tirelessly to make it successful through the death and demise of many. As his blood pressure rose, his thoughts turned to Civantes, who had damaged his face and was probably responsible for this destruction. He thought of all the men he had captured over the years and the time and effort he had spent training them to be successful fighters. Now it was all gone. He scanned the area, fuming at his loss of wealth but, more importantly, his loss of power. Unable to control his fury, he raised his gun, pointed it at the corpse at his feet, and repeatedly fired as the guards behind him quietly took a few steps back. Holstering his weapon, he looked around and saw that no building remained. Every structure had been obliterated!

Walking through the debris, he searched the ground, desperate for any clue. He picked up a thin stick and poked through the rubble of tattered clothes, splintered arena seats, shards of wood beams, and pieces of men and creatures that littered the ground everywhere, covered in a thick coating of blend and muck from the pits.

Searching in silence, he focused on his revenge. He would make it slow and painful, but first, he had to find and capture the culprits. After their explanation, he would exact his revenge on their miserable lives. Wandering through the rubble, he didn't speak. He kept his head down, scanning the ground for any trace evidence he could find.

He came upon papers from his office, including part of his chair; he even recognized the body of one of the twins. Still, he didn't find anything to help him solve the mystery of who had executed this destruction until one of the Rooks approached him carrying a bag in his hand.

"Sir, I found this," said the guard as he handed a sack over to Mullins.

Mullins took the sack and scrutinized it. He had never seen a bag like this before. It was well worn and made of solid plant fiber with two shoulder ropes attached and a pouch flap sealed with another piece of twine. Slowly he undid the rope, opened the sack, and peered inside.

<hr />

The mist from the Basking Falls waterfall rose high in front of the group as if to welcome their arrival. The spray was cooling, engulfing their tired, dirty, and smelly bodies from the long journey. Everyone was anxious to get into the water to cool down, cleanse themselves, and have an opportunity to relax. Snag's quick cannonball entrance into the water spurred the other men to do the same. His loud splash and noisy antics off the large rocks into the pool below got everyone's attention and sent large ripples cascading in all directions. Like a restless child, he continued jumping to the enjoyment of some and the annoyance of others.

Sith, Slas, and Klen quietly slipped into the water and scrubbed themselves clean before leaving to stand guard on the shore. Brill took Jaes, Callow, and Dao aside to talk to them about the next leg of the journey while the pets slept quietly in Callow's pack. Everyone tried to focus, but they were distracted watching Jup swim. The big man used his massive arms to cut through the water with strong, powerful strokes and dive under for so long that no one knew where he would surface. Dwell was interested in something other than Jup. High on a ledge, he sat alone, oblivious to the others, totally engrossed in the tattered book that Callow had seen earlier. Callow saw him rereading it and wondered what was so interesting within those pages that he didn't want to join the others.

Their brief period of relaxation at the water's edge ended when Slas waded into it, frantically waving his arms for everyone to get out of the pool. Those that saw him didn't hesitate and quickly scurried up the bank and out of the water except Jup, who was still diving deeply below the surface. He didn't see Slas' warning, but Dwell did, and he got up and hid back against the wall, away from the ledge. He didn't see any danger but knew enough to heed Slas' warning as he watched for Jup.

The group hurried behind the large boulders lining the Falls and waited for Sith and Slas to join them. Snag stood up and was about to call for Jup when Slas tore at his arm, causing him to fall to the ground with a thud and bump into Callow. He smiled at her shyly and apologized as Slas raised his finger to his closed mouth.

As three prominent men appeared from one of the worn pathways, no one made a sound. Callow gasped when she saw their hideous faces, which announced to everyone that they were sick. Their skin was discolored and shedding from their bodies, and their heads were enormous. Together they walked directly into the pool and submerged themselves in the water up to their necks, releasing a collective sigh. The water soothed them, and soon they kicked up their feet and began to float with their eyes closed. Jup resurfaced simultaneously with his back to them just as the last man tilted his head back to float and close his eyes. Jup didn't see them and silently dove back under the water. The man closest to Jup suddenly opened his eyes and straightened up when he felt the water's surface break up against him. History had taught him to be cautious. In his world, unseen horrors can take you by surprise anywhere, and any time, so he floated while scouring the water's surface for ripples and, more importantly, bubbles. Quietly he alerted the others that someone or something was with them in the water. Immediately, they silently distanced themselves from one another and virtually stopped moving while their fierce eyes darted back and forth atop the water, looking for any movement.

Dwell watched, horror-stricken from the ledge, that the mutants would kill Jup once he surfaced, so he quietly picked up a rock and threw it in the opposite direction to where he thought that Jup would reappear. It hit the water with such a loud splash that the men instantly turned and swam under the water towards the sound in a maniacal fashion creating huge, white-tipped waves. Moments later, they resurfaced atop the water, crying out with shrill yelps of frustration as they looked around frantically for the object of their attention.

When Jup heard the rock hit the water and the commotion from the Snatchers, he thought it was Snag jumping off the rock again, so he decided to swim over and grab him. He surfaced right next to the three men who attacked him with a fury. Snag jumped up to help, but Slas pulled him down again.

Seeing his frustration, Dao turned to Snag, saying, "He's right, Snag, you can't go in there. We don't know if there are more of them out there. If any of us can care for himself, it's Jup."

"He's right, Snag; let it go. Jup can take care of himself," Jaes added.

CHAPTER 5

The Falls

The loud commotion in the water drew the attention of something on the bank that slipped in and under the water. The group watched helplessly as Jup fought for his life against the three Snatchers. His thrashing and twisting created another upheaval in the water, which the men followed, drawing them deeper and deeper into the pool. As they neared the center, Jup dove underwater and grabbed the legs of two men, but he kept losing his grip as their skin quickly tore away from their limbs. Determined and unwilling to give up, he grabbed so tightly around their ankles that he felt their bones break as he pulled them downward. Their thrashing and kicking to release Jup's grip were futile as he pulled them down to the bottom of the pool and held them there until they stopped moving.

Watching anxiously from behind the boulder, the group waited for Jup to resurface. When Jup was sure the men were dead, he released them and watched from below as their lifeless bodies quickly floated up to the surface and launched out of the water onto their backs. The third man saw Jup's surface and frantically started to swim to shore, but Jup's strong swimming skills, composed of powerful kicks and effortless strokes, quickly covered a lot of area. Soon he was close enough to grab hold of the man when the man suddenly disappeared under the water leaving only a tiny ripple behind. Jup spun around in circles, looking over and under the water, but he couldn't see anything. He waited for the Snatcher to return, but he didn't. The uncertainty of what happened caused the hair on his neck to stand straight up just as something big brushed up against his thigh. The contact lasted for seconds before it ended. Jup didn't move

15

until it did, but once it did, he raced back to shore as quickly as he could without looking back.

Dwell also scurried his way down the ledge and rejoined the group, and said to no one in particular, "Let's get out of here; it's getting dark."

"I couldn't agree with you more, Dwell," Brill said.

The group moved towards Jup, sitting on the shore, knees drawn up to his chest and was clearly rattled.

"Jup, we've got to move," Snag said as he touched the big man's shoulder.

"Where did he go?" Jup asked Snag. He held his hands towards the water, waiting for the man to appear.

"I don't know," Snag replied, exasperated.

"There was something else in that water beside the two of us," Jup said, looking intensely at Snag.

"I know, Buddy, but let's get out of here before it decides to find us on the shore!" Snag said as he extended his hand to help his big friend to his feet.

Dao took the initiative, leading the group out and away from the waterfall, heading west. Jup followed and looked back one last time at the pool and saw a large dark shadow under the water. He thought to himself that it was strange that a man that big didn't float.

They walked atop Basking Falls at dusk and then headed west. On the west side of the Falls, they found a cave to rest in for the night. Sith, Slas, Klen, and Jup all took turns on watch. Early the following day, they headed out again. The terrain began to change from the forested, heavy wooded areas to open plains with few trees and flat land; it wasn't pretty; it just was. Snag and Cat shared the stage and kept everyone entertained. Snag with his made-up songs and poetry, while Cat accompanied with its creative dance techniques. The barren landscape provided no cover for the group with its wide-open fields, but they had no choice. Their destination lay beyond this landscape.

The land in this region had been cleared of bush decades ago to plant and harvest cash crops in what was once a thriving farming community. Now, there was no movement of farmers, machinery, or produce. The only things moving were Brill and his friends as they made their way from the barren fields to the dirt roads dotted with farmhouses.

The beautiful, well-kept farms were blanketed in an eerie silence. No longer did birds fly overhead or insects' chirp. The houses stood silently at the end of the driveways as if on guard but unable to resist intruders. Brill, Callow, Dao, and Dwell all stopped when they reached the steps of the first house and listened. There were no sounds of any life. The back screen door was open and swung easily in the breeze, as did the curtains in the opened windows. The group split into two; Brill and his friends went to investigate the farmhouse while Jaes and the men checked out the buildings and barns.

Brill's group entered the house by the back veranda, where rubber boots were lined up against the wall. The clean boots were of various sizes, small and pink to large and well-worn. They entered the kitchen, where the remnants of a meal still sat on the table. The food was no longer recognizable, but the settings remained intact and undisturbed. The pets scrambled onto the chairs at the table and sniffed the contents on the plates before dramatically falling to the floor as if in a death grip. Pictures stuck on a silver surface caught Callow's eye. She examined the photos of a young family with four beautiful blond, blue-eyed children. She continued staring at their faces as tears quietly rolled down her face. She pulled off one of the pictures and put it into her knapsack.

Meanwhile, Dao looked in the kitchen cabinets for anything that could aid them on their journey.

Dwell quietly moved upstairs to the bedrooms. He, like the others, had never been in a traditional house, and to him, it seemed like so much wasted space for so few people. He didn't understand why these people would want to put so much distance between themselves and their loved ones. He was taught to keep his loved ones close and to spend as much time with them as possible, to love and to learn from them. Checking out the undisturbed bedroom of the parents, he moved on to the children's rooms which were in complete disarray. The bedding and mattresses were strewn from their frames, and everything was pulled out of the closets.

"There's nothing here; let's go," said Dao as he walked past his sister, out of the kitchen, and towards the stairs to join Dwell.

"Ya, okay, just give me a minute," Callow said as she stared at the photos a little longer and wiped away her tears before following her brother upstairs into one of the children's rooms. Overwhelming sadness overcame her again as she picked up a doll from a pile of debris on the floor. She held it to her chest before tucking it into her knapsack and turning.

"Is everyone ready to go?" asked Brill as he checked the upstairs bathroom. A mirrored door on a small cabinet was ajar, so he opened it. Inside were hundreds of pills of various colors, shapes, and sizes. He read the labels that listed the dangerous side effects of taking those medications. The side effects seemed more hazardous to Brill than any sickness he had ever heard of. He wondered why people below the tallwoods allowed strangers to control their health and how could pills so dangerous ever make a person well. In the canopy, natural substances are used to cure illnesses and, at the same time, make our bodies stronger. Brill thought that made sense. People on the ground didn't want to take responsibility for their health. He thought that was sad. He felt that everyone in the house must have been extremely sick to need so much medication, and he wondered if they were now healthy. He hoped so.

Dwell came down the stairs with Callow following closely behind. Dog followed, riding the banister but got his head caught in the spindles of the railing when he tried to flip off it onto the floor. Cat found its struggle amusing and rolled around on the floor as Dog struggled to free itself. Dao laughed when he saw the creature and popped him free with his knee before heading towards the downstairs bathroom.

Dao entered the room and asked no one in particular, "Hey Guys, what do you think this is for?" and climbed into the tub.

Dwell walked in with Callow behind him.

"I don't know. Is it a bed?" Dwell asked.

Dao lay down in the tub, which was too small for his muscular frame.

"I don't think so. It hurts too much," and stepped out.

"And what about this thing?" he said as he pointed at the toilet.

"It looks like a water bowl, "Callow answered. "Maybe this is where they get their water from."

"Yea, that makes sense," replied Dao as Dog jumped up on the rim of the toilet, drank from the bowl, and fell gagging onto the floor. Cat, always anxious to help, took the plunger and stuck it onto Dog's stomach before struggling to remove it. Dao watched in amusement before he knocked it off.

"All right, we're done here. Let's go find the others," Brill yelled from the kitchen.

CHAPTER 6

Horror at the Homesteads

They left the house and were heading toward the barn to find the others when they saw Jaes and his group walking toward them. Jaes informed the others that they had checked out the small building and found nothing unusual inside. The group followed Dwell as he opened the large livestock barn's doors to a collective gasp from the entire group. In the barn were the skeletons of about two hundred cows still in their stalls. On the grain sacks near the front door were the skeletons of three cats still curled up as if sleeping. Unsettled, they quickly left the barn and walked towards the other buildings then the group split up again.

Brill and his friends headed to the largest shed, which housed several types of farm machinery. At the back of this building, four wooden bins had been constructed to hold various grain seeds. Brill thought about taking some of the grain but then decided against it and told the others not to take any because they couldn't be sure it was safe. On the way out, Brill found a worn-out tree branch at the door that had been turned into a walking stick, so he took it.

They circled the buildings and heard Jaes' group behind the large cow barn. As they cleared a huge dust-filled pile of dried manure, they saw the men standing in a circle, looking down at the exterior barn wall. When they reached the circle, they followed the gaze of the others, and there on an old bus bench seat sat the remains of a man who had his arm around a woman, and at their feet was the skeleton of a dog. The sorrow of the situation was so heavy, in a quivering voice, Jup asked, "Shall we bury them?"

Brill walked over to him and said, "Jup, I'm afraid we will run into this situation on every farm we visit, and we won't have time to bury them all. I'm sorry, my friend."

Callow approached Brill and asked, "Where are the children?"

"Ya," Jaes interjected. "We didn't see any."

"I mean, where could they be? They're so small?" she exclaimed as she held out the picture from the fridge for all to see.

Brill didn't want Callow to get overwhelmed with the situation, so he firmly said, "I don't know, but what I do know is that we have to get out of here now; we're too exposed."

Dao turned and led them away from that farm and down the road. They stopped at every farm they passed, hoping for different results, but the scene was always the same. Deserted farms with most of the deceased parents either in the house, the nearby fields, the barns or sheds, and missing altogether on a few occasions.

After a while, Callow and the pets didn't go into the houses or any other buildings; the sorrow of the situation was too heavy for her to carry, so she decided to wait at the end of each driveway for the men to return after inspecting the sites.

With dusk approaching, they came upon a massive farm with a sign on the barn that said, "Hasteleads Holsteins."

Snag asked, "What do you think a Hasteleads is?"

"Don't know, but they sure must be big; just look at the size of the barn," said Jaes.

Callow stayed behind and sat near the bare pine trees that lined the driveway with her comforting companions, Cat and Dog. The men checked out the house and then the buildings. They found the farmer's skeletal remains in a cement feed bunker in the shed with a shovel beside him. When they left the barn, Jup was the last to leave and shut the door with a loud bang. The bang was so loud that Callow quickly turned her head towards the noise and saw the men heading her way, but she also saw something flash by the small window in the hayloft of the same building.

Callow met Brill as he came down the driveway. She whispered to him, "There's someone up in the top of that barn Brill."

"We just checked it out, Callow. There's nothing up there, and besides, when we were inside, we checked for a ladder to the hayloft, and there wasn't any. So, there's no way to get up there. We checked; now come on, let's go," he said.

Brazenly she stood directly in front of him, unwilling to let him pass, and said defiantly, "I know what I saw, Brill, and there is someone up in that barn, and if you don't go check it out, then, I will."

Brill caught her arm as she turned to walk back to the barn, "Okay, okay. I'll look. You stay here and behave."

He let go of her elbow and draped his arm around her shoulder, pulling her near him. She looked up into his eyes and smiled.

Brill told everyone to take a break and stay under the trees and out of sight while he returned to the barn. He told them he had left his walking stick near the barn and needed to get it. He touched Dao on the shoulder, motioning him to follow. Dao quickly got up and joined him.

"Where did you leave it, Brill?" Dao asked.

"I purposely left it at the back door of the house. It's with the others; I just needed an excuse to return to the barn. He then told Dao what Callow had told him.

Callow watched the window as they approached the barn. Brill entered first and motioned for Dao to walk down the opposite side of the barn. They walked the length of the barn and were turning back toward the front of the building when Brill motioned for Dao to join him near the front door. He pointed up at the ceiling where the end of a retractable ladder could barely be seen. Brill looked down to see that the dust on the floor had been disturbed. Interlocking his fingers, he motioned for Dao to step onto his hands so he could lift him. Dao reached up, grabbed the end of the ladder, pulled it down to the floor, and started climbing.

At the top of the ladder, he was about to step off and onto the floorboards when he was hit with a shovel knocking him off the ladder into the hayloft. His body rolled until it came up against stacked bales of straw, then lay motionless.

Brill heard the strike and yelled, "Dao, you, okay?"

No response came, so he started to climb, and when he got to the top, he too was met with a shovel across his head, causing him to fly off the ladder onto the floor next to Dao.

Callow waited anxiously for Brill to return. As the minutes ticked by, her concern grew.

"Jaes, come with me," she yelled.

Jaes opened his eyes and got up. "Where are we going?"

Walking ahead of him, she called over her shoulder, "Just follow me."

They quickly returned to the barn, went inside, and saw the extended ladder. Callow quietly explained to Jaes that she had seen something in the top window of the barn when Jup slammed the barn door.

While speaking to him, Slas entered the barn and walked towards them. Callow didn't say anything because she knew how strongly Slas felt about protecting the group. She watched him grab the ladder rungs and climb with Jaes close behind. He rose to the top rung and was stepping off the ladder to clear the portal hole when a spear was thrown at his exposed chest, piercing his heart. He slumped forward with the spear protruding out of his back, blocking the portal hole so that Jaes, behind him on the ladder, couldn't advance into the loft.

"Slas, move it," said Jaes.

Slas didn't respond.

Again, Jaes pleaded with Slas, "Come on, Slas, let's go."

Tugging on Slas' foot caused Jaes' hand to slip; when he pulled it away, his palm was covered in blood, which dripped onto the ground. Jaes scampered quietly down and told Callow that Slas wasn't moving. Callow looked up and, realizing their situation had just taken a turn for the worse; she ordered Jaes to "Go get the others. We need to save Brill and Dao!"

The others returned to the barn as quickly as possible. Callow told them that there was someone up there who had attacked the men and that they needed to get up there quickly.

Sith started to climb the dropdown ladder while Callow and Dwell went outside to find another way into the building. A pipe ran from the barn's roof to the ground at the back of the building. Dwell immediately began scaling it, followed by Callow. The ascent was effortless as their bodies were used to climbing.

Reaching the roof, they carefully made as little noise as possible. Crawling on their stomachs, they went to the roof vents and peeked inside.

CHAPTER 7

The Children

Inside were children of all ages, scrambling amongst the rafters and on the stacks of bales in the hay mount. Many older children were armed with weapons, such as shovels and steel bars; some even held axes. Callow could now see why Slas was not moving on the ladder because of the large spear in his chest. She could also see Dao and Brill tied up and lying on the floor with gags in their mouths.

"I'm going to try to talk to them," Callow told Dwell as she laid back on her stomach and yelled into the vent.

"Hello. My name is Callow. Why are you attacking our friends? We are not here to harm you. We're just passing through." she pleaded.

They waited for a response. Minutes later, the soft voice of a young girl reached them on the roof.

"We have had enough big people pass through like you. They tell us they are here to help us; they steal our children before we know it. We don't need your kind of help," she yelled for emphasis.

"We're sick of you, Snatchers, and we won't let you take us anymore. We will die trying to stop you," said an angry young male voice.

Dwell looked at Callow incredulously, "He thinks we're Snatchers!"

She turned toward the vent, "Please take the gags off our friends; they will tell you that we're not Snatchers. We're hunting the Snatchers!"

Dwell watched a young boy move towards Brill and remove only his gag as a young girl in a pretty, blue summer dress walked across the straw-covered floor in her worn white cowboy boots towards Brill and squatted directly in front of him. Her short red hair framed her young, freckled

23

face amongst her bright emerald eyes, illuminating her face like a beacon as she stared straight ahead at Brill. The fearlessness in her eyes told Brill that she was serious and in charge.

"Talk," was all she said.

"Just like Callow said, we are not Snatchers. We're hunting them because they are hunting us. We've left our homes to find and destroy them because we have been warned that they are coming for our families and us, so we must find them first. I mean, look at us. Do we look like Snatchers," he said as he nodded toward Dao.

"No, no, you don't look like those hideous creatures. Well then, where are you headed?" the girl asked.

"We were told to head west as far as possible until we reach Province II. We were also told that they are on the move and that if we plan our moves correctly, we can intercept them there," he said.

She pulled the gag off Dao's head with the flick of her wrist and cut the ropes that bound their hands and feet with a knife that instantly appeared. The boys sat up with their heads in their hands, trying to clear the cobwebs from their thoughts. The shovels had produced extensive contusions on both their foreheads and throbbing headaches. Holding their heads in their hands, they took a minute before trying to stand, and when they did, they wobbled before regaining their balance.

Callow watched and said, "Please, let us help our dear friend you killed. We need to pay our respects and say goodbye to him."

The young woman motioned for the older boys to take the spear from Slas' body so he could be taken down the ladder. Once the spear was removed, they gently secured a rope tightly around his chest, and with many small hands, they slowly lowered his body down the ladder and into the arms of Jup and Klen. They carried him outside behind the back of the barn, where everyone assembled.

Patiently, they waited for Dao and Brill to join them. As the group mourned the loss of their friend, they watched about twenty children approach them, ranging in ages from as young as six to early twenties, following them at a distance in silence. Brill's group surrounded their friend Slas, who was placed on the ground, and waited for Sith to come over. He bent down, spoke silently to his brother, and kissed him. Then he touched his fingers to his mouth and looked towards the sky before he got up. Brill held Callow as she silently wept. The children stood and watched.

After each had said goodbye to their friend, Dao turned to the young girl from the loft and asked, "What's your name?"

"Will," she said. "That's what the kids call me."

He looked at her quizzically and asked, "Why?"

She looked Dao sternly in the eye and said, "They call me Will because I will not give up. I will do whatever it takes to protect my family and friends. Regardless of how sad and hopeless this place is, I will show them with my words and actions that I have the will to survive, and that survival includes them. I tell them to think as I do and be thankful every day. You see, children, like us, we are good. We are born good, and it takes someone evil to make us bad. So, I'll take care of them because evil can not win; everyone knows that goodness and truth will prevail." She glanced down at the ground and then looked up quickly.

"There is no greater gift than life," she said in a voice just above a whisper.

"Well, Will, I couldn't agree with you more. I wish you would have reminded your kids of that philosophy before one of them put a spear through our friend here. But right now, can I borrow your shovel?" Dao asked as he shielded his head with his arms and laughed.

Looking at him mischievously, she smirked and got him a shovel so that Jaes, Sith, and Klen could bury Slas outback as the others went inside to address the children.

Brill explained the mission to the children and what they hoped to achieve. He read the letter from Dr. Hamm about the Snatchers coming. The children listened intently, and when he had finished talking to them, they moved away from the courier's group to discuss. Callow examined the large bumps on the boys' heads and gave them each a drop from her blue elixir bottle. Soon the headaches disappeared, as did the bumps. Minutes later, Will and the children returned.

"We can help you," Will said in her soft caressing voice. "We can get you safely to the next province, but you must promise us one thing."

"What's that," he asked.

She moved her face to within inches of his and said, "That you kill every last one of them."

25

Brill nodded, caught off guard because he didn't know how to respond.

"We are very sorry for taking your friend's life but have also lost many young, innocent lives. Some were snatched from their beds as they slept, never to be seen again. That's not going to happen again. 'We' won't let it. We won't be fooled by anyone anymore. The last time we were deceived, they took some of our kids, but when we realized our mistake, we went after them and got them back.

So even though you say you want to help us, we know that is untrue. In today's evil world, it is every man for themselves, and we know that. Now get some sleep - we leave in two hours," she declared and was gone.

Everyone dispersed and found a place to lay their head. Callow watched a tiny little girl struggle to climb the bales looking for a place to lay her head. Once she reached the top, she curled up alone without a blanket. Callow climbed up next to the child and stroked her hair until she fell asleep. She removed the doll from her pack and tucked it between her little arms before she laid behind her and held her tightly with the pets tucked between them.

After completing their bed checks, Will and Brill came together in a corner and began sharing their stories. Brill told her about Mullins and the compound, Civantes, The Farm, the competitions, the lab and the experiments on children, and Dr. Swallow. When he finished, she described her encounters with the Snatchers.

"Many times, they have come through here looking for us, but we hid, and fortunately, they have always left empty-handed. But, she emphasized, we may not be so lucky next time. Other groups of children have not been as fortunate as we have. They have lost many from their groups. It's horrible," she said.

"How many Snatchers have you seen?" Brill asked.

"The last time, we counted about thirty that came onto our farm, but we don't know how many there are. We don't know whether there was another group down the road when the others came here or they have a large army elsewhere. We just don't know," she said.

"What do they look like?" Dwell asked as he came over when he overheard them speaking.

"They're big, like the Demonis and ashen. The first thing you notice about them is the size of their massive heads. It's like their heads have never stopped growing. When the sickness first spread, it was because the waters were affected. Some people who lived out in the country and a few from town used that water to wash their dishes and to shower but not to quench their thirst. Instead, they boiled it before they drank it or drank rainwater. Over time, though, the women got much sicker than the men. It was strange because the women eventually died, but some men didn't; their bodies changed. They took on the grotesque appearance of swollen heads, slumped-over posture, swollen limbs, and fingers, and most shocking is their eating habits. Disgusting!" she stopped and pretended to vomit before continuing. "Some of them look like they can't even support the weight of their heads because they are bent right over, and we have even seen some walk with their knuckles dragging on the ground for support."

"Well, they must be slow then if they can't even support the weight of their heads," Brill laughed.

"Don't be a fool. They are quicker than you think and faster than you can imagine," Will replied.

Those must have been Snatchers that we saw at the Falls," Dao said as he joined them.

"I don't know. They may have been. I guess we will know soon enough," Brill said. "Come, let's get some rest. Before we know it, we will have to leave." He thanked Will for her help and, more importantly, her trust.

They went their separate ways to settle down for the night. Dao near the hatch while Brill looked for Callow. He found her and climbed up the bales to join her. Grabbing some loose straw, he placed it around her and the little girl before snuggling behind Callow for some much-needed rest. Everyone turned in except Snag, who watched them from afar.

CHAPTER 8

The Waterways

Get up, get up. " It's time to go," said a fourteen-year-old boy as he shook the couriers to wake them.

Slowly the group gathered their belongings and readied themselves for the next stage of the journey.

Outside was dark; there was no moonlight, only stars in the sky. The group followed Will and three boys to the back of the barn and into the field heading due north. Brill noticed on the walk that the ground seemed to slope increasingly to the left the further they walked. He was glad that he still had his walking stick. Callow saw the benefit of his walking stick, so it wasn't long before she and the others found their own. They walked for hours in the stillness of the night in unfamiliar territory. The youngsters kept their pace and seemed to know every nook and cranny of the landscape. Their comfort level with the terrain was a huge comfort to the group, and no one was concerned about where they were being taken.

After seven hours of walking, the ground sloped so much that everyone struggled to stay upright. Their guides stopped abruptly when they came upon a break in the land that only seemed visible to them. To Brill and his friends, it was nothing more than a small ridge on the surface of some rocks. Will turned back to them and said to the group, "Follow me."

They nodded in agreement, so she turned around and walked right back to the ridge, which was a slight opening in the rock, bent down, and disappeared. Snag, and Jaes followed without hesitation, as did Dao, Dwell, Sith, the pets, and Klen, albeit with some scratches and abrasions from the tight squeeze between the rocks.

Brill and Callow looked at each other and were uncertain whether this was the path they should be on, but they, too, followed Will and the three young boys down the hole. Jup was the last to enter. He placed his feet into the hole and let his weight sink. Immediately, he got stuck. Try as he might, he could not enter further into the tunnel nor pull his shoulders out of the hole. Dao shimmied back up toward the surface, and when he reached Jup, he took out his red potion and handed it to him.

"Just a drop or two on your tongue, and then hand the bottle back to me," Dao said reluctantly.

Jup struggled but managed to get his arm out of the hole, opened the lid with his teeth, and placed a few drops into his mouth before he returned the bottle to Dao's hand. Immediately, he felt the surge of energy blast through his body, allowing him to break up the rock and enlarge the opening. He went down through the tunnel and climbed to the bottom, where the others were waiting for him before the rocks at the surface collapsed, blocking any entry from above.

"Quiet," the young girl whispered. The crashing rocks reverberated off the walls and echoed throughout the canyons notifying everyone or everything down there that they had arrived.

The canyon opened into a labyrinth of caves and recesses. Will was remarkably familiar with this terrain, and she led them with her flashlights downward into the cave until they reached a half-moon beach where three shallow canoes were grounded on the shore.

"Get in quickly; we need to go.

Move," she said while flailing her arms. Then she assigned everyone to their canoe and told them to shove off.

Due to size, the three big men were split up, one in each canoe, along with one of the young boys. The crews were decided by weight. Callow, with the pets under her legs, rode with Snag and Jup. Brill rode with Dao and Sith, and Dwell, and Jaes rode with Klen. Will took the helm of the first boat.

She led the boats down the calm waterway for the first three hours, passing countless caverns and smaller pools. Callow felt that someone was watching them in the darkness, but she didn't see any movement or hear anything other than the sounds from their boats. Slowly, the current began to speed up, forcing everyone except the children to grab the sides of the boat to secure themselves to the vessels. The increase in speed was unsettling to them as they struggled to hang on while the children straddled the stern, relishing the ride. Using the oars as rudders, they steered the boats through the cavernous course without colliding with the enormous stalactites or stalagmites scattered along their route.

The canoes' effortless flight ebbed and flowed with the current and the expert navigational skills of the boys. Their passengers were not as fortunate as their helmsmen. The ride was a frightening and unsettling affair, and some quickly lost the contents of their stomachs.

Under Callow's shirt hid Cat, who was too afraid to watch the water flying by. Dog did the opposite and perched himself on the boat's bow, eagerly looking ahead and solid as a rock. Suddenly, without warning, the canoes started to undulate violently as the walls whizzed by.

Klen couldn't settle his stomach, and in seconds his tanned face turned an ashen grey from the intense rocking of the boat. It took all his strength to remain in the skiff while he held his head over the side, vomiting. His nausea was so intense and came on so quickly that he seriously considered jumping into the water. Eventually, the violent current subsided, allowing the boats to float down the channels gently. It was hours before Klen could pry his grip from the side of the boat. Will steered the canoes toward the gravel shoreline, and the youngsters pulled the canoes from the water. Everyone got out and stood on the shore assessing their stability, except Klen, who was still lulling around on the bottom of the large canoe.

Snag got his footing first and looked around the cavern. "Whoa," was all he said.

All the passengers looked up to see the walls covered in etchings. A few were large, beautiful images painted in vibrant colors, but most sketches were black, depicting brutal scenes of violence and death. The children paid no attention to it; they had seen it all before.

Will took a few moments to watch their reactions and then said, "Follow me." She turned and started to run down a tunnel.

"Hurry. Let's go; we have to keep up," Brill said to the others as he ran, struggling to keep Will in sight. Klen tried his legs, but they weren't cooperating. He knew he could not stand, let alone run, so he slowly dragged himself out of the boat and flopped onto the shore. He tried to stand repeatedly but couldn't keep his balance and kept falling. Tired and unwell, he stopped and shimmed up the gravel on his elbows until he reached the wall, then sat up with his back against it while the others continued running after Will.

One of the young boys returned to Klen when he realized he wasn't with the group.

"Get up; you can't stop here; it's too dangerous," he said.

"Look, I need a minute to settle my head and stomach. Okay. Then I'll catch up to the rest of you," Klen said with his eyes closed.

"No, you can't. If you stop here, it will find you," the youngster stammered.

"What are you talking about? 'It' will find me. What is 'it'?" Klen asked sarcastically.

"I don't know what it is, but I do know what it isn't, and that's friendly. So please get up before it finds you and hunts us all down," he said in a deep, exasperated voice, but Klen wasn't listening.

"Don't you worry about me, young man; I can take care of myself," Klen said as he put his head back against the wall and closed his eyes.

The young man shook his head and said, "Okay, but you're a dead man." He returned to join the others and met Jaes on his way back to Klen.

"Don't go back there, Jaes," the young man said.

"Why not? What's back there?" he asked, surprised.

"You don't want to know, but if you go back there – you will! Turn around, come back with me, and join the others," he said as he took off running down the tunnel.

"Will what?" Jaes muttered to himself as he walked back towards Klen. He looked over his shoulder at the young boy disappearing from sight in the direction he had just come from.

CHAPTER 9

Shadow

Klen sat resting against the wall with his eyes closed, hoping his stomach and head would soon settle down. He didn't see the long black shadow under the water moving towards him. He tilted his head back, trying to stop the spinning and clear the brain fog. It felt good to stop and be on solid ground. He decided that was the first and last boat ride he would ever take.

The wall was so cool on the back of his head, and the cavern silence was relaxing and peaceful. He started nodding off just as the shadow slowly slithered out of the water toward him. Jaes came into view and yelled, "Hey buddy, come on, let's go. We need to catch up to the rest of the group."

Klen slowly turned his head toward Jaes and half-opened his eyes before speaking, "Ya, ya, I'm coming."

Jaes stopped yards from Klen and waited for him to get up, but he made no effort to stand. Instead, he tilted his head back against the wall for a few seconds longer as the black creature weaved its way toward him and tightly wrapped itself around his lower body. By the time the pain receptors in Klen's body could warn him of the danger, he was already in its death grip. It was too late. The creature had slid behind his back and around his neck, squeezing as it went. When Klen opened his mouth to scream, the black shadow was already down his throat, muffling his cries. Jaes watched in horror as the creature devoured Klen, pulling what was left of him into the water and under the surface. Frozen in shock, Jaes watched as the bubbles in the pool subsided then the creature reared its ugly head up high out of the water towards him. He turned and ran for his life.

"Run," was all he could scream at the top of his lungs.

He was moving so quickly that he caught up to the group in no time, even though they were still running.

Jaes continued yelling, "Run," as he shot past everyone, including Will.

"Whoa, buddy," Will yelled at Jaes as she stopped in front of a set of stairs carved into the side of the wall. "We're done running now. We need to climb."

"Follow me," was all she said.

The stairs were treacherous and slick because they were constantly moist and well-traveled. Handholds were carved on both sides of the footholds for support. The climb was hard and slow, but they surfaced outside the tunnel and into daylight atop a large mountain after more than an hour.

"Rest now because we will have to get back on the road soon," she told them.

They emerged from the tunnel, sat, opened their bags, and ate. When the last youngster appeared from the passageway, Brill looked confused as he panned the area looking for Klen.

"Where's Klen?" he asked Jaes.

"Gone," Jaes said.

"Gone where?" asked Callow.

"The thing in the water got him," he answered.

"What thing?" asked Brill.

"The kids told us not to slow down and to keep moving, but Klen wouldn't listen to them, so "It" got him, and he's gone," Jaes said, shrugging his shoulders.

"As in dead?" asked Callow.

"Oh ya," exclaimed Jaes. "It ate him, ya; I think that is what it did, but I'm not sure. I don't know. I don't ever want to see that thing again – ever." He walked away, shaking his head.

Brill went over to Will. "What was that 'thing' that got Klen?" he asked.

Will looked into Brill's eyes and said, "There are creatures that have thrived from all the death around us and have become stronger and more dangerous. I think it may have been a snake before, but I'm not sure. We call it "Shadow," she said as she walked away.

Brill stopped and thought about the Shivers they had met in the river. Knowing that two such monsters were out in the wild didn't comfort Brill. The thought of being eaten by such a creature was horrifying.

Brill called after Will and asked. "Where are we going now?"

"Going to get you as close to the Snatchers as possible," she said.

"You know where they are?" he asked incredulously.

"I know where *some* of them are," she replied, turning away to speak to the youngsters.

A little while later, she came back to Brill with the young man about fourteen years old who had steered Callow's canoe.

"This is Fite; he will lead you on the next part of your journey. I need to return home with the others. Fite is the best guide in the region, and he will get you where you need to go," she said as Brill and the others looked towards the scrawny young boy with no hair standing before them. Brill laughed to himself when he thought of the young man's name. He believed that the only fight this thin, scrawny young man had left in him would be to run in the face of danger.

Will turned to Brill and said, "Don't be fooled by appearances Brill. Many a man have gone to his rest underestimating another. He will get you where you need to go."

Then she walked away but turned back towards Brill, saying, "Remember your promise to me."

Brill nodded and thanked her for all her help, and then she and the two boys left.

Fite sat watching Snag and Jup laughing with one another. He went over and whispered something to Snag, who got up at once and followed him away from the others. They spoke privately before approaching Brill and Dao.

Snag started talking, "He (Snag pointed at Fite) isn't talkative, but he says he likes me and wants me to talk for him. He likes me because I laugh a lot which he thinks makes me wiser than all of you. I told him he was right."

"Ya, ya, just tell us what he said," Dao said dismissively.

"He said that we are close to an arena where the Snatchers go to watch the fights. He said he will take the three of us to scout it out." Snag said.

"When do we go?" asked Brill.

"Now," replied Snag.

"All right, Dao, you, Snag, and I will go with him, and the rest will camp here until we come back," he said.

"I'll go tell the others," Dao said and left. Callow and Dwell were following behind him when he returned, determined to change Brill's mind.

"I'm going with you," Callow said sternly.

"No, you're not," he said, and then he looked sternly at Dwell before he could open his mouth and said, "and neither are you. You wait here with Jup, Jaes, and Slas until we return."

Brill raised his finger to his mouth to silence them before they could protest. They remained that way as Brill ran to join Fite and the others. Dog looked back and forth at Brill, then Callow, and decided to follow Brill while Cat remained at Callow's side, flashing its posterior at Dog before it left.

Fite led the three over and out of the rocky terrain and back into the wilderness of thick forests.

Dao and Brill stepped on rocks, leaves, and other debris to avoid leaving tracks just as they would in their forest. Fite did the same, and eventually, Snag followed suit. They stayed low in the woods as the sun rose high in the sky.

CHAPTER 10

The Arena

As the sun rose to its highest point in the early afternoon sky, Fite motioned for the men to get low and stay behind a large boulder that they came upon. Over the top of the boulder, in the distance, they could see a large building.

Fite whispered to Snag, who relayed the message to the others.

"Fite says this is where they fight, and the Snatchers come to watch," he said.

"We need to get closer," said Brill.

Their guide nodded and signaled with his arm for them to follow.

They crouched through the forest, then crawled in the fields to get within three hundred yards of the building. There they stopped and hid behind large, rusted metal parts buried in overgrown weeds.

Brill took out his map and orientated himself. According to the map, they were one-third of the way to Province II. He felt for the whistle around his neck and tucked the maps back into his pack. When they looked up, Fite was gone.

"Where did Fite go?" he asked.

No one knew.

"We need to get inside that building," said Dao. "So, I'll go." And he got up to leave.

"You can't go alone," Brill said, and before he could speak again, Snag happily volunteered to go and was instantly up and standing tall beside him.

Brill reluctantly agreed to let them go. He didn't think he could stop Snag even if he wanted to.

Dao led Snag along the treeline back toward the building. There was a lot of commotion around the poorly lit, large structure. Men were walking in and out of the building. Vehicles kept arriving. As the boys got closer, Dao took a deep breath when he recognized the familiar smell of the blend at The Farm. Snag nudged him, and when the coast was clear, they hid behind some parked trucks near the building while Brill and Dog watched in the distance.

While waiting for their next move, a man in uniform walked past them to the rotting metal at the edge of the grounds. Snag looked at Dao, and without saying a word, they knew exactly what to do. Snag silently crawled towards the man until he was directly behind him. He could smell his urine and felt warm liquid splash on his arm. Dao waited in the weeds for the man to finish his business. As the man turned to return to the building, Snag suddenly grabbed his ankles, surprising him and causing him to fall forward without a sound. As he hit the ground, Snag used a familiar wrestling move to pin his leg to his back while he pulled back on the man's head. The stress on his neck made it impossible for him to make a sound. Dao ran towards the men, and with both hands, he gripped the man's head and covered his mouth and nose until the man stopped moving. Snag got up and dragged the man behind the metal into the shadows.

"Get his clothes," Snag said over his shoulder to Dao.

They spent the next five minutes removing the man from his uniform, which Dao fit into nicely. Dao dressed and put his clothes into his pack while Snag watched. Snag quietly whistled to Dao, who came over. Snag pointed towards the building where another man was approaching. Dao thought, 'we are obviously in the relieving area.' Quickly, he tossed his bag at Snag and nodded before he got up and walked out from behind the junk.

With his head down, he fumbled with the front of his pants as the man walked past him, then turned and followed. When the man stopped at the edge of the grounds, Dao stood beside him and said, "Big competitions again tonight, eh?"

The man turned towards him and said, "Ya, did ya hear? They shut down The Farm in Province IV, so we are now the biggest arena for the fights. And tonight, Civantes is out of his mind, pissed. He's looking for revenge on the Captain. Rumor has it that the Captain cheated him out of a big win at the last competition."

"Did he?" Dao asked.

"I don't know, and I don't give a shit," the man said.

"You don't like the fights?" Dao asked.

"I don't like anything about this garbage," he said, looking over his shoulder at the building.

"Then why are you here?" Dao asked.

"I used to be a fighter years ago, and because I was good, I gained freedom from Civantes. But he is a devil, just like the rest of them. He might even be the worst devil. They don't give a damn about anyone or anything except for their egos and greed. They can all go to hell for all I care." He said as he finished his business and turned to go.

"Why don't you just leave?" Dao asked.

"And go where? Home to my family? They took them long ago," the man said as he looked into Dao's eyes. Dao felt for the man's loss and sense of hopelessness.

Snag watched, waiting for a sign from Dao to neutralize the man, but it never came, and he was surprised when the two men walked right by him towards the light of the building. Then Dao followed the man right into the building, unnoticed.

<hr />

"We can't just wait here for them to return," said Dwell.

"I agree," said Callow. "Let's try to get closer to them so we don't get separated. Besides, we're stronger in numbers, don't you agree?" She said to the others.

The men looked at each other and nodded in agreement.

"Let's go," Dwell said as he led them in the same direction the others had gone.

The five of them walked in the darkness, staying along the treeline, and just like the others, Callow and Dwell tried to walk on anything other than the ground to minimize their tracks. Jup, Jaes, and Sith did no such thing; they marched on straight ahead, leaving a clear mark for anyone tracking them to follow.

As they neared the halfway mark to the arena, Callow caught a familiar scent in the wind and stopped dead in her tracks. She grabbed Dwell's arm to stop him, and the others did the same. They scoured the area looking for any movement, but with the impending nightfall, it wasn't easy to see amongst the forest shadows. As the scent intensified, Callow's brain registered where she had come across this smell.

She turned to Dwell with terror and said, "It's the wild dogs."

CHAPTER 11

Wild Dog Attack

Dwell remembered the horrifying stories the couriers had shared with everyone in the canopy about the wild dogs they met on their return from the compound and again at The Farm.

"Climb the trees – quickly," yelled Callow.

Cat didn't hesitate and raced up the trunk while Dwell and Jup weaved their hands together to boost Callow onto a large bough. They were used to climbing freestyle. Sith, Jaes, and Jup did the same to Dwell. When Dwell got into the branches, he removed a rope from his bag, tied it to the bough, and tossed it down to Jup, who held it out for Sith and Jaes, who quickly climbed to join the others.

Callow kept looking for any sign of the dogs. Just as Jup began to climb, she saw three massive dogs walk into sight.

"Jup, get up here," she screamed.

The dogs looked at Jup and lowered their heads, exposing their massive teeth while advancing on him. The three animals split up and circled him as he released the rope. The middle dog was the largest in the pack, and it stopped and pulled its lips back, revealing six-inch canines dripping with saliva while the other two dogs slowly made their way around the sides of Jup.

"Jup, look to the side," yelled Dwell.

"I'll help him," Jaes said to no one in particular.

"No, stay where you are. I'll take care of these demons," Jup yelled back and turned to his right to see two dogs creeping toward him just a few feet away. When he turned, the dog on his left lunged and bit him in the lower leg tearing away the flesh. Immediately, he went down on his left knee, cringing from the injury allowing the dog on his right to jump onto his shoulder and bite his ear. Instinctively he head-butted the animal sending it flying backward and onto the ground.

Jup was quick. He grabbed the dog on the left by the snout and pried open its mouth with his hands until the jaw bones snapped and separated, hanging loosely in his grip and threw the dead dog as far as he could. It remained there while the dog on his right attacked again, only to be met by the force of Jup's fist squarely in the chest. The sheer power of Jup's punch caused the dog to fly back into a tree trunk, where it slouched to the ground and was slow to get up.

While the battle raged, the middle dog sat watching the fight. It saw how the two dogs were silenced before it quietly got up and circled Jup, who was still on the ground, unable to stand up. Sith saw Jup's distress and jumped to the ground to help. He landed next to Jup and stepped before him to challenge the middle dog, the pack's leader. The Demoni casually shifted his attention from Jup to Sith and slowly approached him with teeth bared. While its lips were curled back, it launched itself at Sith, hitting him squarely in the chest and knocking him to the ground. Sith covered his neck and face with his arms, but his flesh was no match for the razor-sharp teeth of the alpha dog. The second dog saw an opportunity and joined the attack as Jup dragged himself across the dirt. The two dogs tore up Sith while Jup watched, unable to help his friend.

"Jup, catch," screamed Callow as she tossed her blue vial at him. "Don't drink it all, only a little."

Jup caught the elixir, removed the top, and drank from the vial while watching the carnage before him. He sealed the bottle and tossed it aside. The blue liquid streamed through his veins, repairing his tissues. Feeling better, he jumped up, ignoring the pain, and ran to Sith, now just a mass of tattered flesh. Picking up a large branch, he swung wildly at the dogs, striking one and nearly missing the other. Sith lay dead on the ground as Jup pursued the middle dog who stood, daring Jup to challenge him.

As the two enemies sized each other up, Jup relished his newfound strength as the lesser dog returned to the battle. Jup swung the branch again, but this time it smashed into the dog's head and exploded its jaw. The dog fell to the ground with a thud and lay there shaking. In one swift movement, the middle dog circled back toward the injured dog and tore the throat out of the now motionless animal.

Then it turned its attention towards Jup, who crouched down and placed both hands on the ground to protect his core. The dog stepped over the carcass and walked towards him near the tree and away from Sith's body. Jup held out his hands, taunting the dog to come for him. Dwell understood Jup's plan without speaking a word. With its muscular hind legs, the dog approached Jup and lunged at his neck. Jup caught the animal in flight and, using his rejuvenated strength, clenched it in a bear hug, squeezing the air out of it.

Dwell dropped the rope from above, hitting the dog. In a flash, Jup grabbed it and tied it tightly around the animal's neck until he could no longer tighten it. Within a minute, the dog stopped moving and went limp in his arms. He threw the creature to the ground and crushed its skull with his boot before he untied the rope. Callow and Dwell climbed down to aid Sith, but it was too late; he was no longer breathing. The vials of elixir were of no use to him now.

Jup quickly picked up the bodies of the other dogs and threw them in a pile against a nearby tree, crushing their bones as he went. Then he turned back towards his friend Sith and gently removed Cat, who was lying on his friend's chest licking his face. The big man gently picked him up and, with the help of the others, buried him under the tree.

After Sith was put to rest, Dwell, and Callow scoured the ground on their hands and knees, looking for what remained of Callow's blue vial, unaware that Jup had already found and pocketed it when no one was looking. His eye had caught sight of the vial peeking out from under the brush as he threw the last dead dog in the air. It was then that Jup decided that he would not leave his fate in the hands of the others. When he returned to the tree, he spied the couriers' sacks on the ground and wondered what other goodies they might have in their bags.

"I can't seem to find your elixir, Callow," Dwell said as he bent and swept the ground with his hands. When he got near the dog carcasses, he cut off a chunk of hair and tucked it into his pocket.

"We can't linger here, Dwell. It's lost. Come, we must go," she said to him as she caught Jup staring mischievously at her sack. She also noticed the slight bulge in his pants pocket and realized they were searching in vain for a vial that Jup had already found! She hoped they would meet with Brill and the others soon because enemies seemed to be everywhere.

CHAPTER 12

Treachery

Brill waited quietly with Dog for Dao and Snag to return. As the minutes passed, he wondered if he should join Dao and Snag or return to Callow and the gang. While debating what to do next, he heard Callow's voice.

"What are you doing here?" Callow asked to Brill's surprise.

"What am I doing here?

What are you doing here? I told all of you to stay put."

"Brill, it was too dangerous for us to remain back there. Sith is dead. The wild dogs happened upon us on our way here and killed him when he tried to save Jup. When we got to him, it was too late to use the elixirs; he was already gone. Jup finally killed the dogs with the help of my blue elixir, which Dwell, and I thought was lost, but it's not really. We're just thankful that only one of us was lost. It could have been a lot worse," she continued.

"Are you and Dwell okay?" he asked, concerned.

"Ya, we're fine. Both Dwell and I were up in the tree when the attack happened," she said. She knew that as soon as she said it, Callow wished that she could take the words back. She cringed that she hadn't mentioned that Jaes had also been up in the tree during the attack.

Brill glanced over at Dwell, who had lowered his head when he heard Callow's remarks. Too embarrassed to look his brother in the eye, Brill didn't say a word; his disappointing gaze said it all. Everyone sat down, and for a time, no one spoke. All welcomed the silence until Brill filled them in.

"Dao and Snag are at the building, so we can either wait here or try to get closer," he said.

Dwell's head shot up, "I'll go."

"And I'll go with him," Jup said.

"Are you strong enough?" Brill asked Jup.

"I'm fine," he said in a low drawl.

Callow watched him roll the elixir around in his pocket with his hand. She didn't think letting Dwell go alone with Jup was wise because Dwell was no match for Jup if he turned on him.

"Brill, why don't you go with Jup? Dwell, Jaes, and I will scour the perimeter." Callow said as she turned to Brill and squeezed his arm. Brill caught her subtle nod in Jup's direction. The concern in her eyes told him that he needed to heed her advice because, within the group, the cohesiveness had suddenly changed.

His eyes told her he understood her concern, and he nodded in agreement.

"Sure, but remember to return to this spot after you check it out because I will look for you here. And I'm getting tired of chasing after people who aren't where they are supposed to be," he said while looking at Callow. "Cat, stay with Callow."

He turned to leave; Callow whispered in his ear, "Jup has found my blue elixir. It's in his pocket, and he's been eyeing our knapsacks since the attack. Be careful; it's getting harder to know whom to trust," she said before she walked away.

Dwell looked defeated, but he knew it was no use trying to argue with his brother, so he sat back down and hung his head.

"Remember to be here when you're supposed to be," Brill told them as he began to follow Jup. He hoped Callow was wrong about Jup. He didn't need any more enemies, especially one the size of Jup.

<hr />

Snag waited for Dao to come and get him, but he didn't return. More guards of various sizes came out to relieve themselves. Tall, short, fat, and brutally skinny men filed by but no one to match Snag's physical profile. After waiting for an eternity, a guard about his size finally approached him to use the outdoor facilities. When he stopped, Snag overpowered and held him firmly around the neck until he stopped struggling and fell unconscious. He dragged the body to the junk pile and dropped him near the other guard. Then he stripped the motionless guard of his uniform and put it on. He shoved his clothes and Dao's pack under the rusting metal and walked into the back of the building through the same door Dao had entered.

The interior was brightly lit, and the air was filled with anticipation and tension. The backroom reminded Snag of the other fighting facilities he had performed in. The smell of perspiration, blood, and death was overpowering. For many, the atmosphere was unnerving and terrifying, but it was just another day at work to Snag. He headed deeper into the bowels of the building, looking for Dao. On the left side of the building were rows and rows of holding cages filled with men just like him. Across the aisle were giant cells that had the creatures. He searched the pens for familiar faces but didn't see any until he reached the last row, where he saw a friend from his early fighting days.

He quickly hid behind a pillar so that his friend couldn't see him, not that his friend would recognize him. The young man in the cage had once been a champion, vibrant, strong, and full of confidence. Today, he was a shell of his former self. Covered in catastrophic injuries, the man sat dejected, welcoming death.

Snag fought the urge to free the man and decided not to. He had to stay focused, so he continued deeper into the building. Shaking his guilt away, he avoided the man's cage and kept walking and searching for Dao, whom he found drinking blend with the guards in the room where the blend was made.

The men were drinking the unpleasant smelly fluid from the vat, and he watched in horror as Dao gave his empty cup to another guard, who refilled it and returned it to him.

Snag got closer to the vat to hear what the men were saying.

"So, who's fighting in the big event tonight? One of the guards asked no one in particular.

"A guy named Bile from Province I," said another.

"Who's he with, Mullins or Civantes?" asked another.

"Bile is one of Mullins' best slaves," laughed someone.

"Is he any good?" asked Dao.

"Extremely, maybe the best I've ever seen," piped up the bristled voice of an old guard sitting with his back to the vat and his eyes closed.

"And who is he fighting?" someone else shouted out.

"Not *who* but what," came the old man's crusty voice.

"Okay, what is he fighting?" another asked.

"Death," was the old man's reply.

"Its name is Death?" someone asked.

"No, he's fighting against Death," he said.

The men looked at one another silently, lost in their thoughts of the mutant creatures and hoping that none escaped tonight. All nicknames bore truth, so no one seemed too anxious to meet this contender.

Snag brushed up against Dao, who turned slightly to see who had bumped him. When he realized it was Snag, he faked a coughing fit, so the other men would think the drink had gone down his windpipe. As he continued to cough, he left the group and walked out the back door into the yard with Snag close behind. Once out of the ears reach of the others, Snag caught up with Dao and asked.

"Dao, what the hell. Why did you disappear?"

"Sorry, but I just couldn't hurt the guy. After talking to him, he doesn't like being here any more than you or I. They destroyed his life too. He's a nice guy," Dao explained with his slightly slurred speech.

"Did you ask him about the Snatchers?" Snag continued.

"Ya, he will show me who they are once the competition starts again. He says they are always seated in the arena above Civantes."

Brill, Jup and Dog saw Dao and Snag exit the building. Brill whistled a familiar call, and Dao quickly turned toward the sound, reached into his pocket, removed his black patch, and placed it on his wrist.

"Let's go for a walk," he said to Snag and headed away from the buildings to the brush. They saw Brill and Jup and circled the rusting metal to avoid detection before reaching the others. Brill sniffed the air as they approached and said, "What is that smell?"

Dao looked down at the ground, and Snag spoke up, "It's the drink from inside. Dao has been getting information from the guards, and they made him drink it." he said.

"Are you okay, Dao?" he asked.

"Ya, I'm good," he replied quietly.

"Well, what's going on inside?" Brill asked.

Dao told him everything he knew about the Snatchers and the night's big fight. Snag also told them about his friend in the cage while Jup and Dog listened.

"We have to find out where they're going and how many there are," Brill said as he explained his plan while huddled together.

CHAPTER 13

Death Escapes

Hiding behind vehicles on the right side of the complex, Jaes kept an eye out for the guards. Dwell was quiet behind Callow. She turned to face him.

"Dwell, I'm sorry. I should not have told Brill you were in the tree with me. I'll explain it to him later, but now we have other things to worry about. Jup found my elixir. I didn't see him put it into his pocket, but I could see it there. That's when I knew we couldn't trust him anymore."

Dwell didn't respond.

"Didn't you notice how hard he was looking at our packs, probably wondering what else we had that he could take," she continued.

Dwell wasn't listening. "Stop trying to protect me, Callow," he said as he got up. "I can take care of myself. Now let's go. We need to check out what's happening, and we don't have much time."

He grabbed her hand and helped her up. The pet watched the confusing conversation between the two and wasn't sure if they were happy with each other or mad at each other; it couldn't tell, so falling backward on the ground, it closed its eyes until Callow called for it and it came running.

A small addition had been built on this side of the building but didn't have a door. There were windows at ground level and some high above near the roofline. They all were open. Dwell scurried to the nearest corner, pulled the low-lying windowpane down to the ground, and looked inside. He could see two guards, one short and another very tall, standing on a platform throwing dead carcasses into a big open pit full of nasty-smelling sludge composed of flesh, body fluids, dirt, and lime, which the men threw on top of the carcasses to minimize the smell. It wasn't working.

Suddenly, the men took a break and stopped shoveling; Dwell turned his attention to the pit bubbling and expelling gases. The skin and fresh dirt on top were thick and undulating; it began to surge slowly and then with more vigor. Dwell waved Callow, Jaes, and Cat over. Together they watched the men resume shoveling, oblivious to what was happening below them. The pit's surface bubbled while the men continued to work as the water rolled. Reaching out of the repulsive liquid were limbs, swiping and clawing from beneath the muck until the torso of a creature appeared.

Beneath the sludge, the creature's body was glaring white except for its face, which was a sickly pink hue. Its torso was covered in two to three-inch bumps, even on its underside. It had no ears or a pronounced nose, but it did have big red, drooping eyes and a large mouth that opened to reveal rows of sharp teeth, and it was mad. Its anger was fueled by its slow progress out of the pit and the two men shoveling dirt. The short guard had just tossed a shovel into the carcass tomb when he looked up and caught a glimpse of the creature.

"Res, hey Res, stop shoveling and look over there," he whispered while pointing across the pit.

The second guard stopped and rested his forearm on the shovel's handle. Oblivious to the danger, he wiped his brow and looked up just as the creature exited the liquid and slowly climbed onto the surrounding ledge on the vat. The heavy rotting sludge clung like a blanket onto its body while small chunks slithered onto the ledge and back into the pit. The creature staggered along the wooden walkway, weighed down by the heavy debris attached to it. Unable to move quickly, it stopped and shook itself, covering the room in filth. Feeling lighter, it lowered its head and ran at the two frozen guards with incredible agility. The first guard panicked, dropped his shovel, and turned to run but slipped on the sludge and fell back into the pit on top of the scum, screaming.

Frantic, the tall guard fumbled in vain for his gun before the creature barreled into him, causing his shovel to fall off the platform and striking his fellow guard. The guard's midsection took a direct hit as the creature rammed its head through his torso via his belly button, causing immediate death. Then the beast turned its attention towards the shrieking cries from within the pit. Unwilling to venture back into the sludge, it picked up the dead guard and tossed him directly on top of his colleague, muffling his cries as he slowly sank to the bottom.

A look of horror crossed everyone's face, including Cat.

"We have to warn the others," they whispered in unison, then turned and ran towards the meeting place.

Fully informed of their plans, Dog was sent back to the meeting place. Jup and Brill didn't lie in wait to steal guards' uniforms as no one was as big as Jup. Instead, while Dao and Snag entered the building from the back entrance unnoticed, Brill and Jup circled the building and walked in the front door with the other patrons making sure to keep their heads down. Once deep in the crowd, they stole hats from drunken spectators and wore them down over their eyes to conceal their identities. Jup stole a coat and threw it over his shoulders.

They walked throughout the building and walkways into the arena, where Brill saw Civantes seated high in the stands. They didn't stay long and headed for the staging area, where the fighters and creatures were organized in cages for their upcoming fights. Despite all the spectators, there were few species of either contestant. Brill didn't recognize any of the men from The Farm, but Jup did. At the end of the human cages was a mean-looking, badly scarred man with a bald head. He was covered in tattoos. Jup left Brill's side and went over to the man. Jup thrust his arm through the bars. The man rose and accepted Jup's greeting, returning the gesture. Brill hid behind a post and saw Jup take the blue vial out of his pocket to show the man, who nodded approvingly while Jup spoke. Then they both turned and looked directly at Brill.

Brill started to move, zigzagging past fighters, guards, and spectators. Looking back, he saw that Jup was still at the cage talking with the man, so he ducked behind a panel at the far end of the corridor, glancing back now and then to see if Jup was following. Brill didn't notice the commotion before him until he heard the cries of men trying to escape from the only doorway in the room next to him. The back wall was missing, so the small room only had three divisions, and Brill could see everything from where he was hiding and turned to see a wave of men clamoring over each other and coming towards him. He was unaware of why the men were running until he looked beyond the men and saw a hideous creature enter the back of the room with the remains of 'something' dangling from its mouth.

Brill froze, contemplating what to do next, when Jup stepped past him into the room with his friend from the cage. Brill thought the guards must have given him the keys in hopes that they would stop this monster. When they entered, the two men hesitated and saw the mutant, but the creature did not. It slowly crept closer until Jup realized they had no choice but to do something. Without saying a word to one another, the men separated and got into their fighting posture. It was obvious that these two men were familiar with one another in the battle arena.

The creature looked from one man to the other, and like Brill, it could hear other voices. It slowly turned towards the door and lunged at the spectators jammed in the doorway, forcing them all to fall back onto one another. Then refocused on the fighters, the creature lunged at the man from the cage who was nearest to it, but the man was too quick and moved away. Jup saw an opportunity and jumped onto the back of the creature. Barbs extended from the middle of each bump on the creature's body and pierced through Jup's skin, fastening him to the monster. Jup slashed at the beast's neck with a circular blade slicing through the skin and muscles until the creature violently thrashed about, hurling Jup to the ground. Jup rapidly yanked the barbs from his body that he could reach while his friend taunted the beast, creating space away from his partner. The creature inched towards the man until it had him backed up in a corner, with nowhere to go.

CHAPTER 14

Chaos

Desperate, the tattooed man waited for Jup to cause a distraction to lure the creature away, but he didn't return the favor. With time running out, the man tucked his head towards his chest and ran headfirst at the monster, striking it in the chest and lifting it off the ground. Supported by only its rear legs, Jup's friend pummeled the creature's underbelly with his mighty fists. The punches temporarily stunned the beast as the barbs shredded the man's hands. Exhausted and unable to raise his arms, he fell to his knees and was crushed under the beast's weight before it turned its attention to Jup.

Brill watched the crowd's frenzy as they yelled and celebrated the man's death. The lack of empathy and their unquenchable thirst for bloodshed made him sick. Disgusted and uninterested in Jup's future, he slid from behind the panel and passed through the crowd as the cheers died. Before he left the building, the cheering erupted again. Brill wondered if Jup had time to use the elixir because the crowd's applause grew loud.

Dao re-entered the building and headed directly to the vat room where the blend was made. Snag watched his friend engage again with the guards while sharing mugs of the smelly offensive liquid. Impatient and concerned with Dao's behavior, Snag grabbed and tried to pull him away; Dao resisted. He was enjoying the camaraderie of the guards but, more importantly, the effects of the blend, which were slurring his words and disrupting his balance. Snag continued to try to convince Dao to leave while holding him upright when men came running towards them and began pouring out of the doors and into the night. Unaware of what was happening, Snag stood and watched the men leave until a young guard fell near them and yelled, "Get out; the creature is loose."

Snag started to panic as he continued to try to pull Dao away, but his friend was oblivious to what was happening around him and began to protest Snag's efforts strongly. More men passed them to the outside, except for the old man against the vat. When Dao saw the old man, he stumbled towards him and plopped beside him on the bench. The old man didn't move. He had seen this circus too many times. Dao started to slur something at him, and in no time, he was resting his head on the old man's shoulder, fast asleep.

As much as Snag didn't want to leave Dao, he knew he would have to if he wanted to survive. Just as he left the brew room, he ran into Brill.

"Snag, where's Dao?" he asked.

Snag told him what had happened to Dao. Brill ran to Dao and saw him fast asleep against the old man.

"Dao, let's go," Brill urged his friend while gripping his hand.

Dao didn't move. Brill dug into his pocket, removed his blue vial, and opened the cap. Snag opened Dao's mouth, and Brill placed a few drops on his tongue. Instantly, Dao awoke and sat up, trying to focus on Brill.

"You boys aren't from around here." the old man said to no one as a tear rolled down his cheek. "I was once like you. Go now while you can before the devils get hold of you. Avoid the creatures, but more importantly, avoid the men. Go and take care of each other."

The men turned away from the old man and helped Dao up to his feet.

"Dao, we have to go," he said again. Dao seemed to understand and slowly gained his balance finally. Snag supported him on one side with Brill on the other side as they exited the building. In the meantime, the commotion inside the building continued to grow. Dao inhaled the night air as the three emerged outside and ran to the perimeter, where they collapsed on the ground.

Time was running out. The crowd inside the arena was now in crisis mode, and Brill still had no information about the Snatchers. He needed to act quickly.

"Snag, take Dao back, and find the rest of the gang. Now!" he commanded.

Snag put his arm around Dao and led him away from the buildings and towards the meeting area, where they found Callow, Dwell, and Jaes with the pets. They removed their uniforms, packed them in their bags, and dressed. Snag filled the others in on what was happening inside the building and the ensuing chaos. Jaes told them they had seen the creature escape from the carcass pit and kill the guards. Dwell listened intently and then ran toward the buildings after his brother.

Confusion was everywhere; Brill walked unnoticed while half-listening to the guards' conversations. Most of the spectators had fled. Still hoping to hear something about the Snatchers, Brill roamed around while the guards protected the outside of the buildings. Dwell ran looking for Brill. As he neared the building, a nearby guard looked at him quizzically and asked, "Hey, are you one of those guys that blew up The Farm?"

Dwell slowed and walked towards the man, saying, "Do I look like a tree dweller, you dirty dog?"

The man stared into Dwell's face, took a good look, and said, "A what? Ya, I saw you there."

Dwell came closer and, in a friendly manner, wrapped his arm around the man's neck. Not utterly sure of Dwell's identity, the man relaxed enough to allow Dwell to quickly place a chokehold around his neck, cutting off his air and rendering him unconscious. Dwell held the man up, quickly walked past the parked trucks, and dumped the man behind the vehicles before continuing to search for Brill.

Brill continued to listen and eavesdrop on many conversations until he heard the word "Snatchers" coming from two elder guards sitting on the ground, quietly talking.

Brill knelt near them and listened.

"Where'd they go?" whispered the little man to the other.

Brill could see that both men had the same identification tag on their shirt, Sabre.

"They're headed west to their den, which is quite a distance away," he replied.

"But I thought they had left Province IV for good?" he asked.

"They did. They're not in Province IV anymore. Civantes set up his Lair in Province II, and I think the Snatchers may have a camp near Highpoint, the big rock. I think that's what they call it," he said.

"Have you ever gone there?" the smaller man asked.

"Hell no, they'd kill me as soon as they saw me. Only Snatchers are Snatchers. They don't like us. Hell, they don't even like each other. They are a nasty lot," he replied.

Brill slipped away and headed back toward the meeting place when he looked over and saw Dwell speaking to two guards. With his hat pulled down over his eyes, making him unrecognizable, he wandered over to the men and began acting like Dao on the blend, unruly and belligerent. He realized this behavior was acceptable in this society but was encouraged amongst the men. Dog walked in Brill's shadow towards the men.

"Hey, you guys got any more drink?" Brill said, slurring his words and pretending to stumble.

Dwell watched Brill but didn't acknowledge him as the two guards turned toward his older brother. He was angry that Brill thought he needed his help; he didn't. Brill approached the men while fumbling to remove the elixir from his pocket and held it to the light. The liquid shimmered bright blue. Both guards looked in awe at the bottle.

"What is that?" they asked.

"It's magic," Brill said as he staggered away towards the long brush. The guards looked at one another and decided to strike. They left Dwell and began to follow Brill. One followed closely behind him while the other lagged, making sure that no one else was following. Dwell took off running and got ahead of Brill in the long grass. Brill sang softly under his breath, just loud enough for the guards to hear his jovial tune. Both men smiled as they left the light and entered the shadows, sure that the drunken young man was an easy target.

CHAPTER 15

Escape

When Brill reached the long grass, he glanced to his left and saw Dwell waiting for the men. Brill veered left a couple of steps further, leading the guards toward the labyrinth of debris strewn about where they could be subdued without detection. He staggered past three large tanks, then stumbled to the ground allowing the men to get up close behind him. When they were inches behind him, Brill shot up and landed an uppercut on the man nearest to him, stunning him and sending him flying backward. Dwell came up from behind the trailing guard and jumped him just as he started to run toward Brill. Placed in a headlock, the man's oxygen soon ran out, and so did his energy. Dwell dragged him behind the tank and tied him up with wire. Stuffing a dirty rag in his mouth, he returned to his brother. The men were exchanging blows, back and forth. Dog must have heard the commotion and came to help. The guard had on high ankle boots that Dog latched itself to. The guard was bigger and stronger than Brill and was no longer stunned as he pummeled Brill with all his might. It took Brill's strength to avoid being overwhelmed by the man's power. Dwell watched, and for a split second, he wanted to see if his brother could escape this dilemma on his own because he was the golden child, 'Brill.' According to their father, Brill could do anything, fight, courier, support, and most of all, lead, while Dwell was just Dwell.

Dwell stopped hesitating as his instincts to protect his family overrode his selfish thoughts. Running towards the men, he dropkicked the man in the back of his legs, causing him to fall backward. Once he hit the ground,

Dwell was on him and quickly subdued him while his amazed big brother looked on in disbelief at his little brother's skills.

Brill stumbled to the ground while Dwell dragged the man and tied him up next to his friend between the tanks. He returned to his brother, who opened his blue elixir and placed the last remaining drops onto his tongue.

"Hey, where did you learn to fight like that?" Brill asked, looking up.

"Oh, my abilities surprise you. Well, there are many things about me that you don't know," Dwell said nonchalantly.

"No, really, Dwell. Who taught you?" he asked again.

Dwell just smiled and shook his head when a small explosion went off in the buildings causing a frantic commotion as the creature made its way outside. As the guards scrambled to escape, the beast looked left and right as if deciding whom to attack first. Once it locked on to a target, it would not be dissuaded. The creature set off on a rampage of destruction.

Brill told Dog to stay.

Brill and Dwell watched as panicked men scattered everywhere. They noticed that three buses were leaving the area at a high rate of speed. Brill looked at Dwell, and without a word, they ran towards the buses, through the crowd, and away from the beast until they were at the end of the driveway near the guard shack.

Brill pulled his hat down and approached the guard in the shack in a feigned drunken act.

"Hey, did you see the Snatchers leave?" he stammered.

The guard turned towards Brill and said, "Who wants to know?"

Brill stepped forward and rolled up his sleeve, revealing the black patch on his wrist, "We do," he pointed at himself and Dwell. "Our uncle told us to get a ride back with them, but we're unsure if they're still here."

Brill let out a huge burp and wiped his face with his sleeve before returning to the guard.

The guard ignored the two brothers, sat down on his stool, and continued eating his grotesque-looking lunch until Brill walked over and innocently asked, "Do you know our Uncle Civantes?"

The guard quickly stood up, approached Brill, and spoke without attitude. "Ya, ya, I saw the Snatchers leave, three buses of them not long ago. Five minutes ago, no four. Sorry, but I can't be positive about the time."

"You know where they're headed?" Dwell asked.

"Probably to the Lair over in Province II," he said nervously.

"How far is that from here?" Brill asked.

"Three day's drive or a seven-day hike to the trail along the Crystal Crossing," said the man. "Anything else?" he asked.

"Nope," Dwell said and started to walk away, then returned to the shack and added, "Oh ya, could you drive us over to the Lair?"

The guard did a double take at the brothers with such a look of shock that they burst out laughing and walked away.

Brill and Dwell walked back along the far side of the building into the trees and circled back towards the meeting place, where they met Dao, Callow, Jaes, Snag, and the pets. Brill told the others what had happened to Jup and his friend against the creature and that Jup had turned against them inside. Callow's face held an "I told you so" look that wasn't wasted on Brill. They were both happy that Brill had dealt with the big man and not Dwell, although Brill wasn't sure after watching his brother in action. Everyone else was relieved they wouldn't have to deal with the big man anymore except Snag, who was sad at losing his friend. Allegiances were a funny thing, Snag thought. One moment, you'll die to protect a friend; the next, that friend is trying to kill you. In this world, there were just too many battles to fight and not enough allies to choose from, and he was disappointed with his friend's choices.

"Dwell do you think you can still drive one of those trucks?" Brill asked.

"Sure, with Dao's help," he replied.

"Good, because we need to go right away," and he took off running with everyone in pursuit toward a bank of trucks parked at the yard's perimeter. Dao searched for a vehicle with keys, which he found above the visor in the third vehicle.

Dwell, and Dao jumped in the front cab while the rest of the group jumped into the truck bed, pulled the stiff tarp around them, and shut the tailgate.

Dwell looked at the truck's instrument panel and then turned the key; the engine sputtered but didn't catch. He tried again, but nothing. Dao told him to wait before he tried again, so they paused and watched the bedlam in front of their vehicle. Seconds later, two guards came running straight at them.

"Turn the key, and everyone stay down in the back," Dao yelled.

Dwell quickly turned the key and waited for the engine to roar. It didn't.

"Do it again," he screamed as the men came closer and reached for their guns.

Dwell turned the key again and grabbed the steering wheel tightly with his other hand. Nothing happened. The first bullet ripped through the windshield and out of the cab, narrowly missing their heads as the men approached.

"Remember the brake, the other pedal. You must put your foot on the brake when you start it."

In his panic, Dwell stepped on the brake, and Dao punched Dwell's leg, causing it to slam down on the gas pedal as the engine fired up. Dwell pulled down on the gear shift handle and slammed on the gas, blasting the vehicle out of its parking space at the two men. The truck struck them both, catapulting them through the air and back to the ground as Dwell swerved and fishtailed his way out of the lot and onto the road. Minutes later, they were miles away from the arena and the madness. Dao relaxed, tilted his head against the back window, and closed his eyes. Dwell settled into a steady speed heading enroute to Province II. With all the excitement, no one noticed that Jaes wasn't with them.

CHAPTER 16

Sneaking with the Snatchers

Dwell, and Dao took turns driving throughout the night. No one spoke as everyone was exhausted, even the pets. They stopped once for Dwell to cover the truck's front headlights with dirt to conceal their location in the pitch-black night. In the back, the others slept for hours until Brill banged on the cab window urging the boys to pull over. Before Dao got out, he glanced at the fuel gauge on E, showing they would soon be out of fuel. Everyone got out to stretch their legs and get some fresh air as the sun rose on the horizon. Then it was time for breakfast. The couriers shared the packed meals with Snag while they sat on the side of the road. Brill finished and unfolded the map on the front of the truck for the others to see where they were in relationship to their target, Crystal Crossing. He packed up the map, for they still had a long journey ahead of them. Before they got back in the truck, Dao told Brill that they were almost out of gas, and it was urgent that they find fuel as soon as possible, or they would be exposed and stranded on the road.

Before Callow jumped in the back, she looked around and said, "Hey, where's Jaes?"

Everyone looked around at one another, amazed that no one had noticed that he was missing until now. Everyone was shocked that another friend had been lost.

Snag broke the tension. "Let's stop at the next farm we come to see. They might have gas," he said.

Soon they were back on the road with Dao as the driver. He pulled over at the next massive farm with many buildings and machinery. He was confident that this farm would have its own fuel source.

They parked amongst the other trucks on the property to conceal their vehicle. Everyone stayed aboard except Dwell, who was to look for gas. He shut the passenger door and was walking away when he heard an approaching engine. Peering around the back of the truck, he saw a large yellow bus moving up the driveway. Quickly he jumped into the back with the others and closed the tarp. The bus pulled up alongside a small building, indicating to the couriers that the driver was familiar with the property.

The bus door opened, and a small man with a large head wearing an oversized smock walked off the bus and moved towards the entrance of the small building. He twisted the lock, removed it, opened the door, and stepped inside. Seconds later, he came back out carrying a hose which he continued to pull until it reached the back of the bus. While he was busy with the hose, another man with a much larger head got off the bus, walked toward the more petite man, and removed the gas cap. The smaller man inserted the hose into the bus tank and held it there while his ghastly-looking face scowled at the other man.

"You think the gas will pump itself?" he asked sarcastically. "Get your ass over there and pump, you mindless blockhead!"

Immediately, the other man lumbered into the small building where the tank was housed and began to hand pump sending fuel through the hose and into the bus while the littler man scratched himself. He started at his ears and down his buttocks, rubbing everywhere. Dao watched the men from the side view mirrors and wondered if the man had bugs on his body. Through the bus windows, he could see rows of empty seats and the heads of a few men. About a third of the seats were occupied. He tapped on the window that divided the cab from the truck bed, and within seconds, Brill climbed through the window.

"What's up?" he asked.

"We've got company. What do we do now?" Dao said as he nodded towards the rear-view mirrors.

"I know, I heard them pull up," Brill said. He had seen the two men and the shadows of the other men on the bus from the back. Brill turned and looked directly into Dao's eyes and said, "We need to get on that bus."

"What! Are you crazy?" Dao whispered.

"No, I'm not Dao," said Brill, "The only way we are going to find out where they are going is to join them."

"You're out of your mind. And how do you plan to do this?" Dao asked with dripping sarcasm in his voice.

"We're going to climb into the back of the bus," Brill said.

"Really? Just like that. And how are we going to do that?" Dao asked with even more sarcasm than before.

Brill then explained his plan to Dao.

Brill used Morse code on the cab window to inform the group in the back what he and Dao planned to do.

Dao snuck out of the truck and sprinted to the big shed, followed by Brill.

The shed was full of machinery, farm tools, and supplies, just what they needed. They checked the shelves, workbenches, and toolboxes behind and around the machinery and at the shed's back wall, which was piled with debris. Dao found his needed supplies behind a stack of rusting metal cans and grabbed them. He stacked the six and a half bags of unused fertilizer in a nearby wheelbarrow. Brill searched for liquids he needed along the far wall. Mama Kilee had informed the boys to use the tools on the farms to survive. He opened every container, searching for a specific liquid by smelling the contents. He checked can after can, lifting them and opening the lids without luck until he jerked on a broken handle, sending him backward. He opened the lid and smelt the contents; the smell was strong and pungent; success. He called over Dao. Brill pointed at the can and said, "I think I found it."

"Me too," he said as he bent over and smelt the liquid, "Yup, that's it; Mama said we wouldn't like the smell. Can you carry it over there to the wagon?" he asked Brill.

Dao lifted the handles on the wheelbarrow and parked it next to the flatbed wagon. He loaded the bags in a tower formation on top of the wagon. The open half-filled bag was placed in the middle of the pile and was filled with diesel fuel until it overflowed all over the other bags and onto the floor, trailing to the door. He pulled the rope out of his pocket and told Brill to return to the truck and tell the others to stay put no matter what happened. Brill took off as Dao laid the rope from the wagon to the door in the fuel and poured the rest on top. He threw the empty container onto the wagon, returned, and slightly opened the door. Standing next to the door, Dao took a pack of matches out of his pocket that he found in the truck. With one foot outside, he struck the match, tossed it in the liquid near the door, and ran. The flame raced along the rope, engulfing the fuel and returning to the wagon.

With the bus fully gassed up, the two men stood between the bus and the barn, talking to other men who had gotten off the bus to stretch their legs. They were in a circle laughing and listening intently to the itchy little man speaking quite excitedly while his head bobbed and his hands waved. Dao ran and slid under the frame of a heavy dump truck shielding their vehicle from the shed. He couldn't stop laughing when he saw all the big heads bobbing back and forth in unison with the itchy man. It was the strangest thing Dao had ever seen. As he settled himself under the frame, the flame reached the fertilizer causing a large explosion that blew out the side of the building. Sporadic blasts ensued until all the flammable liquid, and explosive material in the shed had blown.

CHAPTER 17

Bus Ride

The shock wave from the blast rattled the vehicles causing them to rock. When the Snatchers thought the explosions were over, they headed toward the barn to investigate. More explosions erupted, forcing them to run back towards the bus. Dao found the scene hilarious as he watched them from under the truck. The explosions continued until every item in the shed that could explode did.

When relative quiet had returned, and only the sound of the burning building remained, Dao crawled to the back of the truck and peered out. Men were lying on the ground; some were groaning, and others weren't moving. Some struggled, staggered, fell again, and remained there. Using the bus to brace themselves, a few gained their footing and steadied themselves. Dao crawled to their truck and tapped a Morse code message on the window. Brill, Snag, and Dwell heard the tapping, but only Brill left the back and crept into the cab when Dao entered and closed his truck door.

"What do we do now?" Dao asked.

"We get in that bus?" Brill said.

"What do you mean, we get in that bus? We can follow them from a distance," Dao said.

"And how are they not going to see us? If we follow them on the deserted roads, our truck will stick out like a sore thumb," said Brill. "We need to arrive there alive, and we can use our guard uniforms until we figure out our next plan. There are so many dead and injured that they couldn't possibly know which guards survived the incident at the arena. It's our only chance. We've got to sneak onto that bus without being detected, and Dwell will follow us but at a greater distance because we'll keep in contact by patch. Do you have your patch with you?" he asked.

Dao lifted his sleeve, revealing the black patch on his wrist. It was a communication device with GPS location capabilities used by the compound guards. Dao removed his patch and gave it to Brill. He thought Brill's plan was too risky and shook his head when they joined the others in the truck bed. Brill finished outlining his plan to the team and handed Dao's black patch to Dwell with clear instructions on how to use it. He also stressed that Dwell was not to touch the patch at any time during any transmission unless it was an emergency because touching the patch during any message exposed their location to everyone with a patch. That everyone included Mullins.

Dwell confirmed to Brill that he understood the seriousness of the patch and put it on. Instantly, he felt the band squeeze onto his arm. Dao and Brill busied themselves and emptied their packs, choosing only the items that would fit their pockets; they had to travel light. Brill took his red elixir because he was out of the blue. Dao took both of his. They put small balls, the map, Dr. Swallow's and Dr. Hamm's letters, some herbs, and a roll-on bottle filled with a sticky green liquid Brill was anxious to use into their pockets and left the truck. They changed into the guard uniforms and set off. A Snatcher was on the ground near the back of the bus, but he wasn't moving, so while Brill kept an eye out for trouble, Dao gently lifted the handle. The latch quietly released, and he pulled the door towards him and crawled inside. Brill and Dog followed. At the back of the bus, they climbed onto the last set of seats opposite one another. Dao poked his head above the seats and saw a few men seated up front behind the driver's seat and a few standings in the aisle helping the injured sit.

"That's it. There's no one else," the itchy Snatcher yelled. He was pretty disheveled and hunched over as he climbed the stairs, sat in the driver's seat, and closed the door.

"We are getting the hell out of here now," he yelled, turning the key and gunning the engine.

The bus jerked forward, causing two standing men to fall onto the floor, but the driver didn't slow down. He floored the gas pedal gunning the engine, and did a quick U-turn, causing the men in the left seats to slide onto the floor and those standing to crash into the bus wall. Dao braced himself and didn't move, but Brill pinned Dog against the wall. It didn't make a sound, but it did nip Brill in the butt, causing him to move away quickly. The bus flew out of the driveway and onto the road spewing gravel. Brill and Dao hid in the back, tucked behind the backs of the seats, while Dog sat at attention beside Brill. They drove for hours, into the dawn and through the morning. The bus's rear door had two windows, one above the latch and one below. The boys stared out the emergency door's bottom window and watched the flat ground morph into mountainous and rocky terrain. Brill tried to follow the route on his map, but he wasn't sure they were headed in the right direction. His only certainty was that he had no idea where he was going.

"Stay way back, so the driver won't see us," Snag recommended to Dwell as they drove about two miles behind the bus. At times, there was so little traffic on the long flat stretches that Dwell had to pull right off the road so that the driver wouldn't see them in his rear-view mirrors' miles away. At night it was easier to follow but more challenging to see with the blacked-out headlights severely limiting their vision. After fueling up at another abandoned farm, Dwell gave Snag a quick driving lesson. No sooner had Dwell closed his eyes did Snag take out a row of unused rural mailboxes. Before his first hour of instruction was over, he slid the truck into a shallow ditch, curtailing their progress. The three of them struggled but pushed the vehicle back onto the road with Dwell at the helm and Callow at his side. Snag was relegated to the back for some well-earned rest and isolation.

Callow watched Dwell concentrate on his driving. He didn't talk or look out of the side windows; he just faced forward and drove. Callow watched him for about ten minutes before she broke the silence.

"What were you reading back there, Dwell?"

"Nothing."

"Dwell, I saw you reading that same book at the overhang and again at the waterfall."

"It's nothing."

"Don't give me that, Dwell," she said. "That book consumed you. We could have been on fire, and you wouldn't have noticed us. I saw you. Your mind seems to be somewhere else when you're reading that book. Nothing else matters but what is in that book! What is it?"

Dwell looked at her suspiciously, wondering why she was so interested. "It's just a book."

"Well, if it's just a book, can I see it?" she asked.

"No, it's none of your business Callow and don't go making it your business," he snapped.

"Everything we do as a group on this mission is our business," she said. "Why are you being so secretive about it?"

Finally, he said. "Damn, why can't you leave me alone, okay? Besides, I found it."

"Where?" she asked.

"I...." he had just started to answer her when he suddenly slammed on the brakes, causing Callow to bump her chin on the dash.

"Dwell, what the heck...," Callow stammered.

"Look," was all he said.

Callow looked out the windshield, and, in the distance, she could see another bus meet up with the first bus and was now following behind it.

They were miles behind the buses and wondered if Brill and Dao had also seen the second bus.

Brill watched as the second bus pulled in behind them.

"Dao, look," Brill whispered.

Dao turned, peeked through the bottom window, and saw the bus gaining on them. The driver accelerated and was now following directly behind them.

"We need to do something to stop that bus," Dao said.

"I don't know how we can stop it. Whoa, wait a minute," Brill said as he dug into his pocket and pulled out a handful of the little yellow balls.

"Do you know what these do?" he asked Dao.

"No, I don't," he replied curtly.

"Then just watch," he said as he smiled, dropped to the floor, and onto Dao's side of the bus, behind the driver. Slowly he cracked open the door and waited; no alarm sounded. He squeezed one of the balls between his thumb and forefinger until he could feel his fingers touch and threw it at the hood of the bus. His aim was true; it hit the windshield, rolled down the glass between the window and the hood, and stopped. The driver didn't notice the door opening or the ball being thrown at his bus and nonchalantly kept driving.

CHAPTER 18

Separation

Within minutes, a growing plume of smoke engulfed the front of the bus, making it hard for the driver to see. Unfortunately for the driver, the large vehicle's forward momentum continued. His vision inside the growing cloud was entirely obscured, causing the bus to sway from side to side as the driver struggled to keep control. Within seconds the wobble turned violent, whipping the bus all over the road. Unable to correct the situation, the driver left his seat. When he released the steering wheel, the front wheels violently jolted to the left, launching the bus into the air and then onto its side. It rolled multiple times before coming to a stop. Brill and Dao watched through the small bus window as the yellow vehicle slammed into the ground and faded from their view. Brill felt for the yellow balls in his pocket and was amazed at the effect of such a small item. Mama told Brill to use the balls when they needed to hide, but she didn't precisely explain what the balls could or would do, which was produce a very thick smokescreen.

Callow and Dwell watched as the bus flew in the air and rolled multiple times, causing it to rest in the middle of the road blocking their path. When they reached the scene, Dwell pulled the truck over and jumped out to investigate. There were bodies thrown far from the bus and others pinned under it. Snag stayed with Callow in the vehicle. Dwell searched for survivors, but there weren't any. He climbed onto the bus's hood, forced the folding doors open, and went inside. The driver was slumped over the back of his seat. There were no other survivors. Everyone but the driver was ejected. Returning to the front of the bus, he took the driver's portable radio and a map lying on the stairs. He was about to jump out of the folding doors when he saw the hips swaying on a tiny hula dancer attached to the dash. He grabbed her and left.

"Well, what did you find?" Snag asked.

"Not much; no one survived the crash except for her," he said as he held up the tiny hula dancer. He wiggled the plastic doll so that they could see her hips sway.

"Awesome," exclaimed Snag while Callow rolled her eyes and Cat got excited.

"I also found these," Dwell said as he presented the radio and the map for the others to see.

"With the road blocked, I don't think we should try our luck and drive through those ditches. We'll never get out if we get stuck. We need to find another route if we plan to see Brill and Dao again," Callow said. Dwell opened the map on the hood of the truck.

"Look here. There's a parallel road we can take. The road we're on is a major highway, so we'll detour here and catch up to them about ten miles down the road," Snag said while tracing his finger along the map lines.

"Okay, let's do it," Dwell said as he refolded the map as the bus exploded.

Mullins opened the sack and pulled out a water bottle and a cup that stunk of the blend. He found a few pieces of soft, bright yellow unleavened bread in a hidden side pocket. He had never seen that type of bread before. Most breads were hard, had a brownish-grey appearance, and smelt and tasted like dirty socks. He took a bite. It was sweet with a buttery texture that melted in his mouth; it was delicious. Turning to the guard, he asked, "Where did you find the bag?"

"When I was walking through the yard this morning, one of the injured guards was lying on the ground with this on his chest. I had never seen a bag like this, so I asked him where he got it, and he said he found it at our compound last week. I asked him where specifically, and he said in the wheat area."

"Did he get it from someone, or did he find it?" Mullins asked.

"He said that he found it in an empty bin," the guard continued.

Mullins then waved his hand at the guard dismissing him.

He started to piece together all the events that had recently happened. The explosions at The Farm, the dead guards at the compound, the escaped fighters, the now quiet and ever rebellious Dr. Swallow, the unknown hidden person in the lab, and the two young men who had impersonated the compound guards and then escaped. He thought all these events must be related but wondered who was behind it all. They were not locals; he was sure of that. Whoever they were, they were wreaking havoc on his life. Was it the tree dwellers that Civantes had spoken about at their last encounter?

He remembered the incredibly soft and unblemished skin of the impersonating guard. Civantes had said that the tree dwellers were the only known humans still healthy and untouched by the ever-present toxins. Civantes were sure they were the key to saving and restoring the population's health. Maybe not the whole population, but certainly, himself, he thought. Civantes said that his team had conducted experiments on a captured tree dweller, and he used the gained research to cure himself of the sickness. Mullins thought that couldn't be because he was desperate at their last meeting to find these people. It couldn't be true. Civantes' greyish skin tone was evidence that he was still sick. If he had captured a so-called healthy tree dweller, he would have paraded his find in front of everyone because he was such a boastful bastard. The evidence seemed to support Civantes' theory about the tree dwellers; if they were real, he needed to find them before his enemy did. Finding healthy human specimens would make him the most influential person in all the provinces.

First, he had to find out who blew up his building. Walking around the yards were scores of dead and dismembered men. In his frustration and anger, Mullins kicked one or two corpses as he went. As he got closer to the building, he could see many dead men under or near a massive dead white creature slumped on the ground. From the immense destruction done to the creature's head, it was clear the men had used the mutant's head for target practice; what was unknown was whether the onslaught killed the beast or was done for fun after it died. Mullins instinctively felt for his guns to calm himself.

He entered the building, which was deserted, and followed the corridor to the small room where the remnants of a battle littered the room. He walked out onto the arena floor, which no longer had a roof, and looked at all the empty seats. Closing his eyes, he inhaled the lingering wretched scents from the fights, filling his lungs. Opening his eyes, he took a panoramic view of the stadium. It was still silent, which ignited his anger. He didn't stay long and walked to the staging area. There was nothing to see here except the empty and destroyed cages that littered his path. Kicking them aside, he marched outside when he heard a faint cough. Removing his gun from his holster, he listened. Someone was trying desperately to muffle their cough. Cautiously, he made his way along the walls, searching for movement. Moving from room to room, he listened in the deathly quiet building. He crept along, searching for the sound that would betray his prey.

Mullins stepped into the blending room just as the muffled cough abruptly stopped. So did the Captain. He held his breath and waited; it wasn't long before his patience was rewarded. Not far off, a subtle exhalation of air could just barely be heard. Raising his gun, Mullins quietly approached the right side of the large metal cauldron. Unsure of what might be on the other side - man or beast, he slowly crept forward. Beads of perspiration formed on his forehead and trickled down and off his nose as the grip on his gun tightened and his anticipation grew. Face-to-face combat was Mullins' preferred type of confrontation, but that didn't stop him from wondering where his Rooks were. The Captain tried to shake off his anxiety as he gripped his gun.

The explosion crushed the vat, pushing it against the wall and heavily damaging it. Mullins bent low as he rounded the side to see a huge man sitting on the floor, pinned between the large metal pot and the wall. He could tell by the marks on the floor and the cauldron that the man had desperately tried to free himself. He was still trying when he saw the Captain.

"Who are you?" Mullins yelled at the man, pointing his gun squarely at his forehead.

CHAPTER 19

Unlikely Allies

Jup recognized the Captain immediately, and though he was exhausted, he tried again to stand but could not.

Jup didn't answer.

"If you don't answer, I'm going to blow your head clear off your shoulders," Mullins said.

"I'm a fighter, Sir," he said in a deep baritone voice.

"What kind of fighter hides behind a blend pot?" mocked Mullins.

Jup thought about how much he hated the man, but if he wanted to survive this encounter, he had better dangle a carrot for Mullins to let him live.

"I wasn't hiding. The creature got out and went on a rampage, attacking everyone, including myself," Jup said.

Mullins looked skeptically at the man pinned against the wall but showed no other signs of injury from an attack.

"I was thrown back here when the building exploded," he said.

"Were you scheduled to fight because I don't recognize you? Are you one of Civantes' men?" Mullins asked.

Jup wasn't sure what to tell him. If he said to him that he was one of Civantes' men, he would be shot right away, so he decided to tell the truth, sort of.

"I was with the tree dwellers," he said.

The Captain's eyes became large and interested. He moved closer to Jup and put his gun back into the holster. With all his might, he pushed his shoulder against the cauldron, scraping the metal across the floor.

Stretching a hand to Jup, the Captain helped him from behind the vat. The big man was hesitant to take the Captain's hand, but he knew that if he didn't, he would die here in the blending room. Jup's massive hand engulfed Mullins, and together they pulled his enormous body out from behind the vat and up to his full height. The big man limped forward, and Mullins could see the injury causing his limp. His right calf was torn and hanging from his leg, with four large lacerations across his upper right thigh. Jup cleared the vat and leaned up against a nearby wall, dug into his pocket, pulled out the small glass bottle with the blue liquid, and with shaking hands, he removed the lid and poured the remaining liquid into his mouth. Instantly, barbs were expelled through his skin as the tissues began to repair themselves. Mullins watched in astonishment.

"What is that?" he asked.

"I don't know, but they all have it," he said.

"Who are 'they'?" Mullins asked.

"The tree dwellers," he said.

"You know them?" he asked incredulously.

"Yes, and I know where you can find them," he said, smirking.

Mullins told Jup to follow him, and over his shoulder, he said, "We're going to become excellent friends, you and I."

A wave of dread spread over Jup's large body; he had just made a deal with the devil.

Brill and Dao watched the burning bus, and their friends fade from view.

"Whoa, did you see that bus explode?" the driver said to no one as the men aboard quickly turned around to see what the driver was talking about. Black smoke was still billowing and rising in the distance.

Dao looked across the aisle to Brill and mouthed, "We're on our own."

Brill sadly acknowledged Dao's assessment with a nod as the bus continued moving forward.

Dwell pulled out both maps and compared the routes. They were similar. He pointed out to the others their current location relative to where they were heading; they still had a way to go. The bus map had numerous sites that were circled. Snag and Callow stood back and watched Dwell as he immersed himself in the maps, deciphering the data and looking for an alternate route to get them back on track and as close to Brill and Dao as quickly as possible.

Finally, he looked up from the maps and said, "Brill and Dao are on their own now, and so are we."

Callow noticed the sudden confidence in Dwell's voice and his mannerisms as he quickly folded up the maps with authority. With Brill out of the picture, he assumed the leadership amongst their group and took charge of their situation. When he spoke to Callow and Snag, he looked directly into their eyes for acknowledgment and understanding—the sign of a good leader.

Snag turned to Callow and asked, "Do you think we should follow them or return to your home and wait for them there?"

"Jaes, what do you think?" Dwell asked.

The team caught Dwell's error as soon as he said it. As did Dwell.

No one answered.

"There's no turning back now. Brill and Dao need us as much as we need them. We need to find each other," Callow said while Dwell nodded in agreement. "Let's take an inventory of our supplies."

They opened their packs and dumped their contents for all to see. There were elixirs, blue and red, one small pouch of yellow balls that no one was familiar with, some herbs, two small clear containers with different colored lids, water bottles, and food.

Each also had a solar panel, battery, and white cloth roll. Callow's patch fell out, as did Dwell's book, which lay on top of his supplies. Callow stared at the books' cover, trying to memorize the markings while Snag grabbed the yellow balls to inspect them. Dwell attempted to snatch the balls from Snag, but he was too fast and turned away from the others. Dwell followed Snag while Callow slowly opened the book cover. The name 'Ilse Viron' was printed on the first page, and below it was the word – Master.

Callow reached down to flip the next page when Dwell returned, snatched the book from the pile, and put it into his pocket.

"Dwell, where did you get that book from?" she asked him as they gathered their items and repacked their bags.

"Let it go, Callow," he said as he glared at her. "We need to go, so let's get moving," he said as he got back into the truck and slammed the door. Both Callow, Cat, and Snag followed suit and joined him inside.

"Dwell, if that book can help us, you had better share it with all of us," she whispered in his ear.

He ignored her, started the truck's engine, whipped the vehicle around in a U-turn, and headed down the road.

* * *

For hours, Brill, Dog, and Dao lay quiet until the bus wheels began to slow, and it turned down a long dark tree-covered driveway. Sparse leaves and thick branches lined each side of the driveway and intertwined high above the bus, turning the roadway into a tunnel. The day's last sunlight could not penetrate the thick brush surrounding them. Dao moved closer to Brill and whispered, "I'm going to go up front to see if I can find out where we are."

Brill nodded, and so did Dog, cradled in Brill's arms. Dao knelt on the floor and crept forward under the seats to the front of the bus. He stayed a bench back from the first set of legs that he encountered, which was four seats from the driver, when he heard.

"He's here at the Market, so you better not piss him off," the driver said.

"Won't," came a quieter response.

"Well, you had all better shut your mouths and stay quiet; I'll talk. This is our last stop before we head home," the driver said.

"How long will we be here?" asked someone else.

"Only long enough to load," came the driver's response.

CHAPTER 20

The Sales Ring

The bus pulled into an empty spot and parked between another bus and a menagerie of vehicles. The driver and the men who could walk quickly got off the bus. The Snatchers who were too injured to move stayed quiet and waited. Dao was creeping his way to the back of the bus when the back door flew open. Brill was to the right of the open door, and he quickly hit the floor with Dog and hid in the shadows under the seat. Two big men climbed the bus and headed directly for the injured men in the front. The first man grabbed one of the wounded men by his collar, lifted him up and out of his seat, and carried him toward the back of the bus. The other man did the same to the other injured man, and when they got to the back door, they threw the injured onto a cart which was then wheeled away by two people whose faces seemed to be falling off. The men jumped from the bus, slammed the door, and walked away. Dao quickly scrambled towards Brill.

"Where are we?" he asked Dao.

"The Market," was all he said.

Brill and Dao waited until everyone had entered the only building on the grounds or disappeared into the woods before moving to the front of the bus. The bus driver had left the front door partially open, so they slowly descended the stairs with Dog in the lead. He reached the bottom step, ran out of the bus towards the doors of the building, and hid behind the large rain barrels on each side of the entryway. They followed Dog and joined it behind the barrels just as two tall men with large heads approached the far corner of the building toward them and entered the doors, disappearing into the building. Dao caught the door before it closed, and the three followed them into the unknown.

It was very dark inside the building. Too dark for the young men to navigate, so Brill called Dog and told him to lead. The creature chirped, sat on his hind legs and tail, perked up his disfigured ears, and listened. It didn't take it long to pick up a scent and a sound. Soon they were moving again, staying very tight against the dark walls. Dao stumbled once but caught himself from falling, and Brill hit his head on something sticking out of the wall, which drew blood. Dog smelled the blood, shook his head to fight the urge to attack, and continued forward.

They walked in the dark, following the twisting and turning walls until they arrived next to a high wall that encircled the space before them. They walked through this area until they happened upon a steep stairwell that trailed downward. Dog took the lead, and the boys followed, hoping to avoid meeting anyone or anything on the narrow stairs before them. While descending, they could feel deep, long, random grooves cut into the walls lining the stairs. When the stairs ended, Dog continued to the left, following the curving walls until they saw the glow of light up ahead. Hugging the wall, they made their way forward without meeting anyone in the wide corridor.

Dao went to the doorway where the only light appeared and peeked around the corner to see what was so important that it deserved light. Straining his neck, he caught sight of an unspeakable horror that caused him to suck in his breath. In front of him on a raised circular platform were groups of terrified children bound with their arms behind their backs. There were five groupings, each composed of five children. In the middle of the groupings was a grotesque man with a colossal head bent over his cane. He was drooling and yelling something that Dao couldn't make out.

Surrounding the platform were chairs arranged in a circle before the children. Dao counted eight oversized high-backed chairs, all of which were occupied. The lighting was too dim to reveal the occupants; only their shadows revealed their attendance. Each chair had a candle on a small table to the right of the chair. Dao crept closer, enthralled and horrified at the scene before him. The only people present were those in the eight chairs, the children, and the man talking in the middle of the ring. Dao hid behind a high-back chair listening to the ring man speak.

Initially, he couldn't make out what the man was saying until he forced himself to focus on him and tune out everything else around him.

"Well, gentlemen, and I use that term loosely, welcome to sale day. We have five bands of 5 in Lot 30. Let's start the bidding," he bellowed, wiping the excessive drool from his chin with the back of his hand. Then he flung his hand quickly, flinging his drool onto those closest to him. No one was exempt from his grotesque display as his saliva landed on some children and those seated around the ring.

"Twenty pieces for one band," one voice said.

"Twenty-five,' said another.

The man in the center egged on the buyers, "Come on boys, you can't build an army out of the air, bid on these bands, let's go," he yelled.

Some of the younger children cried, but the older ones in their groups quickly comforted and quieted them, so they didn't draw attention from the ringmaster's cane. Soon the room was silent again except for the auctioneer.

"Do I hear thirty for one band? Come on, boys," he barked.

There were no further bids, just silence. The ringmaster stretched his massive head over the platform, staring at each seat, trying to coax another offer out of the seated occupants. Still, his glassy stare and persistence were in vain, for no other bids were forthcoming.

"All right then, one band for twenty-five, it is. Pay the man and pick your chicks. You've got five minutes," bellowed the ringmaster.

Someone from the middle chair stood and walked onto the platform where the children huddled. Someone screamed as the mutant man approached the youngsters, but the bid winner was undaunted. He'd heard it all before and continued his inspection. He stood in the middle of the stage amongst the lots, quickly reviewing his options. He spent a little more time viewing Lot Two, which was made up entirely of boys.

"Bring me twenty-five, now," he said into his patch, then to the ringmaster, "I'll take Band Two," then shuffled to his seat. Dao caught a glimpse of the bidder when he turned under the stage lights. His lower body was grossly overweight, his pale skin seemed to glow, and his beard was long and unruly like his hair. Dao thought the man looked frightening; he must have been a living nightmare to the children.

Taking his seat, he waited for his muscle to appear, and he did from behind the stage with twenty-five guns in his arms. The shirtless man covered in scars dropped twenty-five guns into a cage at the side of the stage, then stepped on stage, untied Band Two, and led them into the shadows. Dao started to panic and returned to Brill.

"Dao, what's going on over there?" Brill asked.

"We are in hell, Brill. These monsters are trading in children. Let's go. We need to follow the kids," then he left.

CHAPTER 21

More Children

Brill didn't have time to agree and took off after Dao. Hugging the back wall directly behind the middle chair, they saw the shirtless man holding a flashlight and leading the children through a large open doorway behind the stage. In his other hand, he was holding one end of a rope; the other end was tied around the waist of the youngest child, whom he was dragging while the rest held hands and followed.

Dao, Brill, and Dog went to that doorway just as the last child walked through, leaving behind the sales ring and entering the blackened corridor.

They trailed quietly at a distance, following the cries of the children and the feel of the walls. Minutes later, they ascended upward and continued until the shirtless man stopped and banged on the large wooden door at the end of the corridor. It opened to the forest.

Dusk had arrived, pushing out the diminishing sunlight as darkness came early and surrounded everyone and everything. The children were led towards an old green pickup truck with a rusting camper top on the back. It was parked in the makeshift parking lot.

"Up," the shirtless man directed as he removed the lock, opened the door and pulled down the portable steps. Slowly and without hesitation, the children stepped up and into the camper. When the last boy cleared the door, the man flipped up the folded step, closed and put the lock back on the door without locking it, and re-entered the building.

Brill turned to Dao, "They must be buying more because he didn't lock it. Come, we must get them out of there before he returns."

"Okay," Dao replied, "What do we do with them when we get them out?"

"We'll hide them on the bus," came Brill's reply.

"What, we are just going to get in that truck, introduce ourselves and tell the children to come with us?" Dao asked with much sarcasm.

"No, we hide them in the back of the bus, just like we did on the ride here," Brill responded.

"And then what do we do with them after that?" Dao asked.

"I haven't thought that far ahead," Brill answered, "but we will deal with that later. Now let's go." He ran to the back of the camper with Dao and Dog in pursuit, removed the lock from the door, and stepped inside. He couldn't see. The darkness reminded him of the compound bin when he found the fighters. Only small shafts of light pierced through the holes in the broken windows. He ran his hand along the windows feeling for a latch until his finger caught a panel. He slid it sideways, casting a faint light throughout the truck bed. Dao and Dog remained outside. The light caused the children to let out a collective sigh. Brill held up his hand and began to speak,

"Please don't be frightened. I'm not here to hurt you but to help. My friend, Dao is outside, and I am going to get you out of here and take you to a safe place away from these monsters," he said as he pointed toward the building.

No one said a word or moved a muscle. Brill bent down to address the children huddled together in the far corner of the camper. Still, no one spoke.

"I saw what those bad people did in there. I am so sorry. Would you like to go someplace safe, away from them?" Brill asked.

A young husky boy, about 12 years old, with a blunt bowl haircut, stepped ten inches from Brill's face and asked, "Just who the hell are you?"

The 'protector' of this lot of boys was speaking so close to Brill that he could feel the boy's breath on his face. Brill held his position and said, "I'm Brill. My friends and I are trying to find the Snatchers. We're trying to stop them from getting to our families, but we also want to stop them from snatching you and hurting yours."

Brill locked eyes with the young man, who didn't move though the other children moved up behind him. The young man felt a small hand in his and smiled, "Okay, what are we waiting for? Let's go." Brill put his hand on the young man's shoulder and squeezed it.

"Okay, but I need all of you to listen. We have a bus on the other side of the building that my friend will sneak all of you onto. But you must promise to be quiet and do whatever he says." The children all nodded in agreement.

A youngster who had been tied with the rope peered around the right side of the husky boy and nestled his head under the boy's arm, looked up at Brill with his beautiful blue eyes, and in his tiny voice, said, "Are you my Daddy because my Daddy said that he would come back and take care of me."

Brill held out his arms for the little boy, who untangled himself from his big friend and ran to Brill, who held him tight.

"No, little buddy. Unfortunately, I am not your Daddy, but I am going to do everything your Daddy would do to keep you and the others safe," he said as he slowly cracked the camper door.

"Dao here is my friend, and I want you to do everything he says. I'm going back inside to help the others. I'll be back soon," he released the little boy from his arms and knocked on the door; it opened. Dao directed the children into the forest as Brill headed back inside.

At the bus, the five boys climbed aboard and laid down quietly on the floor. Five worried pairs of eyes stared at Dog, which Dao saw when he opened the door to leave.

"Don't worry. I'll be back. This here is Dog. He's not a dog. We're not sure what he is, so we call him Dog. He likes it. He's our buddy and will care for you while we're gone. He won't let anybody hurt you. I'm going back to help Brill get the other children. Remember, don't leave the bus and no noise," he said to the five silent faces. Dao waited for some sign of recognition. Finally, the older children nodded, and the little ones held their fingers to their lips. Dao smiled and was gone.

Three lots remained at the sales ring; one was currently accepting bids. The remaining groups comprised boys and girls; some seemed as young as four. The fourth group had already been paid for and was leaving the stage. Brill followed the Snatcher and the children from behind. They walked out of the building and over to a two-wheeled covered wagon attached to a homemade tractor. The three boys and two girls silently waited for the mutant to remove the wooden gate. He lifted them into the wagon, then replaced and secured the gate. Still, the children had yet to make a sound.

When the guard re-entered the building, Brill removed the gate and told the children what they planned to do. Still silent, Dao took the children to the bus and gave them the exact instructions as the first group, and went back to find Brill. The next two lots were also moved into the bus; only one remained. Brill returned to the ring by himself for the last group. Dao remained near the bus, tapping on the side to remind the children to stay calm and quiet. He reminded himself to do the same.

The building's front doors flew open, and an unfamiliar Snatcher walked out, leaned against the building, and pulled a bag out of his pocket. He unwrapped the bag, placed his large nose inside, closed his eyes, and inhaled several times. Satisfied, he dug into the bag, pulling out a fistful of brown hairlike material that he popped into his mouth. Chewing furiously, he suddenly stopped moving and rolled his eyes into his head while leaning against the building. Dao slowly cracked open the bus's back door and whispered to the nearest child, "tell everyone to stay put and be quiet. I've got to get Brill,"

Silence again, until finally, the husky boy whispered back, "I'll make sure their quiet Dao. Go."

Dao quietly closed the door and ran through the forest to the back of the building. Hiding amongst the vehicles, he waited for someone to exit the building; no one did. Dao kept wondering what the Snatcher at the door was doing. Was he the bus driver? Dao didn't know. Perspiration glistened on his forehead; the waiting was excruciating. Impatience overtook him; he couldn't wait any longer; he went into the blackness. He went down into the darkness until he saw a glimmer of light.

CHAPTER 22

The Retreat

When Dao rounded the stage, the last lot of children came into view, dirty and exhausted The buyers were in a bidding war for the last band of children, who were no longer on their feet. They had slumped to the stage exactly where they had stood all day. Dao found Brill staring at the children in the final sale from behind a bidder's chair. Unable to get his attention, he swept the floor with his hand looking for something to throw at his friend; he found pebbles.

The first pebble tossed didn't come anywhere near Brill; the second one hit the chair he was behind, causing the bidder to look his way and Brill to hit the ground. Brill saw the pebble hit the chair, looked in the direction it came, and saw his friend frantically waving his arms.

Brill acknowledged Dao and the need to leave, but he was torn. Waiting to free the last group would jeopardize the four other groups already in safely on the bus. Brill's indecisiveness was now putting all their lives at risk as the escape window narrowed. Frantic to leave, Dao threw his arms up at Brill, who conceded and moved towards him. As they neared the corridor, the ringmaster announced the completion of the final sale, spurring the eight buyers to converge on the stage to socialize and criticize one another.

As the bidders hurled insults at one another while limbering up their grotesque bodies on the stage in a bizarre session of mutant yoga, the children were untied and led away. The boys ran down the corridor, out of the tunnel, and through the forest to the front of the building.

The Snatcher was still against the wall, trying to steady himself. He leaned forward, extended his arms as if flying, and headed towards the bus. Struggling with the door, the man kicked it, entered, and sat heavily in the driver's seat when the boys slid under the seats with the children. The children saw Brill's finger in the moonlight when he raised it to his mouth. Again, the children nodded. Looking over the seat, Brill could see that the driver was the only Snatcher on the bus. He was relieved to be rejoining the children. The driver hummed, started the engine, closed the door, shifted in gear, and pulled away from the Market.

The back of the bus was filled with guarded optimism; the children were no longer sold slaves, only one Snatcher was aboard, and they were moving. The bus did a U-turn and headed toward the driveway when the front doors of the building blew open. A group of hideous men exited, laughing and cheering as two of their companions took turns striking one another in the head.

One man saw the bus leaving and ran after it yelling, "Hey, hold on there." The driver recognized the voice and stopped immediately, unfolding the door before the man. Expecting the worse, Brill and Dao grabbed the hands of the nearest children. The running must have tired the Snatcher as he slowly lumbered up the steps. Brill counted the steps, one, two, three, then looked. He could see the man facing the driver and all twenty children lying on the floor from the back door to the middle of the bus staring at him. If the Snatcher took five steps down the aisle towards the back, he would surely see them all. Brill signaled Dao, and they both got off the floor, crouched behind the seatbacks, ready to strike if needed.

The men outside watched the discussion on the bus, except the two who had been in the punching match and were vomiting in the barrels. Behind Dao, a small child stifled a sneeze by closing his mouth and plugging his nose, but a small squeak escaped. The man standing heard the noise, turned towards the back for a second as everyone froze, then abruptly left. The stowaways on the bus let out a short-lived quiet collective sigh of relief until the two men in the fight boarded the bus, slumped into the two front seats, closed their eyes, and fell fast asleep. The driver began to hum, closed the door, and pulled away from the scene.

<hr />

For hours, Dwell and Snag took turns driving down the neglected dirt roads and back wood trails, fueling up at random farms along the way. As they left the last farm, Snag decided it was time to teach Callow how to drive.

"Callow, I think it's time for you to take over some of the driving responsibilities. Come on up here so I can teach you," he said with laughter in his voice.

Dwell quickly responded, "Snag, do you think that's a good idea?"

"What do you mean? Do I think that's a good idea?" he answered. "Of course, I do. Look at her. She's beautiful, smart, and a brave woman. So, driving should be a breeze."

Callow shot Dwell a dirty look as she climbed into the driver's seat; Cat draped itself across her lap.

"Okay, turn the key to start the engine," he said.

Looking at him confidently, she turned and held the ignition key; the engine screamed.

"Whoa, now let it go," Snag yelled.

'Ooops…." Callow cried sheepishly.

He took his time teaching her the basics of driving. How to put the vehicle in gear, the functions of the two-floor pedals, and reading the gauges.

Snag's tutorial was a success.

Callow quickly sent the truck lurching forward down the road while Dwell laughed and mocked her. Her instructor came quickly to her defense, condemning Dwell's driving abilities. In no time, Callow was driving with confidence and without error. Dwell, feeling confident in her abilities, jumped in back to get a little shut-eye, leaving her alone with Snag, who was hoping this opportunity would present itself. He looked forward to getting to know Callow better.

"Callow, is Dao older than you?" Snag asked.

"Yes, two years older. There's just the two of my Mom and us," she said.

"It seems like all of you are rather good friends. You, your brother, Dwell and Brill?" he inquired.

"Yes, the four of us have always been good friends, especially Brill and I, because we're so close in age," she replied.

He noticed how she smiled, and her voice seemed to rise when she mentioned Brill's name.

"Everything has been so crazy lately. Nothing seems sane or the same. Too many people are doing terrible things, to *too* many innocent people; it's madness. We all just want to return to normal and be with our families and friends in peace. We want these horrible people out of our lives," she sighed.

"Ya," Snag agreed, "Peace would be a nice change for everyone."

She turned to face him, "Where are you from, Snag?"

CHAPTER 23

Snag's Story

Snag turned sideways on the seat, faced Callow, and told her his story. "I'm not sure. I didn't understand what was happening when I was younger. I just knew that sickness was everywhere. I do remember one day that my dad just didn't come home. He left my mom with us three kids, and she didn't know what to do. She drove us over to my dad's sister's place, but when we got there, there wasn't anyone there, so she kept driving until we ran out of gas in the country. We walked and walked for miles. Finally, we came upon a small creepy-looking house. It was the only one. I remember the dim light on the porch, a single bulb with no encasement. So, here's my Mom with three little kids, night coming up, and nowhere to go. She must have been scared to death. So up the steps, she goes and knocks on the door. We wait, holding our breaths. A freaky old guy came to the door and asked us what we wanted. Mom told him we needed gas for our car."

Snag turned toward the front windshield and stared straight ahead as if reliving the scene again. A tear rolled down his cheek.

"He looked my mom up and down and snickered at her. My two little brothers were in front of her, but he didn't even look at them; they were invisible. He told her to come in. She didn't want to, but we needed gas. She shuffled my little brothers inside; I stayed outside. He never saw me on the porch behind my mom. I was only nine, but my dad had taught me to fend for myself and how to fix stuff, so I was handy and tough. I didn't like the look of this guy, so I stayed and waited for her to come back out, but she didn't. I snuck around to the back of the house and waited there.

An hour later, the creep came out by himself, entered the shed, and got a gas can. Then he took off walking up the driveway. I watched him until he was out of sight. I tried the back door, but it was locked. I ran to the front door only to find it locked as well. I tried every window, but they were locked or stuck shut, except for a small one in the basement. I couldn't open it, but a large hole was covered with a folded piece of screen.

"Mom, Mom, I kept calling, but she didn't answer, so I ripped off the screen, crawled on my belly, and fell to the floor. I was so damn scared. It was dark, and I didn't know if anybody else lived there. I felt my way until I found the stairs, climbed to the top, and opened the door. It was dark upstairs also, except for a small light in the kitchen. I was so thankful that there wasn't anyone up there. I checked the living room and the bathroom. I opened another door which must have been his bedroom, because there were men's clothes all over the floor, garbage everywhere, and it stunk like hell. I was quiet inside, but suddenly this dog started barking like crazy. I must have jumped two feet in the air, and the worst thing was, I couldn't see it. It sounded huge, and it scared the hell out of me, but I didn't run. I kept walking into the room. My legs kept moving me forward even though I didn't want to, but my brain told me I had to. The man had blacked out the window, so I turned on the light.

On the far side of the bed, I saw it. A big dog was lying on a large pillow on the floor. It couldn't see me cause its eyes were all white with no pupils. But it could hear and smell me. It kept barking and showing its teeth. I had to shut it up before the guy returned, so I looked around for weapons. I finally saw a few tools and a knife on a little table. I grabbed the knife, jumped on the bed, grabbed a pillowcase, and slipped behind the dog. I threw the pillowcase over its head while I grabbed it from behind. I choked it so hard that I thought my arms would fall off. I wrapped my arms and legs around its neck and held on. It seemed like forever before it stopped moving, and then I slit its throat. I still have that knife," he said matter-of-factly.

Callow sat quietly and didn't say a word.

"I went to the next room, only to find that door closed. Slowly, I opened it. I had to hurry up and find my mom, and it didn't matter how scared I felt. The room was empty. I looked under the bed, but nothing. So, I ran back to his room and looked under his bed, but nothing. I opened his closet, but nothing. Then I ran back to the other room and opened the closet, where my mom and my little brothers were stuffed onto shelves. They were gagged and tied up. I will never forget the look of horror on my mom's face that day. She was so frightened and horrified that I was afraid to remove the gag from her mouth. I was sure that she would start screaming and never stop. I told her I would get her out of there and that everything would be okay. She didn't believe me; I could tell by her eyes. I don't know what he said or did to my mom in that brief period, but whatever it was had terrorized her.

It took forever to calm and reassure her before I could remove her gag and the rope from her wrists. When I did, she was mostly quiet, whimpering. I helped her off the shelf and my little brothers too. I told everyone to stop moving as I could hear a car coming. It was him! I shut the bedroom doors and took them down the stairs into the dark basement. I showed them the broken window and told them they had to climb outside and hide behind the barn as soon as he entered the house.

We saw him get out of our car. He was holding one of my mom's scarves up to his mouth, like breathing through it. It pissed me off that he had her scarf, and right then, I told myself I would kill him. We listened as the back door banged open. I lifted my little brothers, helped my mom out the window, and told them to run. I watched as they ran behind the barn. I was so happy and relieved to know they were safe now.

Now I had to find a weapon. I started looking around the room, but it was too dark. Then I heard a door slam so hard upstairs that the guy must have broken it. Then another, and I realized he knew she had gotten out of the closet. I heard him open the basement door and I quickly moved behind the stairs.

I was terrified. He took his time walking down the steps in the dark. Behind the steps, split logs were stacked with an ax beside them. I grabbed a long log because the ax looked too heavy to lift and waited. When he stepped onto the floor, he looked around like he was looking for something. I could see the shadow of his hand waving in the air in front of me. While he kept waving, I came out from behind the steps and swung the log as hard as possible at his gut. His hand caught something, and as he bent over, he pulled a rope, and a light came on. I saw him fall, so I swung the log repeatedly until he didn't move anymore.

I fell to the floor and cried. I couldn't believe people could do that to others, especially moms and little kids."

Callow looked at Snag with such a look of compassion that it made him blush. "Then what happened?" she asked.

I grabbed everything from the house that we could use, food, blankets, medicines, and water, and put them into the car. I ran, got my mom and brothers, and put them in the car. The monster had already filled the car, so I filled the gas can and put it into the trunk. Mom started screaming that there were no keys. I settled her down by saying I would go get them, but she wouldn't let go of me."

Snag re-enacted the removal of his mom's hands from his arms.

"My brothers helped me peel her hands off me, and I returned to the house. She was crying uncontrollably, I hated to leave her, but I had to get the damn keys if we were going to get out of there. I light was still on in the basement and ran down the stairs. I realized the monster was gone as I stepped down on the basement floor. Immediately, I turned and tried to run back upstairs, but he grabbed my ankle from between the steps, pulling me down. I tried to stomp on his hand with my other foot, but he kept pulling me through the boards.

I was so afraid for my mom. Who was going to take care of her? I started crying. My fingers were sweating and full of slivers from the steps. I remember screaming, "Nooo……. And then I heard a loud blast, and he released his grip on me, and my knees hit the ground. I looked behind me, and he was slumped over the woodpile. I looked to my right, and there was my little brother, Rois, with a shotgun in his arms. He was staring at me. I took the gun out of his hands and hugged him so tight. Then I poked the creep with the gun, but he didn't move because he had a massive hole in his chest. I dug through his pockets, found the keys, jumped up the stairs, turned off the light, and ran out of the house.

My Mom kissed and hugged me, but she didn't ask any questions. I told her we needed to go. While she fired up the car, I checked the shed and found more shotgun shells. Then we headed for my mom's sister's place, which was far away. Her husband was a soldier, and she was a nurse, so they took great care of us from then on. We were safe and well cared for there, but as I grew up, it was just too safe. I felt that I needed to do something to help other moms and kids, so when I was old enough, I left home, and here I am," he said with a big smile.

"Wow, what a story," Callow exclaimed as she wiped the tears from her face.

"I wish it were just a story," Snag said. "Hey, where are we? We've been driving for hours," he said, lightening the mood. Just then, there was a bang on the cab's back window.

"Pull over, Callow; it seems like Dwell has wakened from his beauty sleep."

CHAPTER 24

Silent Support

The crowd sat quietly, listening to the alarming broadcast over Mama's black patch, set in a ring on the table. Talk of death and destruction dominated the airway. The elders, along with Gotl, Jith, and Wirl, listened intently, hoping to pick up any information about the kids. Jith was entirely animated; more than once, Gotl told her to sit with him across the room to avoid accidental contact with the patch, which could divulge their location.

There was no mention of the children or their mission; their fate was uncertain. The elders had faith in the abilities amongst them, as was illustrated on their last mission, but the lack of news was unsettling. The transmissions were coming from the compound guards, the Rooks, Captain Mullins, and others who didn't identify themselves but seemed to upset the Captain every time he heard their voices. Gotl and Mama had a deeper understanding of the seriousness of the children's mission. They knew that their survival rested solely in their own hands. The Clan made it clear they would not intervene in the mission for fear of jeopardizing the canopy's location. Their community would not be sacrificed at the expense of four youngsters.

Jith vehemently disagreed with the Clan's decision. Mama understood Jith's concern, but communicating by patch would reveal not only their location but that of the couriers. As stressful as the situation was, Jith was sure that either her husband or Mama would break their word and help the children - just like she planned to do. They didn't know it yet.

CHAPTER 25

The Ride

Jup rode in the Captain's vehicle to the compound so that Mullins could keep an eye on him. He sat opposite the big man, resting his gun on his thigh, and pointed directly at Jup's chest. The small space limited Jup's movement. If he moved against the Captain, he would be shot before he could kill the man. Jup felt it was best to keep quiet until he could leverage the information; he had to save his life.

As the guard at the compound waved them through, an uneasy dread flooded Jup. He could not recall spending time at the compound other than driving through on his way to The Farm to participate in the competitions. Yet, he could feel that bad things happened here. He needed to leave this place as soon as possible.

The truck parked in front of the laboratory. The guard opened the door while Mullins called for support on his patch. Jup looked around at the garage and outside the lab, and his uneasiness increased.

"Follow me," Mullins said.

Jup followed him into the building, up the stairs to the second-floor door marked "Testing." Mullins unlocked the door and entered; the guards pushed Jup through the doorway to a waiting chair that Mullins swung towards him.

"Sit down," he said. "Now tell me about your friends, these tree dwellers."

Jup looked around the room and back at the Captain; *something* seemed familiar. The white walls, the rooms, more poignant was the smell which brought about memories, bad memories. He turned back to Mullins and began to tell the Captain about Brill and the others.

———◆—◆—◆———

Brill turned the volume down on his patch. His wristband was buzzing and lighting up with multiple transmissions.

"We have to move," Brill said to Dao as he dug in his pocket. "I don't know how much longer the children can stay quiet. I've got an idea. Tell them to stay on the floor when they see the smoke."

Brill and Dao bent and whispered into the ears of the children nearest to them, who then passed the message along to the others. The children turned back towards them, nodded in agreement, and held their thumbs up.

"Dao, I'm going to throw it at the door, and when it starts to smoke, I'm hoping the driver will pull over. Then you and I are going to take out the two guards."

Brill held up his red elixir, which he opened and sipped, then replaced in his pocket. He held up the yellow ball for Dao to see.

"Ready?"

Dao nodded. Brill felt the familiar power surge as he peeked above the seat to gauge the distance to the door. Then he pinched the ball and threw it. Seconds later, the ball landed in the stairwell and began to smoke. Instantly, the bus was filled with smoke causing the driver to slow down, pull over and stop. Unable to see his hand in front of his face, the driver opened the door and stumbled out of the bus, coughing as he went.

While the bus was still moving, the back door was opened, and the two fighters were launched out of the door. They landed about fifty feet away, rolled into the ditch, and didn't move as the door swung back and closed. Dao opened the windows to divert the smoke away from the children, who remained quiet on the floor. Brill ran out of the bus towards the driver, bent over, and rubbed his eyes. Brill didn't realize how strong he was when he grabbed the man's shoulder and spun him around; hard. The little man's body turned while his large head lagged, wobbling and spinning; Brill was afraid the man might pass out, so he grabbed and steadied him. The little man squinted and struggled to focus as Brill stood before him, wiping the water from his eyes.

"Where are you headed?" Brill asked the man.

The man's eyes opened as wide as possible and leaned toward Brill. It took a few seconds for his vision to clear well enough for him to see, and when it did, he jumped back in fear.

"Whoo in the worl are you?" he asked in a low draw.

"It doesn't matter who I am. Who are you?" Brill asked.

Dao had the children and Dog off the floor and sitting in the seats, watching Brill and the little man.

"Daa kall me Nutay," he said. "Whach ya want?"

"I want you to take me to the Lair," Brill said as he flexed his massive muscles before the funny-looking man.

The man jumped back again, and he answered with concern.

"Wi in the worl would ya want to go dare?" He continued in a louder voice while poking his finger at the ground, "Dare ar bad, bad pepol dare ar wonnerful chillans"

"I want you to take us there, Nutay. How long will it take to get there?" Brill said.

Dao walked off the bus and covered half the truck's headlights with mud.

"Who dis guy?" Nutay asked when he saw Dao approach.

"Don't be worrying about him. Just answer the question," Brill said.

Nutay was now bobbing his head up and down and looking quite worried. "It taks bout two days from here if we don't be wast'in too much time talkin," he said.

"Okay, let's go," Dao said as he jumped aboard and sat directly behind the driver's seat. Brill tried to put a hand on Nutay's shoulder, but Nutay dodged him, walked back on the bus, and sat heavily in his seat. He faced forward, then suddenly whirled around when he saw twenty young faces staring back at him. A huge smile overtook his large head and lit up his eyes as he looked from face to face.

"Nutay, we took these children from the buyer's vehicles at the auction. Who were those men, and where were they taking these kids?" Brill asked.

Nutay looked downward, placed his chin on his chest, and quietly sobbed. Dao and Brill looked at each other, unsure what to do; no one spoke until he composed himself. Nutay wiped his face with the back of his hand, looked up at Brill, and explained, "I don't lik whet dey do down der. I trie to help'em - dem chilians once, and I got this." He pulled up his shirt, exposing a large scar down his stomach.

"I almos died dat day," he said. "Now I jus watch'em and cry."

Brill stepped before Nutay and bent down, "We want to help them too, Nutay. That's what we're here for. But we can't help them without your help."

"Well, I do anithin to help the chilians, jus tells me what cha want," he said.

Brill sat down opposite Dao and told Nutay what he wanted to do.

CHAPTER 26

Memories

Jup sat, then walked the chair back against the wall and as far away from the Captain as possible. All his life, Jup had used his size to his advantage. It was rare for him to be frightened of anyone, but sitting in front of the Captain in this place scared him.

Jup told the Captain how he had come across Brill and Dao deep in the forest; he didn't mention what he was doing in the woods. He said that he and his friend had happened upon Brill and his friend while they were sleeping and overtook them. Jup described the tree dwellers as slim, weak, and poor fighters. He didn't mention Callow or Dwell.

The Captain sat listening with a small knife in his hand. He listened, never interrupting or asking questions, and occasionally, he would look up at Jup and smile.

When Jup finished talking, the Captain put down his knife and stared at him. The Captain was about one hundred and fifty pounds lighter than the fighter, but the Captain didn't fear Jup because he could smell Jup's fear and see it in his eyes.

"What part of the forest did you come upon them? Mullins asked.

Jup didn't know the names of the forests or any areas in this province because he wasn't from here, so he hesitated to answer. He knew the Captain had no patience, so he tried to remember the locations Brill had spoken of when Basking Falls came to mind.

"Basking Falls," Jup answered.

"Good, good," replied the Captain. "And where were they headed?"

"The Snatcher's Lair is what they kept talking about, but I don't know this place," Jup said.

The Captain leaned forward, walked his chair up to Jup's until they were only inches apart, and smiled. The two guards behind Mullins also moved and were now standing directly behind him.

"Now, why would they want to go to the Snatcher's Lair?" he asked.

Jup looked nervously from one guard to another and then back at the Captain before responding.

"To stop them," was all that Jup said.

The Captain sat up and chuckled, then stopped before laughing again. He took a hard look at Jup, saw that he was deadly serious, and let out a huge belly laugh that echoed off the walls and windows in the room. Jup fought the urge to snap his neck.

Finally, the Captain stopped laughing and looked up.

"Stop them, really?" he resumed laughing again, much to Jup's annoyance, until he finally composed himself, stood up, and said, "Find him a secure room."

The guards watched Jup get up and walked him down the long hall in the experiment's lab to the room at the end of the corridor.

"Inside," said the guard as he opened the door and nudged Jup from behind.

Jup pushed the door wider and entered the room with a suspended bed, a small sink, an even smaller sealed window, and walls filled with scratch marks. The guards pushed him again, secured the door from the outside, and left. He sat on the bed. He was so tired, and his injured leg still ached, so he fell asleep, but sleep did not comfort him.

Mullins raised his patch. "All platoons are to meet at the front gate in two hours, fully armed and ready to march." Then he went off to Dr. Swallow's lab to pack.

⎯⎯⎯◆◇◆⎯⎯⎯

Alone in her nest, Mama heard the Captain's last message, which alarmed her, but she decided not to tell the others. Instead, she got up, went to her overlay, took out a small box, placed it on the table, and sat down. Mama knew exactly where Mullins and his men were going and who they were after. She didn't want to create hysteria amongst the Clan by sharing the shocking news because sometimes not knowing is better.

She opened the box and rummaged inside until her fingers rested on a tiny latch under the bottom lining. She pulled the latch, and the bottom of the box was released, revealing another narrow, wooden box that held a thin glass flask. Inside the flask was a gas that radiated a glistening deep orange. Mama carefully picked up the flask and cradled the bottle, staring at the contents she wished she had buried long ago.

Her thoughts drifted to her father, her mentor, and her hero. He was so proud of her, his prized and only student. She excelled in all the sciences, especially when making compounds and amalgams using synthesis, fusion, and other multifaceted techniques. He had shown her his methods, and she had enhanced his processes, making them more effective. She kept her secrets when she was taken away, never sharing her discoveries with anyone.

She understood the implications of her success, the risks, and the responsibilities. She placed the item back into the box and secured the latch. Leaning back in her chair, she asked her father for strength and wisdom in the coming days as she would need him now more than ever.

Callow pulled the truck over and waited for Dwell to join them. He was groggy and disheveled when he opened the door and got in. Callow and Cat shimmed over towards Snag, brushing up against his shoulder. She didn't notice the grin on his face when she touched him.

Dwell pulled out his maps and analyzed their progress. "What was the last sign you saw, Callow?" he asked.

"It was Tickleberry. At least, that was the name sprayed onto the sign," she said.

"Okay, well, that puts us a few days out from the Lair," he said. "Snag, why don't you jump in the back and get some shuteye? It's uncomfortable, but at least you can stretch out."

"Nah, I'll hang out with you two for a while. Besides, I'm not tired," Snag said as he pressed gently against Callow's arm.

"Suit yourself."

Dwell shifted the truck into gear and noticed they were low on gas.

"We need to find gas soon," he said as he pulled out and headed south. They were driving through the deserted streets of Tickleberry, where several stripped and outdated cars lined the streets and sat in driveways. The population sign outside of town read "6,945," but it looked more like zero to Callow. Storefronts were ajar or boarded up, their contents pillaged years ago.

Dwell drove by the dark empty gas station and looked at his gas gauge. The needle was below the empty line, the truck was running on fumes. Coasting down the main street, Snag couldn't recall the last town he was in; it was so long ago. Dwell, and Callow had never set foot in a city which was evident by their gawking.

The deserted streets were dimly lit by the remaining solar streetlights whose batteries refused to die. The hazy glow cast an eerie pale on the surroundings. Dwell opened his window to get a better look; the silence was unsettling. The truck began to sputter as the last fuel in the tank reached the motor. Snag also opened his window, and Cat quickly poked its' head out to see. Snag tried to hide the uncertainty on his face.

The truck crawled along while they strained in the dim light to make out the signage above the typical small-town business storefronts, a flower shop, Memere's hair salon, town hall, and a police station. The engine coughed one last time and coasted to a stop. Snag bent down to grab his water bottle on the floor, giving Callow an unobstructed view out the window. She gasped when she saw something moving near the fire hall.

"Get out," she whispered to Dwell.

"Get out for what, Callow?" he said.

"Get out!" she said more forcefully.

Dwell unlocked the truck door and got out.

CHAPTER 27

Tickleberry

"**W**hy?" he replied, trying to get out of her way.

"Get out. There's someone over there," Callow said as she looked at Dwell while pointing towards the large fire hall building. Dwell cast a skeptical look at Snag, which didn't sit well with Callow.

She snapped back, "Remember the kids in the loft? If it weren't for me, we would never have found them," she said defiantly before she opened and pulled Dwell out his door.

"We need to leave our packs here and take only what we need," she said.

They opened their sacks. Dwell put his elixirs in his pocket, and Callow put her patch, red medicine, and a yellow ball in hers. Dwell told Cat to stay and secured their supplies in the truck. Then he ran and caught up to the others on their way to the fire hall.

An old fire engine sat rusting on its flattened tires in the driveway beside a water truck that was missing its tank. The garage doors were blacked out with paint and boarded up with planks. They walked along the east side of the building, where all the windows were boarded up, and even the frames were hidden. Callow was so sure of what she'd seen that she turned the corner and continued around the back and down the alley with the boys in tow. All the windows on this side of the building were blacked out, so she kept walking in the unnerving silence of the night.

Suddenly Callow said, "Listen!"

They stopped. Dwell, and Callow focused on their astute hearing; nothing.

The building's exterior was constructed of cinder blocks and mortar three stories high, capped off by a sizeable ornate tower, missing its bell. A large clock, frozen at three o'clock, sat directly below the bell. The group continued walking. Dwell felt Callow's mounting frustration.

"All right, Callow, let's go," Dwell shouted. "We need to find gas and Brill."

Callow kept walking, ignoring Dwell's plea. She turned to her right, looking upward as she scanned the walls, focusing only on the fire hall while Dwell and Snag lingered behind. Still looking upwards, and didn't see the uneven pavement ahead, tripped, and fell into the station wall. Her right hand shot out to break her fall. Her fingers brushed against the basement window, causing her to fall hard on her right side, bruising her knees and scrapping her palms. Dwell, and Snag arrived as she sat up. They were helping her to her feet as she brushed off her knees. She stood and examined her hands. Her left hand had a minor laceration, so she wiped the blood on her pants, then looked at her right hand; it was all black. Shocked, she looked back at the window where the light was emanating from her hand mark on the window.

Dwell bent down, placed his face inches from the pane, and in the illuminated handprint, he saw another pair of eyes staring back at him.

Startled, he fell backward onto his backside, then scrambled to his feet with Snag's help as Callow walked toward the window.

"Get away from there, Callow! We don't know who or what they are?" Snag said.

"It's fine, Snag, they're friendly," she said. "Only the innocent hide when the world has gone mad," she reminded them as she stared at the window.

The person inside jumped off the table, fell to the floor, and got up and ran with the help of another.

"Wait, please wait," Callow pleaded.

They were gone, and the light went out. Callow ran to the front of the building and tried to pry the doors open, but they wouldn't budge. She pressed every button she could find; nothing. Exasperated and frustrated, she sat on the ground, defeated.

"Let's go, Callow. Sometimes, those hiding get to decide when they want to be found," Dwell said, helping her to her feet.

Back at the truck, with the gear in neutral, they rolled it down the street, looking for gas. Callow pushed from behind, keeping an eye on the station, hoping the "hiders" would approach them. They left the downtown core and moved into a residential area when Callow suddenly took off running across multiple yards, down alleyways, and jumping fences. Dwell, and Snag didn't realize she was gone until they saw her round the corner of a house in front of them, with a young man in tow. Try as he might break free, he was no match for a teenage tree-climbing girl. She dragged him over to the boys.

"Dwell, open the back," she said.

Dazed at her abilities, Dwell did what was asked and opened the back door while Snag looked in amazement. Callow told the boy to get in the truck, and when he refused, she picked him up, threw him in the back, then joined him. Dwell and Snag quickly jumped into the back as well. With Callow's solar panel and battery hooked up, the light was sufficient for them to see each other. Callow looked at the young man's face. He was clean with well-manicured hair and looked to be about twelve years old. The young boy was afraid as he looked back from Callow to Dwell to Snag.

Callow spoke first, "We're not here to hurt you."

He didn't speak, just stared at them.

"Where are the others?" she asked.

Again, nothing.

With a big smile, Snag turned towards the boy and said, "Hey Buddy, we need gas, and then we'll be on our way. Do you know where we can find some?"

The boy seemed to relax a little, and Callow gave Snag a thankful look; she admired his way with people.

The boy started to speak when suddenly the truck's back gate fell open to three men with guns aimed at the friends.

"Out," said the older man in the middle.

The young man was first to jump out, followed by the friends with their packs.

"Let's go." The older man pointed the barrel of his gun in the direction he wanted them to walk. Snag went first, followed by Callow and Dwell and the others.

Back to the downtown area, they were directed to stop in front of

"Postma's Flower Shop," a boarded-up storefront with a dilapidated name plate hanging loosely from brackets above the door. The door was opened, and everyone followed inside. The friends waited inside the door as the men busied themselves. Callow noted that they must have done this before because they were well organized; one man got chairs, and another brought candles without speaking. The older man pointed the barrel of his gun forward, and Callow led the way. They sat in a circle, and no one said a word. Suddenly Callow's impatience got the best of her, and she spoke.

CHAPTER 28

Puppa and Bumma

"I don't know who you people are, but we just need some gas," she said, exasperated.

The older man didn't sit; he walked over to Snag, picked up his hand and looked at it, then did the same to Dwell and Callow. Next, he gripped their thighs just above the knee and squeezed. Snag jumped and giggled while Dwell tried unsuccessfully to remove his hand. Callow was grabbed so quickly and briefly that she didn't have time to react. Walking around the circle, he took note of Snag's rough skin and scars compared to the unblemished, tanned skin of Callow and Dwell. Tenderly he ran the back of his hand on Callow's face so gently that she didn't resist.

"Why are you here?" he asked no one in particular.

"Sir, we just need gas for our vehicle," Snag said.

"Where are you headed?" he asked quietly, confidently.

"West, Sir," came Snag's response.

"Nothing good comes out of the West," he added.

"We know, Sir, that's why we're headed there," Snag answered.

"And who are you?" he asked, looking at Snag.

Callow interrupted, "We're just people who want to be left alone to live in peace, but some people don't want peace for us or anyone else."

"I know who you are," he said, looking back at Snag. "I know you're a fighter, a free fighter. Good for you."

Then he turned to the others, "You two are tree dwellers. Your glowing faces and strong bodies betray you. Around here, we say that the tree dwellers have been kissed by the sun; looking at the two of you, it sure does seem that way."

He sat down with his gun across his legs and stared at them.

"Who are you?" Callow asked.

"They call us the Watchers. I'm called Puppa," he said while gently looking into her eyes. The young boy she caught stood beside him and lovingly put his arm around his neck.

"These are some of my sons, Lev, Mose, and Rep," he said as he pointed to the young boy and the two men. "I am very grateful for my children. Not only do they keep me young and active, but they bring me extraordinary joy."

"How many are you?" Dwell asked.

"Not too sure. Guess we'll have to show you," Puppa said and got up.

⸎⸎⸎

Initially, the children were quiet on the bus ride, but as time passed, restlessness set in, seating arrangements changed, and whispers could be heard behind the backrests. Family members celebrated reunions; others searched in vain. The husky boy moved up and sat behind the driver with Dao.

"I remember you," he said to the driver.

The driver glanced up into the slanted mirror above his head and stared at the boy, trying hard to remember who was staring intently back at him. They continued staring at each other without saying a word until a smile exploded onto Nutay's face.

"Flippy dat you?" he asked.

Flippy smiled back, grabbed the steel pole, stood beside him, and proudly said. "It sure is."

Nutay let go of the wheel and embraced the young boy affectionately.

"Whoa," yelled Dao.

"Oh, don't ju all wori, I bin drivin dis bus all day wit juss my legs. I've bin doin this so long I be doin it in ma seep," he said. Dao and Brill laughed nervously as the smooth and steady bus continued down the road. The boy sat down, smiling from ear to ear. Full of joy, Nutay raised his arms, and using only his legs, he weaved the bus through the yellow lines on the road, much to the chagrin of Dao and Brill; the children loved it. Dog was

109

so excited that it jumped on the dash! Dao and Brill remembered the last time they saw a bus weave and wobble on the road; it wasn't so pleasant.

After an extended period of his driving antics, Brill said, "Okay, Nutay, we get it, you're one talented driver, but could you now please drive with your hands?"

Nutay laughed, removed a gun from his pocket, placed it on the dash, and smiled at Brill.

Surprised that Nutay had a gun, Brill asked, "Is that loaded, Nutay?"

"It sur is, but not for you," he laughed and placed one hand back on the steering wheel, much to the relief of Dao and Brill, who settled back in their seats to review the maps. With a long journey ahead of them, Brill's concern turned to the children. He needed to find a place far away from the Snatchers and hidden from Civantes, but where?

Civantes lowered his patch. He heard Mullins, transmission mobilizing his men to prepare for battle. Laughing, he thought about Mullins, diminished forces waging war against the machine he had been building for years. Success over the Captain would grant him control of the provinces, commodities, fighters, security details, and, more importantly, the medical data available from Mullins's labs. He called for his messenger.

"Contact the Snatchers by wire. Tell them that Mullins is heading this way and to stay off the patch. I want to surprise the Captain when he arrives. I don't want him to know I am expecting him. Then notify all district principals to meet here tomorrow; no excuses, and they better not be late. If they are, they might as well slit their own throat because I will. Tell them to prepare their defenses, including the children, who will be our first defense line, as shields.

"Go now; he's only days away." The messenger nodded and bolted out of the room.

Civantes sat back in his oversized, hand-carved chair. It was cushioned with the pelts of long-extinct animals and decorated with the feathers of exotic birds. He was thinking about Mullins, whom he didn't see at the last competition because my incompetent guards couldn't tell the difference between dead and alive creatures. Idiots, I'm surrounded by them, he thought. The Farm was our last meeting when he tried to cheat me out of my elixir. Fool, I will get my revenge the next time we meet. I'll make damn sure of that! I messed up his head last time; maybe I'll remove it from his shoulders this time.

He chuckled to himself again.

"Come, Captain, my old friend. I look forward to seeing you again."

Civantes' instructions were noted, and twelve messengers were given a copy of that notice to deliver to their principals. A loud screech could be heard above as they departed on their dirt bikes. The envoys looked up, saw a large shadow circling overhead, lowered their heads, and sped away from the Lair.

In the meantime, the patch on Mullin's wrist remained silent, to his surprise. His message was the last transmission, and he found that very odd.

CHAPTER 29

Preparing for Battle

Two hundred guards stood in formation, assembled at the front gates of the compound as commanded. Supply trucks were loaded by the men and stockpiled with a menagerie of armaments, ready to go. Mullins' security force, the Rooks, was also present, and like their Captain, they relished and upheld their infamous reputation as ruthless and barbaric men.

Mullins reviewed his troops standing at rigid attention in their combat fatigues, staring straight to maintain formation and hoping to avoid any eye contact with the Captain. He had donned a disturbing black face covering to conceal his injured cheek and eye, making him appear more sinister.

He approved of the menacing black uniforms, precision training, respect for authority, and most of all, the allegiance to him. As the afternoon sun blazed down, making it difficult for the men to hold their positioning, Mullins' wrath was an excellent motivator to do so.

He walked amongst the rows of men, weaving in and out, unnerving them. They kept their eyes forward and dared not move. The Captain caught movement to his left, not a blatantly obvious sign, just a hand flinch. Sauntering toward the man, he was happy to see a steady stream of perspiration dripping down the man's face. He passed the guard, turned back, and struck him squarely between the shoulder blades. The guard collapsed and fell to the ground. Not a single other guard moved.

Mullins placed his boot on the man's neck and said, "Today is your lucky day. I am going to let you live. Now get back in line and hold your position until I instruct you otherwise."

Slowly the man got off the ground and stood at attention while Mullins parked his face inches from his. Seconds passed, and the only thing that moved was the sweat dripping down his nose. Satisfied, Mullins moved on, climbed in his truck, and addressed the men while flanked by four of his largest Rooks.

"Today is a good day. We are heading west to visit my old friend and nemesis, Civantes. He's not my friend, and we won't visit him. What we are going to do, is destroy not only his Lair but also him. And we are not going to quit until it's done. Please speak up now if anyone here feels they can't join us on his mission."

A very tall guard in the back row was being bothered by a gnat flying up to his nose. Maintaining his posture quietly, he forced air out of his nostrils, trying to deter the persistent pest. When the Captain finished speaking, he saw the man wave his hand in front of his face, trying to swat it away; Mullins didn't see the gnat; he saw a man unwilling to commit, so he pulled out his gun and shot him.

He turned to the guards and said, "Load 'em up."

The guard barked out the orders while personnel loaded into the vehicles and waited for further instructions. Mullins walked back into the building to get Jup, who was awakened by the gunshot. He was sitting on his cot with knees drawn up tightly to his body.

It was a fitful sleep. Jup had nightmares of people in white coats putting wires on and needles into him.

He screamed, but no sounds came out. He saw the same happening to other children; they didn't wake up. When the gun went off, he realized he wasn't dreaming, just remembering.

Remembering the lab, the experiments, the children, and his family. With his feet on the floor, he cradled his head. Seconds later, he heard someone coming and removed his hands from his face. Grabbing the pillow beside him, he wiped away the tears, then slapped himself hard several times to awaken from the sadness.

Footsteps approached. One door, then another opened. Mullins stood smirking at him.

"Let's go," was all he said.

Jup got up and followed the Captain down the hall.

"I need to take a piss," he said.

"Down the hall on the left," Mullins said. "Do I need to go with you because I don't have any patience today?"

Jup assured him that he wouldn't do anything stupid. Mullins watched him walk down the hall, shut the door hard, then turn around. Quietly Jup cracked the door open, looked in the hallway glass, and saw Mullins' reflection; he was moving around the office. Jup snuck out of the bathroom and into the file room where Brill had found a ledger. The broken lock still hung from the top of the cabinet; he slowly opened it and flipped through the files. He recognized a handful of the children's faces from the pictures attached to the files. His younger brother, Rile's image, was on a file. He took both and placed them in his pocket. He didn't know if his brother had left the lab, as he did. He never knew what had happened to him. Closing the file drawer, he returned to the bathroom, flushed the handle, and opened the door with a loud bang.

Mullins was opening drawers in his desk, looking for something.

"Lose something?" Jup asked.

Mullins turned around and straightened himself up, "None of your damn business. Let's go."

Mullins placed the sketched pictures found in the backpack into his pocket.

Directing Jup into the hall, he locked the door, and they continued down to Dr. Swallow's lab, which they entered.

"Stay here," the Captain said to Jup and walked by him to the accomplished laboratory table.

Jup looked around the room; he saw cages, flasks with fluids, the desk, books, and pictures of people smiling and holding one another. Mullins grabbed a rigid container into which he placed two flasks with clear liquids and secured them. Jup looked closer at the pictures; he wondered why they were so happy. He wondered who they were and wished he were with them. He took a picture of a couple and a man with his arms around a young girl and put it into his pocket.

Mullins strode to the door and into the hall. Jup followed. He locked the lab and said, "Let's go hunting."

Jup led them down the stairs out of the building to the waiting truck and got in. He was glad to be leaving that place. He was also hunting, just not for the same prey the Captain was interested in.

CHAPTER 30

The Extended Family

Mose and Rep peered through the storefront windows and motioned for the others to follow. Hiding in the shadows, they walked down the street toward the back of the fire hall. Callow looked up, certain again that she saw a shadow moving in an upper window. Through the alley, they followed Mose to the fire hall's back wall. He told them to turn around. Locating a nondescript brick, he pressed it, and a door slowly opened, which he entered. Puppa and Lev followed, as did Callow and Dwell. Before Rep stepped in, he brushed the ground before the door with a tree branch erasing their footprints. Inside he pushed a button and closed the door, sealing them in. He saw the look of helplessness on Callow's face and said, "We don't hurt people here; we help."

Callow saw the look of compassion in his eyes, and without fear, she followed them deeper into the building. Snag and Dwell were ahead of her.

Lev ran ahead of his father into the glowing corridor, which banked left and right for many yards. About every fifty yards, a small glass window would appear on the top of the tunnel. Callow looked upward to see pairs of tiny eyes staring back at her. They continued walking until they reached a large steel door with a keypad. Puppa stepped forward, placed his hand on the pad, and his eye to the optical reader, then stepped back. He instructed Snag and Dwell to do the same while Callow searched for Lev, who was gone.

The heavy door opened from the left side and swung wide open so everyone could enter immediately. Within a short distance, another door made of thick opaque glass appeared. Again, Puppa stood before the door, blew into a tube, and stepped back. The seal on the door automatically released and swung open for them to enter.

Puppa turned sideways, swept his arms forward, and said, "Welcome to our home. We affectionately call it 'The Refuge.'"

They slowly moved forward, amazed at their surroundings, and were met by a beautiful older woman in a long, flowing dress.

"Well, hello. My name is Bumma. It's not Bumma, but that is what everyone calls me," she said with a warm smile. Around her legs were the arms of laughing children. She held out her hand to Callow while stroking the hair of the children. Puppa came around the friends and lovingly placed his arm around Bumma's shoulders. Callow shook her hand, as did the others.

"Follow me. You must be hungry," she said. The friends all nodded and followed. Callow thought about Cat.

They passed many open doors until they arrived at two large wooden double doors, which Bumma opened simultaneously. The friends were shocked at the scene in front of them. In the large room were tables full of food surrounded by hundreds of people of all ages; young, old, men, and women. When those seated saw Bumma and Puppa, everyone stopped talking and turned toward them.

"Hello, everyone. I want to introduce you to our new friends," she said, pointing her outstretched arm toward Callow.

Callow responded, "Hi, I'm Callow, and these are my friends Dwell and Snag." Snag and Dwell waved to the crowd, who applauded and cheered while escorted to a round table next to Puppa and Bumma.

Men and women placed food on all the tables, but no one touched it. Instead, they bowed their heads and patiently waited for Puppa, who stood and gave thanks for each other, their health, and the food on their plates. Once seated, people began to talk and eat. Adults assisted the children in making their plates, and everyone ate together.

Snag knew he had never partaken in such a wonderful feast with such kind hosts. The sharing of food, the magnificent surroundings, and the charity of Puppa and Bumma and their families reminded Callow and Dwell of back home.

The conversation during dinner was light, nonspecific, and full of laughter. Bumma ended dinner with a general prayer that signaled the male and female teenagers to clear and wash the dirty dishes. The younger children helped the women gather the extra food in the kitchen. There was no arguing, yelling, or fighting amongst the people, just community. Bumma and Puppa asked their guests to follow them down the corridor to a large sitting room without a door. Dwell couldn't get over the size of the home; it seemed to go on and on. The youngsters took their seats while Puppa stood waiting for Bumma to sit before he sat beside her. She touched his hand and smiled kindly at him, which he returned.

"Do you have any questions?" he asked.

Dwell looked at Callow, who raised her eyebrow, prompting him to ask, "Who are you, and how did you do this?' he asked, raising his hands above his shoulders.

Puppa laughed and said, "Well, many years ago, we lived in the cities isolated from one another, ignoring our neighbors and taking care of ourselves. We became isolationists in our homes and greedy with our time; we kept it for ourselves. When the sickness hit, we saw how much those poor people in the country suffered. Their fate was not their fault; they used the chemicals on the land they were told to use; they were farmers, not scientists. As the sickness progressed, some of us shed our selfishness and went out into the country to see if we could help. At the farms, we found many adult corpses and a few children's corpses; too few children. It didn't matter how hard we looked; we couldn't find the children, so we widened our search area to look for them. We found a few toddlers, but most children were within the age range of four to fourteen. Some older ones refused to follow us, so we left them alone and took those who wanted to join us.

At first, we kept the children in our townhouses, but when their numbers became too large, my friends and I built this place here, and others like it throughout the different regions. We raise, love, and protect these children. When investigating a farm, we use a grid system to ensure no one is left behind. We work on a radius system searching a broader pattern from a pivotal point, farther and farther from our homes. In the beginning, we didn't find many children, and then we found out why by chance.

We came upon a truck that had crashed in a field. Inside the truck's front seat were two dead men with large, swollen heads. In the back was a truckload of bound deceased children. We were horrified at the loss of life and buried them in the forest. Only then did we know who had taken the children, but we didn't know who these large-headed devils were and why they were snatching them. That's when we started to call them Snatchers.

We took what we could from the truck and buried it too. We didn't know where these horrible people came from, but the information in the vehicle gave us a good idea of where they were taking the children. I will share this information with you later in my office."

Bumma patted Puppa's hand while he told the story.

"How many Snatchers do you think there are?" Dwell asked.

"I don't know for sure, but there must be quite a few, and I'll also show you why I think that later. For now, why don't the three of you get acquainted with our family and relax a little before we get to work," he said. Then, he stood up, shook each of their hands, and they left.

CHAPTER 31

A Little Heaven

"I'm going to check it out," Dwell said as he left.

Callow and Snag remained seated as they watched Bumma and Puppa leave.

"This place is amazing!" Callow said as she looked around the room.

"Ya, I can't believe they've built this. Come on. Let's go check it out, too," Snag said as he held out his hand to help her.

Callow took his hand and stood; Snag didn't let go once she was up. He walked with her in tow out the door and down the hallway. They passed the kitchens, the reading room, sleeping quarters, and the most fantastic room of all, the playroom. It glowed from the walkway!

Standing in the doorway, they gazed into the room. The scene was surreal. The space was filled with happy, laughing children of all ages. After seeing so much death and destruction, seeing the happy children was a blessing. Slides, rides, climbing ropes, mazes up the walls and onto the floor, and homemade toys everywhere. Callow stood in the doorway with her mouth wide open until a little girl took her hand and pulled her into the room. Others soon joined them and pulled her deeper into the room to a maze cart on the floor, where they all sat in, one in front of the other.

A young, petite redhead came over, strapped them into the cart, and pulled the handle, sending their coach forward on the rails as the little girl snuggled closer to Callow. The cart moved slowly at first but soon picked up speed. Callow pulled the little girl closer and held her tight while she laughed with delight; soon, Callow was doing the same. They rode around the room up and down the walls amongst the colors and mazes. Callow heard Snag laughing like a little kid behind her. The ride ended, and Callow and her new friend got off, as did Snag, laughing and high-fiving one another in their excitement, which spurred more children to join them. With their arms full of children, Callow and Snag fell to the floor as the children climbed over them. They stayed there for hours.

Snag spent most of his time watching Callow interact with the children, full of happiness and carefree. He thought that she was the most beautiful sight he had ever seen. He wondered why everywhere couldn't be like this instead of the dark, death-ridden society that life had become.

Dwell had also taken a tour of the building and returned to meet Puppa in his office. Puppa was seated behind his large, clean desk. Behind the desk was a wall covered in children's drawings from floor to ceiling. Dwell walked in and was drawn directly to the wall. There were stick pictures of Bumma and Puppa with notes written by noticeably young hands. Dwell read them, 'i luv u bum and papa, luv u bunce.' Another wrote, 'thank you for saving me, Puppa,' and 'I love my new mommy and daddy,' amongst many others. Overwhelmed with the beauty and joy of their love for one another, Dwell stopped reading to wipe the tears from his eyes. Puppa walked around his desk and directed him to a chair. He sat and covered his eyes with his hands; Puppa waited. Dwell wiped his face with his hands and then his shirt.

"Sorry," he said to Puppa when he looked up.

"Don't apologize to me for having compassion and recognizing the gift of love, Son. This world would be much better if everyone had what you have. If more people had the gift of tears, we wouldn't be in our mess," he said with all seriousness. "Did you take a look around, Dwell?"

"Yes, Sir, I did," he replied.

"And what did you find?" he asked.

"I found many happy people living together in a wonderful place away from a crazy world,' he replied.

"Exactly. And do you know why the people here are happy?" he asked.

"Because you are a family?" he answered.

"Exactly, and family means children," he replied. "If there are no children, there is no family, and without family, there is no joy.'

Dwell nodded as he agreed with Puppa. Everyone here was so happy and respectful of each other, just like at home in the canopy.

"All right now, let's get to work," Puppa said as he opened his desk drawer and took out a map and a book. He set the book down and spread out the map.

"We have a region map, including the nearest four provinces. There seems to be a concentration of camps in Provinces II and III. See all these crosses. They are at very distinct locations. We checked out this cross here," he said, pointing at the marking close to their location. "We found a camp there full of Snatchers. I figure that hundreds of men and many children are at each location. I found this map in the truck with the children, *and* I also found this.," he said as he rolled up his sleeve to reveal a black patch on his wrist. Dwell's eyes lit up! He rolled his sleeve to show his patch, and they both laughed.

"So, you know about the messages?" he asked Dwell.

"Yes, we know that the Captain and his guards at the grain compound use them, and we think that one of the pharmacists, Civantes uses it to transmit messages," Dwell said.

"Ah, Civantes, I have read that name many times," Puppa said as he tapped the book beside him.

Dwell looked down at the book and saw that it looked remarkably similar to the book he had in his sack. Puppa watched Dwell eye the book.

"Later tonight, we are going to check out a camp. Would you like to come?" he asked.

"Yes, of course," Dwell said, not taking his eyes off the book.

"I'll show you to your room now so that you can get some rest," Puppa said as he folded the map and put it with the book back into the drawer. While showing Dwell to his room, they saw the others in the playroom from the doorway.

Callow and Snag didn't see Dwell and Puppa watching in the doorway. Music was playing. Snag affectionately grabbed Callow around the waist, spun her around, and caught her in his arms while her golden hair shone in the lights as they danced with such ease; she was mesmerizing. To Snag and Callows' delight, children returned to tackle them when the music stopped. Dwell thought to himself that he had never seen her so happy. Her smile never left her face.

Puppa stepped into the room, "All right now, it's time to settle down so our guests can rest."

The children moaned with disappointment but followed Puppa's instructions, said good night to everyone, and quietly went to their rooms.

Everyone left the playroom. Callow left with Snag's arm securely wrapped around her waist. Dwell couldn't help but notice how happy they looked together.

Bumma soon joined them, carrying a sleeping Cat in her arms, and ushered them to their rooms.

"How?" said Callow when she took the pet.

"My boys are very resourceful," she said. "Now, sleep quickly. Puppa will be gathering you soon for the night mission. Please get some rest; he will be calling you sooner than you think," she said and was gone.

CHAPTER 32

Night Raid

Everyone fell asleep quickly in the comfortable beds and soft bedding. Soon Puppa was at their bedside, waking them to go. They ate the small meal that Bumma had prepared while Puppa briefed them.

"You three will follow us and do as we do. Cat' will stay here. I am sure you are all skilled hikers, so we won't be doing anything you haven't done before," he said.

"Puppa, we need to stop them," Callow said.

"What do you mean 'to stop them'?" Mose asked.

"They are coming for us, so we need to make sure that they don't find us, and the only way we can do that is to destroy them before they destroy us," she said.

"And how do you propose we do that, Callow?' Puppa asked.

"We have some tools but not enough. What do you have?" Callow asked.

Puppa explained the capabilities of the weapons in their possession. By the time they left half an hour later, Callow had realized that Puppa had a vast arsenal with enough firepower to stop every Snatcher's camp in this province and every other. After Puppa's talk, Callow was feeling better about their odds.

Traveling through the hideaway, they exited on the outskirts of town near the quarry, where the men revealed their hidden vehicles. They loaded up in the darkness and followed the quarry's ridge to the caverns at the gorge. They parked on the rise, concealed their vehicles, and hiked to the top of the hill. Looking down the north side of the flat slate wall, they could see the faint glow of a fire at the mouth of the cavern. Puppa gave the order for Mose and Rep to get ready. Dressed in all black, the men secured their ropes and waited for their orders. The remaining men, also in black, spread themselves out along the ridge, tied themselves off, and waited. In the darkness, no one could be seen. Puppa signaled for the men to put on their night goggles and scatter.

Puppa turned to the three friends and said, "Watch." In a pouring motion downward, he turned and signaled to the men.

Slowly Rep poured a container of liquid down the rock face wall. The silvery liquid shone in the darkness and quickly spread downward into the cave entrance. He opened a second container and poured its bronze contents on the rock face to chase the first liquid. The combination of the two fluids created an intense flash of white light that spread toward the opening and into the cave blinding the men inside. Puppa and his men knew that the induced blindness was only temporary, but the Snatchers didn't, so they came stumbling and screaming out of the cave, fell off the cliff, and were swept down the river and over the falls to their death. The foot traffic coming out of the cave stopped within a short period. Puppa gave the sign triggering the men to rappel down the side of the rock face and onto the cave's ledge below. Concealed by their dark clothing, they reached the cavern floor unnoticed and unhooked their harnesses.

Five Snatchers sat rubbing their eyes at the front of the cave, straining to see. At the back of the cavern stood other Snatchers with weapons raised, utterly unaffected by the light flash.

Mose signaled the plan to the others. The point man moved closer to the opening, bent down, and crawled into the cave. Puppa nodded to the friends because he knew what was coming. A second man knelt and ducked into the cave, followed by the rest of the team until all the men were inside. The blind men continued to moan and falter around the cave, making it easy for the team to neutralize them and toss them into the water after taking their weapons. Once the front of the cave was secured, they made their way towards the back to those men who were straining to see what was happening to the Snatchers upfront.

Again, the light flash liquids were poured onto the rock floor and lit, causing the guards to drop their weapons and grab their eyes. The team grabbed these men carried them onto the ledge and tossed them into the rapids below with the others. Some men with the most oversized heads remained on the water's surface for long distances before disappearing.

Rep whistled, signaling the release of the remaining ropes from above. Puppa, Callow, Dwell, Snag, and young Lev joined them. Mose instructed five of the men to remain in the cavern on watch and led everyone else deep into the cave, where four descending tunnels appeared. Puppa bent down, surveyed the rocks' wear, and chose the second tunnel. Without hesitation, the men jumped in, followed by their new friends. Snag held Callow's hand as they quietly made their way out of the tunnel into a corridor that split in two separate directions. The group also split, half into each passage which converged into a large open area, with huts, small buildings, and three large tents with people milling about.

Puppa's group was composed of friends and ten young men. He could see Mose and his group of ten across the large open area on another ridge above the huts. They aimed to get the children out of the tents and back to their safe places. All the men quietly climbed down to the lower level of the makeshift town. Mose and his men knew exactly what to do, relying on the experience they had gained while on other successful raids.

One of the smallest men in the group initiated the next part of the mission. He separated himself from the group, sat on the ground, and opened his sack. The small metal device he removed had two antennas that emitted red lights. The man placed the antennas on the ground and signaled the men to scatter. The men took off running towards the outside perimeter of the lower-level camp.

The soft fire of the pits poorly illuminated the detention camp. As the men got into position, Rep's unique whistle notified the small man that the team was in place and ready. The high-pitched sound also reached the ears of everyone below, and they turned toward the unusual sound. The children practicing fighting techniques, as did those working in the makeshift fields, stopped. Even the cooks at the firepits stopped stirring and looked up. Guards throughout the camp also stopped what they were doing and looked. When the young man was sure he had everyone's attention, he turned on his device.

The machine emitted a painful and deafening noise to only the Snatchers, who immediately stood up and clutched their ears. The captive children also looked up without any apparent discomfort. Puppa and his men moved in a little closer as the device dial was turned up, increasing the high-frequency noise and causing the panicked Snatchers to run around, bumping into everything in their path while holding their heads. The confused children watched their captors in their frenzy and moved away. The frequency was increased a second time to the machine's full pitch and, within seconds, caused the heads of the Snatchers to explode right off their shoulders.

The children watched with shock as their captors' heads randomly blew up. One Snatcher had been eating when his noggin exploded all over the table into the food of the others, much to their short-lived annoyance. Another played with his slimy creature when his head exploded, burying it with his juices. More and more heads exploded until the scene resembled corn kernels popping in a pan. The children ran to the cliffs to escape the spewing noses, ears, and other body parts raining down on them.

The building guards came running out and soon met the same fate. When no Snatchers remained, the team entered the camp. Puppa instructed the small man to turn off the device. Most of the children were on the perimeter, but some confused little ones hadn't moved and were still standing where they were before the device was turned on. Puppa and the men gathered the children in a circle and had them sit down before he spoke.

CHAPTER 33

Liberation

"Hello, little ones," Puppa said softly.

No one responded or moved. The children were not used to speaking without permission.

Puppa and the others looked around, but still, no one spoke.

"We have come to take you away from here," he said, waving his arms around the area.

But the scared wide eyes of the children were a sad reminder to Puppa of the horrors experienced by the young innocents in front of him.

Callow came up behind Puppa, walked towards the children, knelt before them, and said, "Hi, my name is Callow."

A beautiful little girl with long blonde hair walked up, put her arms around her, and said, "Momma."

Callow slowly put her arms around the little girl, who buried her face in Callow's hair as Callow quietly sobbed. The other children came to her, comforting her gently and whispering, "It's okay."

Puppa dispersed some men into the buildings and tents to collect supplies. He directed the rest to find any stray or hiding children. Puppa checked the Principal's office for helpful documentation; there was little.

Once everyone was out of the cavern, the men rigged up the upper ridge to the mouth of the cave with explosives. The blast sent rock down into the cavern, sealing the entrance as the children watched from a distance and said nothing.

They returned home in the dead of night; Bumma was waiting. She always waited for the children and her loved ones to return home. She welcomed the children, fed them, gave them clean pajamas, and put them to bed; the adults also turned in for the evening. Everyone was looking forward to a good night's sleep except Dwell, who got up in the middle of the night and entered Puppa's office. The office wasn't locked because it didn't have a door. He lit the candle on the desk and sat down. Quietly, he slid open the drawer and took out the book Puppa had shown him earlier that day. The book was just like his, except it had the number three on the cover and the letter "D." Dwell's book had a number two and a symbol like a letter "M" on its surface. The pages were filled with written entries of dates, names, and descriptions, just like his book; there were also a few maps. Flipping through the pages, he saw multiple entries of dates against numbers, which he also had but didn't understand. The last few pages were filled with writings and symbols he didn't understand, just like in his book. There was only one difference between the two books. Dwell's book had lists of potions and elixirs, their ingredients, and their uses. Dwell studied Puppa's book until he heard, "You just had to ask."

Dwell jumped out of the chair, startled to see Puppa standing in the shadows.

Puppa took another step forward and said, "We don't sneak around here, Dwell, because we trust each other and don't keep secrets. If you wanted to see the book, why didn't you ask?"

Dwell cast his eyes downward, ashamed of himself for not trusting Puppa after all he had done for him and his friends, especially the children.

Puppa walked around the desk and said, "Sit down and tell me what you need to know."

Exasperated, Dwell sat down and said, "Puppa, when I saw your book," he couldn't look Puppa in the eye, "I got excited because I have a book just like yours, but I don't understand what's written in it. I hoped your book would help explain what it all meant."

"Why didn't you ask me?" he said.

Dwell didn't respond.

Puppa moved closer to the desk and looked down at his book. He turned to the first page and explained the contents to Dwell.

"The first section lists the name of the purchaser, the lot number, and the number of children in each lot. Notes indicate where the children were snatched from and their sale date. The second section details the health of the lots, whether the children were sick or not, and if they were, the symptoms they experienced. The third section details the experiments conducted on many children and the results of those tests. Section four describes the sale of children who have undergone experimentation, who bought them, and where they were sent."

Puppa closed the book, tapped his finger on the leather cover, and said, "This ledger is an account of one of the local Principal's purchases of snatched children over the decades. Your ledger must be the same type of information but from your area."

Puppa pulled another book out of the pocket of his robe. It was like the book on the desk; it had the number six on the cover with the letter L.

"I found this one in the cave tonight, and it has the same information as this one here," he said as he pointed to the book on his desk. "This is the gorge Principal's ledger."

Dwell removed his ledger from his pack and set it beside Puppa's books on the desk.

"May I?" Puppa asked. Dwell nodded as Puppa picked up the book and leafed through it.

"Where did you get this, Dwell?" he asked.

Again, Dwell looked down, ashamed, "I took it from someone's nest in our Clan."

"You took this from someone in your Clan who is no longer with us?" Puppa asked, raising his eyebrow.

"Yes," Dwell said, looking up.

"A good death?" he asked.

"No, he was killed," Dwell answered.

"How did you get this?" Puppa asked with a concerned look on his face.

"I searched his nest after I knew that he had passed. Before he died, everyone trusted him; he was one of our elders. We listened to him, and he was lying to us the whole time. We only found out about his identity after his death. I was so angry that he betrayed us all and risked our lives. He did this to participate in fight competitions with his freak friends. He put us at risk every day, so I went through his things and found this," he said.

"Did you find anything else?" he asked.

Dwell removed a white cloth from his sack and unfolded it to reveal six sleeves, each holding a small glass bottle. Puppa came over and looked at the bottles. He didn't know what they were, but they had a familiar marking on the bottle: "C."

"Civantes," Puppa whispered.

"Civantes?" Dwell asked.

"He is a ruthless, horrible man who has done atrocious and unspeakable crimes to others, especially children," Puppa said. "He is one of the evilest men living in our world. You may know one of the others," he said, looking at Dwell.

Dwell looked up at Puppa and said with venom on his lips, "Mullins."

"Yes, you know this devil also?" asked Puppa.

"He controls the fighters who compete against Civantes' men in the competitions at his Farm. My brother told me about the lab at his compound, where they experimented with kids—horrible stuff. My friends and I just blew up his "Farm" and many of his men, so he's not very happy with us," Dwell laughed.

"Have you shared this book with your friends?" Puppa asked Dwell.

When he didn't answer quickly, Puppa added, "Oh, I see. You are trying to be the hero. You are going to save the day, are you? Well, let me explain something to you. Heroes are exceedingly rare in this life, Dwell, and heroes' chance of a long life is even shorter. Are you planning to live a long and happy life, Dwell?"

Puppa returned his books to the desk and approached the room's entrance. He stopped before leaving the room and said, "I will let you decide what you tell your friends; they are your friends, after all." And walked out of the room.

CHAPTER 34

An Oasis

As the hours passed, the children slept while Nutay drove on, but they became restless when they awoke. Not one child asked for food or complained, but Dao and Brill could hear the rumblings of their empty stomachs. Dao moved next to Brill and whispered.

"We need to feed them, Brill."

Brill nodded and tapped Nutay on the shoulder, "Nutay, do you know where we can find some food for the children?"

Nutay was petting Dog when he smiled at Brill, "I gonna git you dese chillians somethin good," and gave the bus a little more gas. Within the hour, they were pulling into a long driveway that crested a high hill, then dipped down. He parked the bus behind the large farmhouse and turned off the engine as dusk began. Brill looked out the window to see a row of large glasshouses just a short distance from the house.

"Why are we here, Nutay?" Dao asked.

'Com, I sho you," Nutay said as he got up, opened the door, and walked off the bus.

Brill looked at Dao, waiting for Dao's approval before following Nutay.

"I'll go," Dao said as he passed in front of Brill and stepped off the bus.

Nutay hobbled down the lane with his head bobbing in the dim light. Dao ran to catch up to him, and they quietly walked together down the lane. Nutay didn't stop at the first glasshouse or the second or third; he never hesitated or broke his stride. Dao turned to watch him, but Nutay kept his head down and his feet moving. Dao wondered if Nutay was planning to ambush him and instinctively felt for his pack strap, but his pack was in the truck. They passed the last of the large glass buildings; still, Nutay didn't slow down. Dao needed to understand where they were headed, so he stopped. Nutay kept walking and said, "Fraid of a ole man?" and laughed a funny, cackling chortle. His remark relaxed Dao, who caught up to him, and they walked side by side in the shadows amongst the naked trees courtesy of the marvelous moonlight.

Dao listened to the silence of the night and kept glancing behind, wondering if Brill would come looking for him, when Nutay slowly turned left from the pathway to a blackened-out door in a blacked-out building. The building camouflage made it undetectable behind the glasshouses.

"Her, com'in her," he whispered.

He opened the door, and they stepped into the blackness. Most of the roof's glass ceiling panels had been blackened except where tree branches had scratched away the paint allowing sparse amounts of moonlight to enter. Dao could make out Nutay's shadow as he shuffled over to the wall and picked something up. Still suspicious, Dao braced himself for whatever was coming and backed up towards the door, looking for something to use as a weapon. In a beam of moonlight, he saw a small bar near the entrance which he picked up and held by his side. Nutay turned and started to walk toward Dao. As he came closer and closer, Dao saw him raise his hand. He did the same, ready to hit Nutay with the bar. Suddenly Nutay turned on a flashlight, illuminating the space. Dao's arm stopped midair as he looked around, astonished at his surroundings.

The building was full of an incredible array of fruit trees in bloom. Dao's jaw dropped, as did the bar, as he watched Nutay pick a piece of fruit from a small bush and pop it into his mouth. With his eyes closed, he passed the food over every taste bud in his mouth, savoring every bite. Dao watched him consume the whole fruit; nothing was wasted. He could only describe Nutay's reaction to eating the fruit as complete joy. Wiping his mouth with a handkerchief, Nutay looked at Dao and said,

"It's safe," and waved his arm around the room as if introducing him to the fruit and trees.

"Dis fruit it gits only rainwater fro da sky, and as you can see da roots ain't posed to any dirt t'all. Dese trees grown hydroponically, wit no soil. Da walls I blacked out so dat others can't find it. I painted da walls years ago and have been comin here to eat ever since. I haven't tole a soul, not one cept you." He said as he flashed his flashlight upon a ripe red delicious apple.

Dao had seen pictures of apples and other fruit in books in the canopy, and elders had spoken of eating such fruit as youngsters, but he had never seen an apple. Unsure the fruit was safe, he stared as it glistened in the light. Mesmerized by the brilliant red color and unable to stop, he picked up an apple and held it in both hands. It was smooth and without a flaw on its flaming red skin. Rolling it repeatedly in his hands, he smelled it, savoring the new aroma. He could almost taste it through his nose; it was that fresh.

Nutay leaned against a nearby trunk shining the light on Dao and watching him dance with the apple in his hands. He pressed it to his lips but didn't take a bite, feeling the texture of the unbroken fruit's skin on his tongue. His hunger and the ripe fruit triggered his salivary glands to overproduce saliva, which he had to keep swallowing or begin drooling. He looked at Nutay, who nodded in a kind, gentle manner as if he was giving him the approval, he needed to eat the fruit. Dao acknowledged Nutay's nod, put the apple to his mouth, and bit down hard, triggering an explosion of wonderful, sweet juice and flavors into his mouth. Unable to chew and swallow quick enough, the taste sensation was such a surprise to his taste buds that his body's physical response was to produce even more saliva, which kept rolling out of the corners of his mouth. Nutay watched and chuckled to himself. Dao saw the humor in his actions and also laughed. He quickly finished eating the apple, core, and all!

Nutay looked up, smiling at Dao, "Shall we go and get the others?"

"Yes, Sir, " said Dao, who belched and headed to the door.

CHAPTER 35

Permissible Fruit

Minutes later, Dao was on the bus with a big smile.

"Dao, what is it?" Brill asked, genuinely concerned.

"Come on, everyone, Nutay and I have a surprise to show you," he said.

Nutay led the older children, and Brill carried two younger children, as did Dao, who assumed the rear with Dog. Brill was uneasy walking out in the open, especially so late in the day when visibility was limited. Nutay opened the door to the blackened building and let the children in. Brill hesitated at the door as the hair on his neck stood up. He looked around; the wind and shadows dancing in the surrounding forest played tricks on his eyes. Finally, he stepped inside. Dao closed and locked the door. Uneasy seconds passed until Nutay found and turned on his light, triggering the children's collective cry of astonishment when they saw the magnificent garden.

"It's okay. It's safe to eat," Dao said as he explained the growing process. Brill picked cherries from the tree before him, popped them in his mouth, and bit down. Smiling with his mouth open, the fruit exploded in and out of his mouth until he bit hard on a pit, causing him to cringe. Dao and the children laughed.

"Don't be eatin' dem pits," Nutay advised as he flipped a switch on the wall that illuminated the orchard. The noise level increased as the children ran, picking and trying all types of fruit; even Brill, in his excitement, ignored the commotion. Soon activity levels decreased as the full-belly moaning increased. With their bellies full, the children lounged in the branches, on the floor and benches, and along the walls, too tired and full to move. Dog entertained everyone by belching in between bites of fruit. Brill relaxed and sat beside Dao and Nutay on the bench, looking at all the happy faces. It dramatically changed from the frightened and somber faces just hours earlier. What a gift to watch the joy of children being children.

Dao jumped up, "We need to go."

"Ya, we've been here too long. Hurry up, get everyone up," Brill said.

In no time, the kids were lined up in front of the door with pockets stuffed with fruits; even Dog had a menagerie of fruit skewered on his tail barb.

"Otay, let's go back quiet," Nutay said, with a finger to his mouth. The children silently marched into the night towards the bus until one of the younger children whispered, "I don't feel very good."

Brill and Dao understood perfectly, as their stomachs were rolling as well. The group slowed as the fruit raced through their intestinal tracts creating rumblings of uncertainty in their bowels. Nutay continued at the same pace without missing a step. Brill's concern heightened as their trek back to the bus took longer than expected in the fully exposed moonlight. Brill's anxiety rose as the group's vulnerability on the open pathway increased when the children's pace slowed even further.

"Hurry, everyone. We need to get on the bus. Please, we must go faster," Brill was pleading now and trying to corral them into a line towards the bus. Unfortunately for Brill, the children's only concern was their upset tummies. No longer would the Snatchers hurt them, so they didn't have any worries, only their tummy aches. Struggling to convince his young charges of the urgency to move, Brill tried to make them understand that he could help them feel better, but only if they were on the bus. Some of the smaller children decided they couldn't go on and stopped. One even sat on the ground. Dao stood him up, trying to get him to walk, but he would have none of it and sat down again, crossed his arms and legs, and refused to budge. Dao gave him a slight push, but it didn't help.

They were two glass buildings away from the bus when Brill and Dao smelled it, that distinct moldy rotting smell with which they were, unfortunately, all too familiar. Brill looked around as he picked another child off the ground and yelled at the children, "Run, everybody, run! Get on the bus." As he was herding them forward, he caught wind of a familiar smell on his left near the forest's edge. A Demoni pack was running silently alongside the treeline about two hundred yards away, following them and watching them. Dao screamed, "Run, the dogs are coming." The children picked up the pace as they ran toward the bus.

Nutay was already at the bus with the door opened as the children sprinted in, including Dog. Bringing up the rear were Dao and Brill, each with two young children in their arms, racing for the door when the dogs broke from the tree line directly towards them. Everyone had safely reached the bus except for them and their little ones as the dogs gained on them. They could hear and see the children hanging out of the bus windows screaming for them to hurry. Dao was in the lead, but they were still a glasshouse away.

It broke Nutay's heart to see the children so upset.He looked to the dogs, which were dangerously close within yards of the boys. They would not make it, so he opened the door, left it ajar, and went out. The lead dog was just inches away from taking a bite from Brill's leg. Brill's speed was no match for the wild dog. He tried to go faster than his legs could carry him when his toe got caught in a hole, causing him to stumble and fall. Somehow, he managed to keep hold of the children.

The lead dog stopped running, sauntered to where Brill lay on the ground with the two children and lowered its head. Brill quickly stood, helped the small ones to their feet, and pushed them behind him. Dao kept running and made it to the bus. He didn't know Brill had fallen until he put the two little ones into a seat and looked out the window. He raced off the bus towards his friend when he heard.

"Stop, Dao, stay where you are. I'm going to let the little ones come to you. Okay? Call them." Brill locked eyes with the lead dog.

Dao stopped and called the names of the children clinging to Brill's legs and sobbing.

"Bree, Kip, come here. Come on. It's not going to hurt you, okay? I won't let it. Turn around and look at me. Okay. Come on," he said with his arms open wide towards them. Slowly, the children made their way to him. He wrapped them in his arms and placed them in Flippy's seat, and got back off the bus.

The lead dog walked around Brill while the other dogs sat on their haunches behind it. The lead dog stopped and stared into Brill's eyes. Brill stared back and recognized the animal; it was the alpha at the overhang that Callow had stabbed. Brill knew this was no ordinary dog but a cool and collected killer. Brill looked and reached for anything within arms' length to help him, but there was nothing. He checked his pockets and felt his red elixir, a yellow ball, herbs, and the roll-on bottle.

The dog barred its teeth and swung its head from side to side as if tearing apart flesh. Brill wanted to tell Nutay to take off, but he was afraid to take his eyes off the dog, which yawned, exposing a mouth full of razor-sharp teeth. Instead, he crouched in an attack position and waited for the dogs to move, and the alpha did. Coming so close, Brill could feel its breath on his skin before it lunged at him. Brill dove, but the dog caught his forearm, tearing the skin and exciting the other dogs with the scent of his blood. The lead dog lunged again, tearing the skin from his shin. Brill realized that his situation was deteriorating quickly, but there was still time to save the children, so he yelled at Dao, "Dao, get on the bus and get out the kids to safety. Go."

Dao heard Brill and made his way over to his friend, close enough that Brill could see him. "Not a chance Buddy," was all he said.

CHAPTER 36

Good and Bad Therapies

"**D**ao, you don't understand; this is no ordinary dog. It's the Demoni that Callow stabbed at the overhang in the forest," Brill said, and as he did, the dog started snarling at Dao, exposing its teeth before it refocused on Brill. The animal seemed to understand their conversation and then dove at Brill, catching hold of his foot. Trying to pull his foot away was fruitless as the dog's grip, and Brill's exhaustion increased.

"Brill, can you catch something if I throw it to you?" Dao asked.

"Dao, he's not going to let me catch anything," he said, focusing all his attention on the dog.

The dog released his foot and bared its teeth at Dao again. With its head held low, it moved directly in front of Brill, gauging the distance to his neck when a rock flew near its head. Brill ducked, and for an instant, the dog lost his concentration on Brill. An onslaught of rocks followed; Brill covered his head. Curious about where the stones were coming from, he saw Nutay chucking rocks at the dogs, hitting them more than he missed. The support dogs jumped around, trying to avoid the incoming projectiles but not the alpha dog. It held its ground unwavering even as it was struck as it kept its focus on Brill. The other dogs reacted viciously to Nutay's attack and turned toward him. The alpha ignored the bus driver until a large rock came crashing down on its hind leg, causing it to jump; then, it took off after Nutay alongside the other dogs.

Dao yelled, "No!" as the dogs converged on their friend biting and tearing at him. At the bus, Dao got Nutay's gun and rapidly fired off all the shots remarkably close to the dogs without hitting them. Hesitantly, they backed away with bared bloody teeth and withdrew to the forest but not before the alpha dog stared down Brill, turned, and was then swallowed up by the forest. With his elixir in his hand, Dao reached Nutay, who was barely breathing and poured Mama's magic into his mouth, instantly triggering the regeneration of tissues in his body. Nutay watched in astonishment as the formation of new tissue on the lacerations in his abdomen, arms, and legs repaired his injuries. Brill held Nutay while he kept his eyes on the forest, expecting the lead dog to return and finish them, but he didn't.

"Let's get you into the bus," Brill said as they lifted Nutay onto his feet just as a spine-tingling howl was heard from the forest. They quickly got him into a seat amongst the children, most of whom were crying. Nutay struggled but sat up and, with his soothing words, assured the children that he was all right, but one child was inconsolable. Nutay picked him up, sending excruciating pain throughout his body, but he held the child tightly. The small child nestled in his arms and was soon asleep. Dog sympathized with Nutay and started licking his wounds, but his rough tongue was like sandpaper; Nutay, appreciative of his friend, petted him while pushing him away.

More children surrounded Nutay with concern on their little faces.

"Hey, looki, I's fine tinni ones," he said.

He heard a little voice between sobs, "But I saw those bad dogs hurt you and make you bleed."

Nutay looked at the little girl and said, "Lok, I's fine, not a tooth marc on me."

The little one wiped her eyes, smiled, and hugged Nutay hard.

Brill placed a few drops of Dao's blue elixir on his tongue.

"Dao, can you drive?" he asked.

Dao jumped into the driver seat, started the bus, and slowly pulled out of the driveway and onto the road. In their haste, they didn't see the dogs following them from a distance.

<hr />

The Principals' vehicles started arriving bright and early the following day, hours early to avoid being late, and they didn't come alone; it was too dangerous. A handful of their guards accompanied them for self-preservation. They were aware of their master's volatile and unpredictable behavior. Safe passage home for anyone after meeting with Civantes was not a guarantee as his health continued to deteriorate. His hollow eye sockets and ashen and sloughing skin were evidence of his faltering health.

Time was a luxury he could not afford, so he scheduled all his scientists, pharmacists, and biomedical researchers to work both day and night to find a cure. None of the testing, therapies, or experiments had been successful; promising but not unsuccessful. He would never announce those results to anyone, especially not the Captain, who was in the same health race for the restoration and regeneration of tissues as Civantes was. At the compound, rumors persisted that more than one scientist had gone missing after a promising new therapy failed. These weren't rumors, just like at the Lair. Those working in the lab did not do so voluntarily; instead, they worked under indentured servitude, and their fates were tied directly to the success of their work.

Civantes opened the door to his massive state-of-the-art research laboratory. As the doors opened, everyone inside the room quietly stopped working and dropped their eyes to hide from his gaze. He leisurely strolled through the various departments making small talk with anyone in a white lab coat. He didn't notice that most researchers were taking off their coats and hiding them in cupboards. Panning the room for someone in a white jacket, he randomly asked,

"Well, what are the results of the newest therapies and recent test results?"

He was too familiar with and bored of the same generic bullshit answers. He had heard it all before, too damn frequently. "The trial results seem *positive*, and the treatment looks *promising* because the initial stages are *encouraging*, but we won't know for quite some time if the therapy will work 100%." Civantes was sick of the same verbal garbage. A mature female with the nametag Dr. Christ pinned to her white coat continued working undeterred by Civantes' disruption. She was one of the few lead researchers who was not afraid of Civantes, at least not outwardly.

"Well, Dr. Christ, what wonderful news do you have to report?" he snidey asked.

"Well, the treatment looks promising from our initial stages. We have only cultivated positive cell growth from one healthy child out of the thousands of samples we have harvested for testing. We have been working on this specimen cell line for the last three months, and the results look tentatively positive. The problem is that the induced cell lines get overwhelmed by the infected host much later, months after induction. Initially, the healthy cells take control of the mitochondria spurring antibody production and creating new healthy proteins to replace the damaged ones at all cellular levels. At the time of cell invasion, the hosts experience the shedding of the infected cells at an accelerated rate. Weeks later, we find the healthy cells become exhausted from dumping the toxic waste from the cells and collapse. Once overwhelmed, the healthy cells suspend production and functionality, initiating loss of control and deterioration of the therapy and the host-vector."

Angrily, Civantes asked, "What positive effects have you witnessed?"

"We have seen an increase in healthy blood cell and host antibody production in the research subjects. The skin returned to a healthy hue, resulting in a decline in the severity and scope of the body's self-eradication of the dermis and epidermis layers. Preliminary results have also shown a decrease in the size of the skull due to a reduction in the amount of fluid in the cranium. Transitorily, we have also seen a continuing solidification of the skull cavity to a level of customary standard dimensions, albeit for only short periods," she said.

Civantes lifted a scalpel off the counter and twisted it until the light caught the blade. He moved closer to Dr. Christ.

"So, Doctor, what do you think it will take to get us to the next level to have positive, long-lasting permanent results?" he asked sarcastically.

In a firm voice, Dr. Christ moved nervously back away from the counter but said, "A 100% healthy specimen to utilize in adult stem cell therapies is the only plausible solution I see now."

"And where would I find a 100% healthy specimen, Doctor?" he asked.

Without wavering, she said, "Possibly in a tree dweller."

Civantes started to chuckle at first and then psychotically. The doctor backed away from him, as did everyone else in the room, as his explosive and deadly behavior was well known to all. The lab did not have enough hiding places for everyone.

"And where am I going to find a tree dweller?" he asked with an elevated voice.

She pulled a small notebook out of her lab coat and opened it. A folded piece of paper fell out and onto the floor. The Doctor slowly bent down and picked it up, never taking her eyes off Civantes. She defiantly stood up as Civantes gently took the paper from her hand and unfolded it. The paper had grey pencil shading over it, revealing white letters. Civantes read the note, which was a printed copy of the letter that Dr. Hamm had sent to Dr. Swallow years ago. As he read the message, his eyes opened wide. He folded the note and put it into his pocket.

"Well, Dr. Christ, I guess I need to go hunting in Province IV, where we will find those tree-dwellers so that you can find an answer to my health problems, or you're going to have severe health problems yourself," he said as he walked away from her. She didn't respond. On his way out, he planted the knife in a young researcher's hand resting on a counter without breaking his stride.

Once outside, he turned sharply towards his most trusted guard, Vile, and said, "Put a group of Snatcher fighters together for a hunting trip to Province IV. Ensure that only the best is recruited and tell them they leave in an hour. Call them Takers because they will take those tree dwellers and return them to me. Oh ya, pack a bag for yourself. You're going too. And tell them that they find the tree dwellers or don't bother coming back." Civantes started walking away but turned back to see Vile standing behind him.

"Why the hell are you still standing there? GO. Get moving. NOW!" he yelled, and Vile took off running.

CHAPTER 37

Unknown Horrors

Feeling tired and wanting to sleep, Jup remained quiet in the back of the truck, unsure if it was safe to snooze with Mullins so close. He knew he was expendable, just like everyone else, so he stayed awake as the convoy of trucks sped down the road with Mullins vehicle leading the way.

Mama listened to the latest patch transmissions from someone named Vile, notifying specific Snatchers to get ready to go hunting. He said the message was from Civantes. She knew that Mullins was heading to Province II to find Civantes. Vile was told to send the Snatchers; he called 'Takers' to Province IV to find us. Mama heard all the messages, unlike the other members of the Clan. She didn't feel a need to tell them what she knew; it would only panic them. Sitting at the table, she wondered where the couriers were when Jith stopped by to ask her a question.

"What's going on, Mama? How are the kids?" she asked.

"I don't know, Jith. They were told to stay off the patches to ensure their safety, and they have. They are good kids. I don't know if they're safe with so many predators and obstacles in their path. I pray they are. I do know that there are young, smart, strong, and determined – that is their strength," Mama said.

Jith sat down next to Mama and grabbed her hand. "Mama, it's time to help our kids."

Mama looked up into her deep blue eyes but never said a word.

Dao drove all day and night while the children remained quiet and well-behaved. Before he went to sleep to heal, Nutay told them where to find gas. In the middle of the night, they passed out of Province III into Province II. According to their maps, they were still a day and a half away from the Lair and lots of time for things to go wrong. They drove, hoping to meet up with their friends sooner rather than later.

Members of The Refuge gathered in the dining area to say goodbye to their newfound friends. Dwell spoke up on behalf of the group explaining the importance of leaving as soon as possible to find their friends and destroy the Snatchers before they found them. Puppa assured them that he and his men would do the same and continue to destroy every encampment they could find.

"Take care of your friends and family, Dwell. Go in truth, stay together, and stay strong together because nobody needs a hero," he said as he winked and shook Dwell's hand. Dwell smiled back.

Sad to leave so soon, Snag and Callow hugged and thanked Bumma and the children and promised to return in the future. Cat peered out from under Bumma's dress unbeknownst to her. As the friends walked away, it pranced after them in an array of colorful ribbons and bows courtesy of the children. The warm hugs from their newfound friends encouraged and energized the team more than the family could ever have known. With their packs on their back and tears in their eyes, they followed Mose, Rep, and Puppa to their vehicle in the early dawn light. The truck had gas, water, food, weapons from the cave, and a shotgun hidden behind the seat. Puppa explained that the sound weapon only worked in enclosed spaces, but the liquid light could be used anywhere.

Puppa took out his map, and they reviewed the safest route to take and which areas to avoid. He pointed out the Principal sites on their way and described the terrain in those areas. Again, Dwell thanked Puppa for all his help and was about to get into the truck when Puppa put his hand on his arm and said, "Dwell, I would feel a lot better if I sent Mose and Rep with the three of you. They are great fighters and experienced trackers."

Dwell didn't know how to respond. He knew he could care for his friends and himself; he already had. Callow overheard Puppa's offer, and before Dwell could refuse, she spoke up, "That would be great, Puppa. Thank you so much."

Instantly, Dwell could feel the anger rise in his throat. Puppa saw the frustration on Dwell's face and handed him a small bag saying, "Take this; it might come in handy." Dwell gently placed the bag under the seat while Callow, Cat, and Snag jumped in the cab, and Mose and Rep climbed into the back.

"Don't worry, Dwell; you won't even know they are there. They're not heroes, just great men," Puppa said as he walked away. Dwell thought about Puppa's words and then took off after him.

"Thanks, Puppa. I am so grateful for all your help and understanding. Your family has done so much for us; we appreciate it and hope to see all of you again." Then he shook Puppa's hand and ran back to the truck. Before he got in, he turned back to him and yelled, "Hey Puppa, I'm no hero either. I'm just trying to do the right thing, so nobody gets hurt," then jumped in and pulled away.

Puppa nodded as they pulled away and said to himself. "Aren't we all Dwell, aren't we all? The problem is, it's hard to protect your family when you don't know whom you're fighting. Never will understand why humans spend more time pushing each other down when they should be lifting them up." Then he turned and walked away.

They drove the full day towards the border of Provinces III and II. As dusk fell, the sky turned a magnificent orange. The men opened the flaps, lay down, and watched the sunset. Dwell surrendered his driving duties to Snag, and Callow jumped in the back to relax and rest. The terrain gave way to gently sloping hills and deep valleys as the majestic sunset illuminated their surroundings and draped them in beautiful colors. No one spoke, each lost in their thoughts as the surroundings changed with each passing minute. Suddenly the landscape changed. There are vast fields of thousands of markers in rows upon rows, field after field. 3

Dwell sat up, interested in what all the sticks could mean, so he asked Mose and Rep.

"Graves," replied Mose.

"Was there a battle here?" Dwell asked, astonished by the vast numbers.

"Well, not really," Rep replied.

"Well, then who died," he asked as he turned to look at Rep.

Rep turned from Dwell to the fields and spoke, "In the beginning, the farmers got sick and died because they worked directly with the land chemicals. Then the wives passed. The Snatchers came and scrounged around at the abandoned farms looking for stuff to steal, eat, or do whatever they do. That was when they found the children and snatched them. Some children became enslaved, some became fighters, and who knows what else? We couldn't stand by as our most precious and vulnerable were taken, so we vowed to help because we had a moral duty, which became our mission. We organized into groups throughout the provinces and trained men to fight because, in the beginning, there were many battles between our two groups everywhere.

It was a horrible mistake; we were no match for the Snatchers. These creatures are strong, barbaric, and live in the wild like animals; we are soft and slow. We didn't know how to protect ourselves, let alone others! We were easy pickings for them. Spending years on couches playing games and eating junk food made us sedentary and obese, and it finally caught up with us. We paid dearly for it with many lives and the lives of our loved ones. So, in the beginning, we were a miserable failure.

See, throughout the history of the world, the strong have always survived and thrived, and we all know this. In a free society, the people's success was due to the mental and physical fortitude of both men and women to care for themselves and the most helpless and susceptible in their tribes or societies; the young and elderly. That is how successful communities are built, grown, and protected. Over time attitudes changed, cultures lost empathy for one another, and the most basic human instincts of survival didn't matter as many became 'soft' and pathetic.

We tried to train our weaker members, but over time, they were too unmotivated, unskilled, and out of shape, and they knew it. They knew they were no match against the muscle of the Snatchers, so they didn't even resist. In their world of self-pity, they thought that the Snatchers would understand their weakness and have pity on them as society had; they were wrong. Their lack of pride and helplessness infuriated the Snatchers, and the opposite happened; it was a slaughter.

If only generations ago, parents could have seen their children's futures; surely, they would have focused more on teaching them survival and life skills. Physical labor and lessons on morals and respect build up the body and soul with character and integrity. Men need to be strong, not only for themselves but for others."

The fields passed, and the markers faded as the truck rolled on. Dwell sat lost in his thoughts. He couldn't understand why so many people could make so many bad decisions that affected many others. He was sad for all the lost souls who didn't have someone care enough about them to save them or at least try. He was so thankful for his family, especially his parents, whom he could always count on even when he disagreed with them. He saw their love every day in their words and actions.

CHAPTER 38

Callow's Concerns

The back window suddenly slid open, and Callow's smiling face appeared. "We need to get fuel at the next farm."

"If the light on the fuel gauge just went on, we should be good for quite a while. We don't have to stop at the next farm because the tank still holds quite a bit of residual fuel. We can drive another thirty minutes before we need to stop," Dwell said.

"It has been on for quite a while now. Snag and I were talking, and we forgot about it and lost track of time, so we must stop, or we're going to run out," she said sheepishly.

Dwell shot her a "really" look as she turned around and closed the sliding window slowly.

He got up and sat on the wheel well across from Mose and Rep, looking around at the barren landscape, not a house or a farm in sight, only vegetation and dirt. Minutes passed before Snag crested a hill, and they could see a building at the bottom. Dwell banged on the window and mouthed the words to Callow as he pointed toward the building.

"Pull in there."

The vehicle coasted into the long driveway towards the solitary building. Mose and Rep pulled the tarp over the truck bed, concealing themselves as Snag stopped next to the building. It looked abandoned. Callow got out and was joined by Mose and Rep, but Cat remained inside sleeping. Dwell also got out and was joined by Snag on the driver's side.

"We won't be able to get up the next hill without fuel," Snag said.

Dwell shot him a dirty look for being so irresponsible and walked ahead, saying, "Stay here with Callow and Rep. Mose and I will go and check it out."

Mose followed Dwell, who tried the front door of the building. It was locked. They circled the corrugated metal building looking for open windows or doors, but there were none. Checking the ground around the building for tracks, Mose found none.

Mose told no one in particular, "There's no way to get in."

Dwell stood looking at the front of the building, wondering if he could get on the roof, but there were no ladders or footholds on the exterior.

"Let's just break the door down," said Snag.

"Let's not. We don't know what's in there or who's out here," Callow said as she scanned the yard. Her eyes landed on a rusted piece of machinery on the left side of the building, and she noticed that the dirt under the machine had been disturbed. She walked over, dug in the ground with her toe, and hit something hard.

"Guys, come here. There's something here," she said.

They came over and uncovered a door. Callow jumped back when she saw it.

"Don't open that, Dwell," she cried.

Using his hand, Dwell wiped away the remaining dirt uncovering a metal ring attached to one end of the door. He grasped the ring and started to pull.

"Don't," screamed Callow.

Dwell stopped and looked at her.

"Hey, what is your problem?"

"Humonsters, that's my problem," Callow said while moving back from the door.

"Callow, the Humonsters are in the drains. We don't know if this is a drain. There might be buried supplies under this door. We must look. We're out of gas!" he said as he was losing his patience.

"Don't go in there, Dwell. I'm telling you, whatever is in there is not good," she said defiantly.

"Come on, Callow. We're in the middle of nowhere. There's nothing in there, you'll see," he said quietly and more empathically than before. Snag placed his arm around Callow holding her tight.

"Mose gives me a hand," Dwell yelled.

Mose came over, bent down, and helped Dwell lift the door; it didn't budge. He noticed a steel pin under the dirt just in front of the ring along the edge, dug it out, and pulled. The seal on the door released the door just a fraction. Mose looked at Dwell, listening; nothing.

Dwell took hold of the ring and pulled upward, opening the door without a sound. The heavy smell of must and dust flew up and settled on them as they looked at one another. Dwell returned to the truck to get his solar panel and battery and returned to the others. The light exposed a ladder and shelving in the shaft stacked with cans of food, clothing, supplies, and tools. Dwell was relieved when he saw the fuel cans and looked up at Mose, who gave him a thumbs up.

Dwell turned back towards Callow and mockingly said to her, "Callow come and look, no Humonsters down here, just tools and tomatoes."

But Callow didn't move; she glared at him and remained where she was near the truck, unconvinced.

"I'll go down," Mose said as he took the light from Dwell, climbed into the hollow, and proceeded down the ladder.

"Just pass the stuff up," Dwell said.

Mose stepped off the ladder and onto the dirt floor at the bottom of the shaft and passed the light around, inspecting the cache. Grabbing the cans of food, he threw them up to Dwell, who threw them to Snag, who threw them to Rep in the back of the truck. Inspecting the fuel cans, Mose took off the caps to smell the contents, it was gas, but the containers were too heavy to carry or throw up the ladder.

"The fuel cans are full, but I can't throw them up," he yelled up the ladder. He then threw up a rope and told Dwell to tie it off on the truck; he did. Mose attached the cans for Dwell and Snag to pull up. Callow and Snag filled the truck while the men pillaged the supply shaft.

"Let's go, Dwell. Those footprints are not old. Someone was recently here," she said worriedly.

But Dwell ignored her as Mose continued to send items up the ladder limiting their sitting space in the back of the truck.

"That's enough, Dwell," Snag said. "There's isn't any space left in the back for us to sit."

"All right, Mose," Dwell called down the ladder, "That's enough. The truck is full. Come on back up."

Dwell got up and leaned against the truck wiping his hands on his pants.

Mose didn't respond; he continued inspecting the shelves. Behind the ladder, he removed a few items from the shelf and found a door directly behind.

"Dwell, hey Dwell," he called out. Dwell peered down the shaft.

"There's a door down here behind the ladder," Mose said.

"Well, open it," Dwell called back.

"I can't. The ladder is in the way," he replied.

CHAPTER 39

Reoccurring Nightmare

While Snag and Callow continued to load the gas tanks, Dwell inspected the top of the ladder. It was hanging by brackets. Dwell pulled upwards and lifted the ladder out of the hole with Rep's help. Mose shone his light at the door and saw that the steel panel could be lifted entirely off the wall. Putting down his light without saying a word, he grabbed the door and lifted it from the slots in the wall. Mose covered his mouth and nose as the smell of rot shot out of the hole and into the shaft. Once the smell dissipated and no noise could be heard, Mose poked his head and light into a long cement tunnel hole when 'something' suddenly jumped him from above.

Its white eyes and translucent gray skin shone in the light, now lying in the tunnel. It attacked Mose, who could not fight back with his legs in the shaft and his upper body through the panel. The creature was relentless, and within seconds, Mose stopped moving and lay dead. Dwell scurried away from the hole to get a weapon while yelling at Mose, who didn't answer. Rep jumped out of the truck and ran to the shaft; he couldn't see very well, but he could undoubtedly hear something scratching and scurrying in the dark. The light inside the tunnel cast a faint glow into the shaft when Rep saw the horrid creature blast through the small door and clamor up the shelves in the shaft.

He flew backward onto the ground, crawling on his backside and hands as Dwell and Snag stood at the trap door, ready to attack.

"It's the Humonsters," Callow screamed as she headed for the truck's cab.

The creature crested the opening, struggling to focus in the light. Motionless, it stood sniffing the air until it located its nearest prey. Rep tried to stand but kept slipping in the dirt. The creature lowered itself on its stumps, revealing long sharp teeth, just before it launched itself at Rep. Rep put his arms up to protect his head and neck when the gunshot rang out, and the Humonster fell dead at his feet.

Dwell and Snag looked back at Callow, standing with the shotgun in her hands. Stunned, she didn't move as Dwell went over and kicked the creature to ensure it was dead. He ran to the hole and called for Mose, but there was no answer.

Snag took the gun from Callow's hands.

"We have to check if he's still alive," Callow said disbelievingly. "We can't just leave him."

Dwell, and Snag watched Rep walk to the hole's edge and peered downward. His brother's broken body lay motionless between the tunnel and the storage cellar.

"He's gone," Rep said and walked away.

Dwell threw the ladder and the Humonster down the shaft, grabbed the door, sealed it with Snag's help, and placed the machinery directly on top.

"Let's get out of here," Snag said, jumping into the driver's seat.

Callow and Snag joined Dwell upfront while Rep jumped into the back alone, shaken and silent. Within minutes they were back on the road and up the next hill headed to Province II. Cat awoke from sleep, had a big, disjointed stretch, curled back up in Callow's lap, and went back to sleep.

<hr />

The Principals sat nervously around the table, wondering when Civantes would arrive. There were thirteen seats around the table, and some were still empty. The sound of the clock ticking on the wall was deafening in the anxiety-filled room. A short man with a huge head came running down the hall and tried to enter the room, but the momentum of his large head didn't allow him to stop in time to turn into the meeting room. Instead, he turned his head sideways, in the direction of the room as his body continued sliding past and down the hall until he stopped. Gathering himself, he turned around, frantically entered the room, sat down, and tried to disappear. The others in the room snickered but didn't look up or speak.

Minutes later, guards appeared in the hall with Civantes in the middle of them. They stopped in front of the door but didn't enter. Instead, Civantes stood quietly at the door facing into the room, watching. The Principals thought he was straining with all his might to listen to their discomfort, which was palpable. Slowly he placed his hand on the handle as the Principal Snatchers painstakingly watched and waited. Turning the handle, he opened the door, holding it for only a second until the guard behind him reached out to hold it. The guard strained to hold the heavy door ajar in a backhanded position while Civantes took his time to enter.

The guard's arm began to shake uncontrollably while Civantes stood under the doorframe, but he dared not let go of the door; his life depended on it. He was on the verge of collapsing when Civantes finally entered the room. Walking around the table, he made mental notes of who should have been in the empty seats. He made his way to the head of the table as another Principal member turned the corner in the hall, quickly entered the room, and sat down in his designated seat while Civantes watched. The man turned and looked towards Civantes, hoping he hadn't noticed him arrive, but he did. His perspiration and bobbing head deceived him, garnishing more attention to himself. As the seconds passed, a puddle of anxiety silently formed on the table under his bobbing head.

The Principal next to him watched and started to giggle. Soon his giggle turned into a stifling laugh, and then he lost the ability to control it. Civantes glared at the man, and he immediately composed himself so abruptly that he swallowed his tongue, causing him to gag.

"You're late," Civantes yelled.

The late man hesitated to respond. Mustering up the courage to do so, he said,

"Sir, the note I received didn't have a start time for the meeting, so I assumed 6:00 am would be early enough. Was I wrong?" he mumbled.

"Yes, you were wrong," Civantes said as he fired his gun. He grazed the gagging man. Knowing he had missed his target, he adjusted his aim and fired again. This time he hit the tardy man in the head, causing him to fall backward onto the floor. The other Principals moved away from the dead man, turned with strained looks towards Civantes, and remained silent. The man wasn't laughing now, as all his attention was squarely focused on Civantes.

"I'm glad to see that I have everybody's attention now though we are still missing some bodies. Does anyone know where these fine gentlemen might be?" he asked with a sinister tone.

No one spoke. As soon as the question was asked, Principals dropped their heads, did not look up, and slid further down in their chairs, hoping to become invisible.

"Freaks," he said under his breath. "Listen up. Company is coming. I don't know how many of you have met my friend Captain Mullins, but he is on his way. I expect him to arrive in the next day or two, and I want you to welcome him with all the hospitality we can muster. I want him to be so overwhelmed when he gets here that he never leaves and stays here forever, IN A HOLE IN THE GROUND!" he said as he pounded his fists on the table for emphasis.

Because it was in their best interest to do so, the men overemphasized their cajoling and laughter in support of Civantes' attempt at humor.

"So, we need to prepare for his visit, and this is what we will do."

We need to consolidate and transport all our weapons to my Lair immediately, along with any creatures, fighters, guns, Snatchers, and children who can be used for defensive purposes.

The Principals scattered as soon as Civantes finished speaking while Civantes lingered in the room wondering why all the seats weren't full.

CHAPTER 40

Where to Hide the Children?

Brill's concern for the children's welfare grew as they drove on. He didn't know where they were going to hide them. Soon they would be crossing into Province II. He looked over at Nutay, who was wakening from one of the many naps his battered body desperately needed. Nutay caught Brill staring at him, came over and sat beside him without waking the children.

"Watcha tinkin bout?" he asked Brill.

"Nutay, I've got to get these children someplace safe. I don't even want to take them into Province II, let alone anywhere near Civantes," he said with great concern.

"Ril, yo jus gotta ask. I no wher we tak'em dat's real safe an not too far from here. I no someon who luv tak'in care uv chillans, you gon see," Nutay said with a smile on his face.

"Please, Nutay, no surprises," he pleaded.

Nutay turned to look Brill straight in the eyes and said, "I not a bad perso Ril. I got taken when I was a little boy. They tok me from mi hom and mi brothers to, an send me to work for'em. I din't hav dis big head as a boy but wheir da tak us, da waters bad we drinc it all day long an then we look lik dis," he said as he pointed the finger at his head.

"I luv chillans. I do anthin to help'em. I got no prises for you n Dao. You saved mi life, but I do no a plac dat we can hid'em an it isn't too far from here. Wher's yo map Ril?"

Brill pulled the map from his pocket. Nutay scoured the map from side to side and up and down until he found what he was looking for.

"Dar, dat's wher we go'in," he said with his finger on a spot close to their present location. This route would take them off the secondary highways onto tertiary roads made of gravel, dirt, and uncertainty.

Brill took his time to scrutinize the directions that Nutay had described and asked, "How much time will this cost us?"

Nutay looking at him quizzically with a big smile, said, "You ain't gon loos no time Ril, dis way goin' get you more time. It's shorter goin' on dese dirt roads, so you be dere early to meet Civantes, no worries."

"We're not going to lose any time; that's great, Nutay, but where are we going, and who's going to take care of these wonderful children when we get there?" he asked with compassion and sorrow.

Nutay looked up at Brill and, with a tear in his eye, said, "We not al baad. Moos's bin made baad, but som of us stil ver good. I take you to a place where ther's nothin' but good, and the chillians goin' luv it dare. We kno dat dey a gift an we treat'em dat way."

Brill nodded at Nutay and placed his arm around him. "Okay, Nutay, you show me."

Nutay walked to the front of the bus and spoke quietly to Dao, who slowed and moved out of the driver's seat so Nutay could drive. The bus picked up speed, waking Flippy, who got up, sat in the seat behind Nutay, and leaned forward to place his hand on Nutay's shoulder while he drove.

Brill showed Dao on the map their current location and the location of Province II, three hours away. He had a couple of yellow balls in his pockets, half a bottle of red elixir, the letter, herbs, and the sticky green roll-on.

He forgot about the thin silver item he had clipped to the inside of the letter. He took it out and looked at it. It had a button on one end and a hole at the other with a clip on the side. Pointing it at the opposite wall, he pressed the button, emitting a bright red laser light from the hole that shone on the wall. Within seconds, smoke arose as the bright red light burnt into the wall melting the steel with incredible ease. Enthralled by the power of the small light, he began etching a tree into the side of the bus. Dao found a small note tucked deep in one of his pockets. The letter was from Callow. He opened it and read,

'Dearest Dao,

If you are reading this letter, then you are safe. I do not often tell you how proud I am of you and how you care for Mom and me. We have always looked out for one another, and I hope that will always be the case. I am so grateful for our closeness. I do not ever recall us keeping any secrets between us, and for that, I am also thankful. Please take care of each other. I can't wait to see both of you again.

Love, Your sister, Callow.'

Dao folded the note and looked across the aisle at Brill, who was etching designs with the laser all over the back of the bus.

"Brill, knock it off and put that thing away," he told his friend.

Brill pressed the button extinguishing the light. He glanced over at Dog, who was being used as a pillow by the children. Brill laughed to himself. He put the light away into his pocket.

"How much farther, Nutay?" asked Dao.

"Nother hour or so we pull'in in," he replied. They continued down the highway with clear skies and high hopes.

CHAPTER 41

Unwanted Guests

As the bus drove on, Dao finally asked, "How close are we to the Lair, Nutay?

"One mo day," he said, and suddenly a massive dog flew onto the hood, causing him to step hard on the brakes sending everyone to the floor. Scrambling quickly to his feet, Dao ran to the front of the bus with his red elixir and virtually drained it. Instantly his muscles grew in strength in front of the amazed children. Dao winked, opened the door, and climbed onto the hood to join the growling, Demoni. They sized each other up. Dao took advantage of the dog's hesitancy and lunged to grab its front leg but missed as the other two dogs sat patiently in front of the bus waiting for instructions. Dao ignored them and concentrated on the alpha dog.

Dao struggled to keep his footing on the narrow hood, so he braced himself against the windshield. The dog waited for Dao to make an error which he did when he caught his foot in the groove below the wipers. The dog launched, and Dao struck its head with his forearm, causing it to slide backward on the hood. Its eyes glowed with hate as it regained its balance and attacked Dao again, knocking him back onto the window. He grabbed the animal by the neck and wrapped his fingers around its throat. Quickly he discovered that the dog's neck was too thick, and his fingers began to slide. Struggling to maintain his grip, he threw the dog backward onto the ground, where it landed on its feet and paced in front of the bus.

Nutay, Dog, and the children watched Dao from inside the bus while Brill climbed out the back door and onto the roof, crawling as he went. He was halfway to the front when he saw the dog thrown to the ground, so he stopped as the dog paced, looked up, and disappeared out of sight. The dog stood with its back to the bus between the two other dogs. Dao did not understand what the dog was doing, but as Brill edged towards the front behind his friend, he instantly knew what the dog was doing. He had seen this communication method before.

The lead dog walked past the other dogs and circled back towards the bus while the other dogs moved into position and waited. The pack leader moved towards the bus staring at Dao, and jumped up, placing its front paws on the bumper. Dao watched it look away at the other dogs and growl at Dao, which triggered the dogs to jump onto the hood. Overwhelmed, Dao fell back onto the window but not before he smashed the head of the dog on his right sending it somersaulting onto the ground with a thud, where it remained. The dog on his left attached itself to his left thigh. He ignored that pain and concentrated on the pack leader, who had his forearm in his jaws and was thrashing its head, trying to break the bones. Dao dug his right hand into the flesh under the dog's throat and clenched his fist with all his might. The pack leader stared into Dao's eyes, but neither the dog nor Dao released their grip. The flexing caused Dao's muscles to bulge to an enormous size. The dog clamped down harder on his arm.

Brill slid next to Dao. The left dog saw Brill but did not react quickly enough as Brill slit the dog's neck. Dao felt the pressure on his thigh lessening as the dog's jaw released him. The dog bled out and slid onto the ground, dead. The lead dog saw what had happened and went crazy, thrashing and flaying its head, more determined to break his bones; it worked. The increased stress shattered Dao's bones. Dao repeatedly punched the dog on top of its head, but it would not let go.

Brill stretched over Dao, attacking the dog with his knife, but the dog would not release him. The dog's desire to kill Dao was more significant than its desire to live. Brill realized the dog would not stop until it ripped off Dao's arm. In agony, Dao violently kicked at the animal, but it did not relent. In desperation, Brill stood and jumped onto the back of the dog, wrapping his arms around its neck, attempting to cut off its air supply. The dog watched Brill jump and felt him land on its back. It immediately released Dao's limp arm, jumped off the bus, looked back at Dao, and ran.

Holding his broken arm, Dao jumped off the hood and tried to follow, but he could not keep up as he watched his friend and the dog disappear.

Breathing heavily, he returned to the bus.

"Nutay, you said you have a safe place for these kids. Could you take them there now? Don't stop until you get there."

Nutay just looked up at Dao and nodded. Dao drank from his blue elixir and addressed the children.

"Nutay here will take all of you to a safe place. No one is ever going to hurt you again. I promise you, and so does Brill. Okay?"

The children sat with their arms around each other and responded, "Yes."

Dao pointed at Nutay, "We promised to take safe care of you just like your parents would want. Just remember that you are the most important thing on this earth. Nothing is more valuable, wonderful, or beautiful than a child. So do not forget that, okay? That is what we believe. I will get Brill, so you children must help Nutay."

Then he turned and spoke to Dog,

"Dog, you help Nutay and the children here and stay out of trouble." Dog walked over to Dao and rubbed himself against his leg; Dao rubbed its head before jumping off the bus. He raced in the direction where he had last seen his best friend.

Nutay closed the door, turned towards the children, and said, "I promise to take care of yu al. Ain't nobodig gonna hurt any yu evr a'gin."

Flippy, who stood beside the driver, faced the children and said, "I know he will take good care of us cuse he took good care of me before."

Nutay fired up the engine and headed down the deserted highway as Dog watched his friend vanish into the forest. Hearing the engine, Dao turned back and watched the bus disappear.

CHAPTER 42

Uneasy Allies

Jup watched as the Captain shook his wrist patch, which sat quietly on his arm. He shook it, hoping to spur it to life, but his efforts were fruitless. Soon the interest in his patch waned, and he turned his attention towards Jup.

"So, you were a fighter. Were you any good?" the Captain asked snidely.

Calmly, Jup turned towards him and replied, "Yes, good enough to live to see today."

Mullins smiled at his response.

"Did you ever fight at The Farm?" Mullins asked.

"No, I fought in the outlying provinces," he said.

"Yes, you must have because I don't remember you, and I don't ever forget a face," Mullins said.

He looked at all the guards marching to battle around him and wondered what type of hell the Captain was leading them into. Jup shifted uncomfortably in his seat, trying to get comfortable while the Captain watched him intently. He closed his eyes and let his mind wander about how to kill the Captain if the opportunity presented itself. Mullins broke his concentration when he said, "We got a long ride ahead of us, Big Man, so why don't you tell me a little about yourself."

Jup slowly turned toward the Captain and confidently replied, "Ain't much to tell. I fight, I win, and I live."

"Ha, ha." mused Mullins. He was remarkably familiar with the details of a fighter's life. Not so long ago, he did have a stable full of them. He had seen many men maimed and killed by other men or eaten by the creatures. He had even cheered on the demise of his fighters. He felt no allegiance to his men and bet almost exclusively on the monsters to win. He looked at Jup and thought that he might have bet on him. He had no compassion, loyalty, or sympathy for anyone. Eat or be eaten was his motto, along with a win-at-all-costs creed, regardless of who paid.

Mullins saw that the middle finger on Jup's left hand was missing and wondered how he lost it. Jup noticed the Captain looking at his finger. He had enough of the Captain, turned toward the window, and watched the moving landscape.

Mullins knew there were two types of quiet men; those who had size but lacked confidence and shied away from others. They could only be provoked into action after a great deal of persuasion. The other quiet type was highly confident in their abilities and, without provocation, could kill a man in seconds. He wondered which type of man Jup was. He decided it would be in his best interest to expect the worst from Jup. The worst from a man like Jup would certainly involve his best.

As they slipped into the mountainous terrain of Province II, Snag, Callow, and Dwell traveled in silence, lost in their thoughts. Menacing skies cast shadows along the rocky road cut out of the mountain. Dwell drove cautiously along the incline, avoiding the periodic rock falls as he went. Those same falling rocks woke Rep from his sleep in the back. Callow slept with her head resting against Snag's shoulder and breathing softly.

It had been a long time since Snag had felt the softness of a woman. He felt so comfortable with Callow that he placed his left hand on her right knee. In the dashboard light, Dwell saw Snag's hand resting on Callow's knee, and anger rose in his throat. He knew, as did everyone in the canopy, that Brill and Callow had a special relationship. He was unsure if they were more than friends, but he knew *he* didn't like Snag touching or invading her personal space, especially as she slept. His eyes traveled from the window to Snag's hand and back again and again until he couldn't hold his tongue anymore.

"Hey Snag, she's sleeping, so take your hand off her knee," Dwell said.

Snag heard the bitterness in Dwell's voice and wisely decided to tread lightly in the proximity of the cab.

He did not want to wake Callow, so in a very soft voice, he said, "I'm sorry, Dwell. Does it bother you that I have my hand on her knee?"

Dwell did not like the ease with which he spoke of Callow like they were long-time friends when they had just met days ago. Dwell tried to take the sting out of his response, but Snag felt his prickly reply.

"Ya, it does bother me," he said.

Snag looked over at Dwell and said, 'Why?"

Dwell didn't know what to say. Glaring at Snag, he did not say a word, then turned back and stared out the window. Snag silently removed his hand from Callow's knee, placing it on his lap. He needed Dwell, and as much as he wanted Callow, he was no fool. It was best to keep everyone happy, at least for now.

Mama stood in the watchtower, admiring the view of the canopy. She wondered if she would always have this view. She had been coming up to the lookout for decades and loved every minute of her time up here alone. She whistled into the night sky and waited for the sound of rustling wings to draw near her. With her back against the railing, SheShe came into view just before he landed softly on the watchtower floor.

The giant bird settled himself and looked at Mama, who was now just inches from its head. She raised her hand, gently stroked it, and whispered into its ear. It cooed until Mama slowly stepped back, removed her hand from its face, and took off in flight.

Brill hung on for dear life as the Demoni sprinted for the treeline. The animal's smell was so overbearing that he thought he might pass out from the horrible stench. He held his breath. he had to stay conscious because it was much safer on the animal's back than on the ground. Digging his hands into the thick, coarse hair on its back, he intertwined his fingers into the fur in an unyielding grip. The dog was incredibly fast, and in no time, he could see that they would enter the Dead Forest, which he had seen on the map. The Dead Forest was a forest named for its lack of life. The trees had long ago died, causing their trunks to splinter in all directions. The limbs hung low as if too exhausted to hold themselves up. Many touched the ground, making the forest floor a labyrinth of limbs. The dog's experience in the forest was evident from its skillful dodging of the tree limbs while avoiding injury from the sharp branches. Living in the canopy helped Brill to do the same. He stayed low behind the dog's large head, avoiding scratches and potential impalements from the blur of trees as the dog continued running deeper into the forest.

Dao will never find me, Brill thought. Some of the trees had sunk into the moist, soft black ground leaving the lowest-lying branches lying on the ground. The dog did not let up as it headed farther into the forest. Brill knew the Demoni could have killed him long ago if it wanted to. Desperate to save himself before time ran out, he stood upon the dog's back as it ran towards a large tree and launched himself onto a branch before the beast realized what had happened. The dog slid to a stop when the weight on his back lessened, so he whipped back towards the tree, where it saw Brill high above on a bough. When Brill saw the Demoni, he climbed higher to ensure he was safely out of its reach. It watched him scramble upwards.

CHAPTER 43

Help from Afar

Digging his hand into his pocket, Brill pulled out his red elixir, yellow ball, herbs, and the green roll-on; he put back everything but the herbs. Mama said to use them when you need extra time. He snapped off some branches closest to him and made a small bundle that he wrapped and secured with the herbs. The dog watched calmly, except for its upper lip, visibly quivering in anticipation. Brill knew the dog was too clever to chase the stick if he threw it, so he planned to drop it accidentally.

The information sheet on the herbs stated, "Do not eat, smoke, or put on your skin for an extended period. Use of this item: ingestion - will cause any living thing to fall unconscious immediately - body size and amount of herb exposure will determine the length of unconsciousness - use with extreme caution."

Brill checked the knots on the herbs, then wiped his hands on his pants. Holding the bare end of the stick, he pretended to be stacking the sticks on the nearby branch when they fell to the ground. He gasped as they fell directly below him, right before the dog. Brill jumped up and down on the bough, frantically motioning with his arms for the dog to leave the bundle alone, and for about twenty seconds, the dog did. As Brill became more animated, so too did the dog as it sniffed at the herbs. Brill continued to shoo the dog away in vain as the dog became more and more intrigued with its find. Brill moved down the tree trunk for effect. Slowly the dog got up off his haunches and sniffed at the sticks nuzzling the bundle, turning it over and over in front of itself. Brill started to yell and toss branches at the dog to pique the animal's interest, and it did.

The Demoni picked up one of the bundles in its mouth, clamped down hard with its powerful jaws splintering the sticks, chewed, and swallowed. Brill continued his protestations spurring the dog to move onto the remaining branches, chewing and consuming the herbs and part of that branch. After it had swallowed the third mouthful, it sat down on its haunches and resumed staring at Brill, who was now straddling a thick branch and leaning against the trunk, watching. It did not take long for the properties of the herbs to take effect as the dog's eyes struggled to stay open, and its head began to sag.

In no time, Demoni was asleep on the ground. Recalling Mama's advice, Brill scrambled down the tree and headed back in the direction they had come. Thankful to be away from the horrid animal's rancid smell, he kept going, but it was slow going in the bog with no end to the forest. Sometimes clearings would appear, making it easier to run, but most of the time, it was easier to crawl to avoid the sharp limbs.

Fatigue was setting in, so he stopped in the mud for a rest. He knew it was dangerous, but he was exhausted. Lying on his belly with his head on his forearms, he thought of home, his parents, his brother, and Callow. It was comfortable in the wet soil, but he needed to move. He kept telling himself to do so, but his legs and arms would not respond. His mind convinced him that it was easier to go to sleep. Then all his worries would be gone.

He closed his eyes again and relaxed until his eyes shot wide open when his nose recognized the now too-familiar smell of the dog. The cold, wet ground was causing his legs to cramp, making it difficult to get up, so he crawled, and his progress was slow and painful. His mind told him to 'Hurray up, you fool.' Exhausted and discouraged, he laid down again and placed his forehead onto his crossed forearms, defeated. The scent was powerful now, and nearby, Brill cried out weakly, "Dao, help me, I'm here, I'm here," he said as his voice trailed into the forest's silence. He raised his head again and pleaded, "Please, someone help me."

The lifeless surroundings of the forest magnified the all-consuming feeling of hopelessness and disappointment. Brill's thoughts returned to those he loved. Smiling as he thought of everyone who had played a significant part in his life, he said goodbye to them and apologized for letting them down. As the first tear ran down his face, he closed his eyes and stopped moving.

Dao was far behind the Demoni when it entered the forest. As fast as the forest would let him, he moved in the general direction the dog had headed. Low-hanging intertwined branches slowed down his efforts and stifled his progress. Frustrated, he stopped to use his heightened sense of smell to isolate the dog's distinctive odor. Within seconds the wind delivered the clue he needed, and he headed off in that direction, hoping to find his best friend still alive.

Dao noticed the paw tracks of the dog on the soft wet ground, and he followed as fast as the forest would allow him. According to Brill's map, he remembered that the forest was not very long but wide. Flying through the woods, Dao ran for Brill and the entire Clan, whose survival depended on their success. In the distance, he could hear branches breaking, and he strained his eyes to see in the dim light. The commotion ahead grew, along with growling and hissing. Still infused with the powers of the red elixir, he was not sure what lay ahead of him, but he thought it must be Brill even though he couldn't see him. Frantically, Dao scanned the woods, looking for him, when his eyes caught something moving through the trees to his right at about five hundred yards.

He waited to see if anyone or anything else was following behind the moving object before he took off after it. As he ran, he could hear noise coming from his left. He could not see it, but he could listen to its breathing. He struggled with the forest's decay and dying foliage but kept running, ignoring the whippings from the branches and the ensuing gashes. In the distance, what he was following had stopped and now seemed to be lying on the ground. Cautiously, he observed, unsure of who or what it was. As he got closer, he could see that it was Brill who was on the ground and was no longer moving.

Up ahead, he would have to turn right to stay on Brill's path. Just as he was about to turn, a black blur flew by him, heading toward Brill. Dao jumped back when the Demoni flew by him. Suddenly he realized that he would have to reach Brill before the dog did or lose his friend forever.

CHAPTER 44

Fight to the Death

Taking out his red elixir, Dao drained the remaining drops into his mouth and waited for the now-familiar sensation. The double dose caused his body to swell more than ever. Confident of his abilities, he blasted through the forest, breaking branches and uprooting trees barreling towards Brill, oblivious to everything around him but his friend. Saving his life was all that mattered.

Unable to defend himself from the quickly approaching Demoni, Brill closed his eyes, unable to move. Yards from Brill, the Demoni zeroed in on his neck, peeling back its lips to expose its massive teeth in anticipation of the kill. A yard away, it lunged at him. Brill did not see the dog, but he heard the smashing and crashing of branches from behind. Airborne, the dog flew looking toward the sounds when Dao slammed into its torso, hurling it away from Brill. Skidding to a halt quickly, it refocused its anger on Brill, but Dao was now crouching just in front of Brill, so it stopped.

Both combatants were ready for the battle, knowing one would not leave the forest. Dao moved away from Brill towards the dog, who watched him with glowing red eyes. Dao felt the same blinding rage toward the dog it had towards Brill. Infused by the elixir coursing through his body, Dao was ready to explode.

"Brill, get up!" Dao yelled.

Brill opened his eyes and lifted his head when he heard Dao's voice. He was unsure if he was dreaming or if they were dead. Then he heard it again,

"Brill, get up NOW! You've got to get out of here."

Brill could see Dao behind him as he struggled to get up. He slowly got to his feet, staggered, and fell backward against a splintered rotting tree, jabbing his back on a sharp protruding stake just as the horror of the death match began.

Dao swung his fist, trying to punch the dog in the head. The dog casually dodged the punch and tried to bite Dao's newly repaired arm as it flew past its face. Missing his mark, Dao pulled his arm back quickly, avoiding the dog's teeth as it changed its strategy and ran circles around Dao. The dog's movement made Dao dizzy and disoriented. When the dog saw Dao begin to sway, it stopped running and bit him on the left side of his torso, tearing the flesh. Dao cringed and covered the wound with his hand. The dog quickly lunged again, ripping a large swatch of flesh from his right thigh, causing Dao to stumble but not fall. As Dao was still trying to get his bearings, the dog lunged a third time at his neck. Dao grabbed the dog's head with both hands and twisted it forcefully in both directions to break its neck, but the dog lashed out with its paws across Dao's chest, tearing open his clothes and the skin underneath. Blood soaked the front of his shirt as he released his grip on the dog.

Suddenly the Demoni heard movement and turned towards Brill, who had got up from his slouched position and taken a step away from the tree. In that split second, Dao grabbed the animal's back legs, picked it up, and spun it around. The g-force of the spinning motion created a whistling noise from the dog's mouth that echoed throughout the forest. Before launching the dog, Dao screamed a deep guttural cry and threw the dog into the brambles of a nearby tree. It tore away at the branches with its teeth to free itself. Finally free but full of barbs, the dog jumped at Dao. Dao caught it in the air and wrapped his arms around it as it tore up Dao's arms, creating deep lacerations that bled over them and heightened the dog's senses even more.

Dao pushed past the pain and pummeled the animal with his fists. His adrenaline surged at the sound of the bones breaking and whimpers from the animal. Punching in rapid bursts at such speed that his fists were a blur, the dog fell dazed but not dead. Dao picked it up by the tail and swung it around his head before releasing it with another primal scream. Its eyes grew large as it headed towards Brill, who had moved back against the tree. Brill did not have time to get out of the way as the dog crashed into the tree with such force that the tree moved. Dao looked in horror as his eyes met Brill's.

The animal hit the tree while Brill sucked in his breath. Suspended from the tree, it did not move, nor did Brill. Horrified that he had killed his best friend, Dao collapsed to his knees, overcome by grief and his injuries. Seconds passed in the deathly quiet forest until the silence was broken by Brill loudly sucking air into his lungs. He slid down the tree behind the dog onto the ground, uninjured and alive.

The Demoni remained on the tree, impaled by the significant stake sticking out. Brill rose, slowly walked over to a sobbing Dao, and joined him on his knees. He hugged his friend and then helped him to his feet. Together, arm in arm, they headed towards the open road stopping only to rejuvenate themselves with Dao's remaining blue remedy. Brill looked at the near-empty bottle in Dao's hand, then shifted his eyes to Dao. Both boys realized that the drops of remaining elixir would impact their actions in the future; it was a shocking realization. Dao extended his hand to his friend, which he took, cementing their allegiance to one another, and resumed walking.

Brill's thoughts turned away from the elixir and back to Nutay and the children, wondering and hoping they had made it to the safe place.

CHAPTER 45

An Unwilling Mentor

The truck convoy roared along the roads, stopping only for gas and to let the men stretch their legs. Mullins took the opportunity to walk amongst the men terrorizing them with his silent presence, searching for dissension and deserters; he wanted to cull those men from the herd personally.

Small groups of men stood around eating and talking. Everyone noticed the Captain, but no one addressed him; most made wide berths around him to avoid any contact. Isolated from the others, he found himself alone behind a tree, eavesdropping on the conversation of a group of men.

"How many more days of travel do we have?" one of the men asked no one in particular.

"Not sure, we just got into Province III," came a reply.

"Who is Civantes?" asked a young man who looked more like a boy with a hairless face and huge dimples.

All the men looked at the youngster. They were not surprised that he had never seen him, but they were surprised he had never heard of him.

"He is a devil of the highest order," piped up an old guard while Mullins chuckled.

"Why? What has he done?" asked the youngster.

The men started to laugh, including Mullins. The men turned towards the tree, so he stepped out of the shadows joining the circle of men. As he stepped forward, all the men stepped back, widening the perimeter. Only the inquisitive young man did not move. When Mullins approached, the young man stood alone in the circle.

Mullins approached the young man and placed a hand on his shoulder.

"He is indeed evil. Now, what has he done?" Mullins mocked and looked around the circle. The other men stopped moving and focused on the Captain.

"Does anyone here know what Civantes has done?" he asked again.

No one spoke or moved as Mullins surveyed their silence and turned back towards the young man. He moved close to his face and whispered, "See my face. He is trying to kill me. So, I want to beat him to the punch. And you, my young man, will help me do just that."

Mullins placed his arm around the boy's shoulder and began to walk him forward. The young man did not resist but was very nervous now. He turned around to look back at the men; they were shaking their heads. It did not take long before they arrived at the Captain's truck. They found Jup eating and the driver cleaning the vehicle.

"Jup, look. I found an innocent young man!" said The Captain with laughter.

Jup looked over at the youngster but did not acknowledge him. The Captain tussled the young man's dark hair and said, "Jup, you are going to train this young man to fight before we get to Civantes' Lair. Sending an unskilled man into battle does not seem right, so I want you to teach him. You two ride behind me in that truck," he said, pointing to the vehicle behind them. "And train him how to survive. I like him, Jup, so do not kill him."

The kid looked at the big man, scared to death.

Jup thought about arguing with Mullins but decided against it. It was better to follow his orders for now.

"Okay," was all he said, and he realized that this was an excellent opportunity to get away from Mullins.

They climbed into the back of a personnel carrier and sat together on one side of the wooden benches that lined both sides of the truck. The men inside slid down to the farthest reaches of the benches when Jup's massive bulk entered. Some men wore hoods concealing their faces. Once everyone settled in and was sure that Jup would not eat them, a few went to sleep while others just closed their eyes. In the silence, the young man turned to Jup.

"My name is Aden."

Jup did not respond, tipped his head back against the truck, and closed his eyes. He thought about killing the young man but realized that he needed rest more than a confrontation with Mullins, so off to sleep he went.

———◆———

Mama stood up in the watchtower, scanning the sky for any movement. For hours she stayed until she saw black dots high in the sky moving against the white clouds. Satisfied, she turned and left the tower.

———◆———

Aden turned sideways on the bench to watch Jup more clearly. His eyes traveled over the deep scars on his neck, forearm, hands, and arms and the newly healed fresh laceration on his left calf. Aden stared in awe at the sheer size of Jup. He had never seen such a large human being. Compelled, Aden raised his right hand towards the scar on Jup's arm as if he were drawn to touch it. He did not want to wake him; he just wanted to feel it and be sure what he saw was real.

"Do you want to wake the sleeping giant?"

Aden turned and looked directly across at the seated men, who were all motionless.

"Who said that?" Aden whispered.

No one responded or moved. Aden strained to see which man had been watching him when the man directly across from him slowly raised his arms over his head, pulling back his hood. Aden looked at the young man, who seemed much older than his biological years. Aden saw large scars on his neck and face as the hood fell to his shoulders, just like Jup's. He had suffered more wounds than Jup, which did not seem possible.

"They are real, and I strongly advise you not to touch them. " This was said while nodding in Jup's direction. "He is not a man to be toyed with," Jaes said.

Aden looked downward. Embarrassed that the man had been watching him, he felt stupid. Jaes saw the young man's embarrassment and decided to give him advice.

"Do not punish yourself by worrying about the thoughts of others. Stand up for yourself. This age cares little of you and even less for your thoughts," Jaes stated. "Why did Mullins send him back here?"

"I guess because the Captain has taken a shine to me and has asked him to train me," he said.

"Train you? You had better hope he doesn't kill and eat you," Jaes snickered.

Aden's face erupted in worry at Jaes' response.

"Relax," Jaes whispered back. "I know him well. Just listen to him and do not give him a reason to kill you, and you will be fine."

Jaes' words brought no comfort to Aden, and the stressed look never left his face. Jaes looked around the truck and saw the men sleeping, so he motioned for Aden to sit beside him.

"There are a few things you need to know about Jup," he whispered as Aden drew in close enough for only him to hear.

CHAPTER 46

Shadows in the Night

As the truck rumbled down the darkened road, the Captain suddenly awoke from his unsettling rest. A nagging, uneasy feeling caused his arms and legs to cramp, causing him painful spasms. He was disoriented momentarily and then remembered that he and his men were marching toward Province II.

He opened the window to get some fresh air. The calm wind touched his face like a whisper, soft and refreshing. Resting his head half out of the window, he closed his eyes and sighed. As the air gently fluttered against his closed eye in the stillness of the night, he tried to relax and clear his mind. He remained like that for some time and felt better until the air gradually became more vigorous and forceful. The pressure was so intense that it forced his mouth and eye open. It increased so forcefully that it threatened to blow the patch from his face.

He thought that his driver had sped up but looking down at the road, he could see that the truck had maintained the same speed as earlier. Glancing upward into the sky, he saw a stream of intermittent shadows passing in front of the half-moon. He wondered what could make such large shadows at such a distance before he pulled his head back from the window, closed his eyes, and hunkered down in his seat.

While Snag drove, Dwell took out the map from Puppa and spread it out in the front of the cab. He located their position and saw they were close to one of the Principal's locations, which Puppa had indicated on the map with an 'X.' Dwell told Snag to pull over and drive down a tree-strewn driveway. Hesitantly he did, slowly moving down the brush-covered, overgrown foliage covering the pothole-laden driveway. Callow woke in the back from the jarring motion, and Rep helped her.

"Seems like we're off the main road," Rep said to Callow.

Callow pulled back the tarp and looked down the laneway, which was disappearing before her eyes, swallowed up by the dying greenery. They were no longer on the road, and she wondered why. The truck stopped; the road was no longer passable. Snag and Dwell got out, opened the back, and let Rep and Callow out. He waved everyone toward the front of the truck, where he unfolded a map on the hood.

"We're right here, and this is a Principal's location," he said as he placed his finger on the red 'X' on the map. He indicated another X close to the first with his other pointer finger.

"And this is another Principal's location right next door. It looks like there are two here." The locations were right on top of one another on the map. He looked up at their astonished faces as he removed his fingers.

"So, what are we doing here?" Callow asked with a concerned tone in her voice.

"We need to destroy this Snatcher position. We're heading to Province II to destroy Civantes and his mutants, so we may as well start here. If we do not eliminate these monsters now, they'll come after us here or at the canopy. Let's do it now while we have the element of surprise on our side."

Reluctantly, everyone nodded in agreement.

"So, here's what we're going to do," he said while folding up the map, placing it back into his pack, and putting the items he needed from Mama Kileee and Puppa in his bag. Dwell explained his plan as they concealed the truck with dead branches and vegetation.

Callow and Cat followed Snag, with Rep and Dwell following. As they journeyed deeper down the lane, a wall concealed in plants and vines arose. Dwell pointed to his right, and everyone followed, probing and pushing the stones for an access point. Rep checked down low while Callow searched high along the top of the wall. The others checked the middle, hoping to find a doorway or opening to get inside. While everyone searched, Dwell kept watch, looking for signs of trouble.

The thick underbrush pulled and grabbed at their clothing. Cat led the group forward, with its tail straight up at attention, sniffing and scouring the wall for any smell or sign of life or death. The further they walked, the thicker the brush became until their progress slowed to a crawl. Snag got ensnarled in the branches stopping everyone's forward progress. Callow was closest to him, so she removed her knife, freeing him from the clutching branches. Rep and Dwell inspected this area while Callow helped Snag. Rep followed the vines to the top of the wall and saw that the brush was less thick and seemed to be flattened.

"Lift me," Rep asked Dwell.

Interlocking his fingers, Dwell offered his hands to Rep so he could stand on them. Everyone in the canopy was exceptionally good at making makeshift lifts with their bodies using their hands, arms, legs, backs, and even their heads when needed. Dwell lifted him high enough to grab larger branches higher up on the wall, allowing him to climb to the top and peer over the ledge.

Inside the camouflaged wall existed a small village like the Snatchers in the cavern; they had stormed with Puppa. There were buildings and a large open area with many people. Some were children, and others appeared to be Snatchers. Rep took a good look at the area's layout before he climbed down to the others.

"Well?" Callow asked anxiously.

"It's another lair. I can see children working amongst the big heads," Rep answered.

"Can we climb over safely?" Callow asked.

"I think so. The vines are thick enough to hide in them on top and drop down behind the closest building, but we need to follow the wall for about another twenty yards to do that without us being seen," Rep said.

Cat took off down the wall leading the crawling group behind it and abruptly stopped at a section with a different vine color covering it. The vines were not as dark or dead as other parts of the wall's foliage. Cat disappeared into the foliage while everyone else anxiously waited. Callow pulled on the vines, and they quickly pulled away from the wall. Soon, Cat reappeared with an article of clothing in its mouth that it dropped in front of Callow. She picked it up and affectionately petted Cat as it cooed contently.

"Follow me," she said as she ducked down into the foliage and was gone. Deep in the vines, she found Cats' opening.' It had used its barbed tail to cut through the greenery, finding a small swing door. Callow pushed on it, and the door opened quickly, giving way to the inside of the lair. She wondered who would have use for such a small door, certainly not the big-headed Snatchers. Peering through the hole, she saw children and a few guards sitting in front of a nearby building. She crawled through the passageway, ran behind the building, and was closely followed by the other friends.

Once there, Dwell took two of Mama's yellow balls and was about to throw one when Callow grabbed his arm.

"Don't! Let's hear what they have to say first," she whispered.

Dwell nodded and followed her around the building. They stopped moving forward when they heard voices.

"When did he leave?" asked a very gruff voice.

"He and Dreg left yesterday. They're supposed to meet up with the other Takers at Highpoint and then head east to find the tree dwellers," said another.

"I don't think they exist. That story is all just a bunch of crap to give us hope and make us think they exist, so we keep working for them," said a younger voice.

"You think you have a *choice* to work for them?" another said while struggling to contain his laughter.

"Well, I don't know if they're real, and I don't give a damn either. I know that Flug is gone, and I am grateful for that. He is the meanest upright animal I have ever seen, and I hope he never comes back," said the man with a gruff voice. "You know, the other day when that little kid accidentally hit him with a rock, I thought he was going to eat him. I think he would have if he had been alone with that kid. It scared the hell out of *me*."

The others nodded in agreement.

Then a squeaky high-pitched voice added, "I sure hope that the tree dwellers are real because I want my family to be healthy again so we can be together."

The others looked towards the speaker with a look of incredulous surprise as if he had just made the most ridiculous statement they had ever heard.

"You idiot, Civantes is not trying to find a cure to help you. The cure is just for him and his friends. No, wait, he doesn't have any friends. Don't hold your breath waiting for your medical miracle because you'll die trying," he said with a chuckle.

Callow turned to Dwell, "They're already trying to find the canopy!"

CHAPTER 47

Another Principal Location

Callow pointed at the yellow ball in Dwell's hand, indicating it was time for him to use it. He nodded, stepped before her, held the ball away from his body, and pinched it. A tiny wisp of smoke slowly rose from his hand. Stepping close to the front of the small building, he tossed the ball into the window, waiting for a reaction, but nothing happened. Peeking over the sill, he could see the ball on the floor undisturbed. He took the second ball out of his pocket, pinched the sides together forcefully, and tossed it into the window.

Instantaneously smoke engulfed the room, causing the men to smash and bang into the walls before finding the exit. They congregated together outside, straining to see while Dwell ran around them, pouring the first flask of liquids in a circle around them. Snag followed, pouring the second liquid on top of the first and then returning to the back of the building. Everyone covered their eyes from the flash, which was more intense than the flash at the cavern. The brilliant light instantly blinded the Snatchers. The children cupped their hands tightly over their ears and closed their eyes to block out the light and the cries of the men.

Snag, Rep, and Dwell neutralized the guards and then spread out, looking for others in the buildings. Callow with Cat called the children to them. They ran to her in their ragged clothes and dirty faces. They hadn't seen a 'normal' woman in some time and held on tightly to Callow as tears ran down her face. Cat danced and pranced for the children, bringing smiles to their weary faces.

Once the grounds were secured, the men joined Callow. Rep bent down on one knee and addressed the children.

"Hello, everyone. My name is Rep. This here is Callow and Cat," he said while pointing at his friends. Callow smiled, and Cat somersaulted for the audience.

"This here is Dwell, and that guy with the big smile, that's Snag," he continued as the young men waved.

Rep's gentle voice and non-threatening demeanor put the children at ease.

"We are going to take you away from this awful place and bring you to a place where no one will ever hurt you again. Now, I want all of you to go and grab your stuff and come back here as quickly as possible. We will be leaving soon," he said as he pointed to the wall surrounding the grounds. A little boy with his thumb in his mouth and wearing only trousers ran through the crowd of children directly to Rep, and without saying a word, he wrapped his two little arms tightly around his neck. Dwell bent down, took the little boy in his arms, and brought him to Callow.

"Let's go, everyone. Go get your stuff, or stay here with me," she said. Very few left her side. Those who left returned with single items, like a piece of a broken toy or a ripped piece of cloth.

Dwell returned to Rep and asked, "What will we do with these children?"

Rep looked into Dwell's eyes while placing his hand on his shoulder.

"Dwell, this is just one of many groups of children my family, friends, and I rescued. I will ensure they will be taken to a safe place."

"Puppa's?" asked Snag.

"No. Puppa's place is not the only safe sanctuary for children. We protect them at various locations throughout the country. I will notify a local contact sworn to protect all children at any cost. He and I will arrange for their transfer and settle them. But before we do, you need to search the buildings for any information that may help us," he said.

Dwell and Snag were relieved by Rep's words, so they took off towards the other buildings while Rep and Callow got the children ready for travel. They rummaged through the smaller outer buildings but found very little helpful information. They heard a strange noise when they entered the last building on the site. Pulling a small cabinet away from the wall, they found a gnarly little man fast asleep. Snag bent in front of the man and gently tapped him on the shoulder to awaken him. Cat sat directly in front of the man and watched him wake. Dwell held Cat back from jumping on the man, who slowly began to stir. It took minutes for him to open his eyes fully, and when he did, he looked at Snag and Dwell but made no effort to get up. Instead, the man's hands went immediately to his neck, ensuring that what was hanging from it was still there.

"How did you get in here, and who are you?" asked the Snatcher in a high-pitched voice.

"What's in there?" Dwell asked while pointing down at the pouch.

"What's in where?" asked the little man, agitated.

"In the pouch, old man. The pouch," Snag said.

"Nothing, nothing at all. " There is no pouch," he stammered, desperately trying to break the cord to hide the small sack.

Snag moved so quickly that the little man didn't react when he tore it from him and handed it to Callow, who had joined them. Inside was a sealed letter.

An eerie demonic voice whispered, "Don't open that if you want to live. Civantes won't like it if you open his mail."

"Civantes will never know," she said.

Callow opened the letter and scanned the message that Civantes had sent to all the Principals before she read it aloud.

"Principals, each of you are to release your two best Takers (Snatchers) to join up with fellow Takers from the other provinces. They will rendezvous at Highpoint in two days. From there, they will seek out, locate and capture the legendary tree dwellers we know exist. And mark my words; you had better return with them. Tell each of your band of misfits to use any weapons or any means possible to find them.

I have information proving that these tree dwellers do survive and live in the far eastern forests of Province IV. Their bodies are the living, breathing specimens we need to return to health, so capture them and bring them to me unharmed. The more samples we have, the more we can return to our health, appearances, and families. This is what we are living for! The laboratory tells me that we need at least one hundred strong young adults for the experiments to be successful, and the stronger the bodies, the better the results. If some of them do not fit the criteria, they are expendable. DO NOT FAIL AS YOUR LIVES DEPEND ON IT.' It was signed, Civantes."

Horrified, Callow folded the letter and tucked it away in her pocket. The shock at the news was evident on their faces. Knowing that the death squads from every province had been dispatched to find them was shocking, and Dwell got angry. His rage became visible when he approached the little man with fists raised and anger on his face. Cowering back against the wall and fearing for his life, the little man tried to hide. Then Callow came to his rescue. She stepped in front of Dwell and placed her hands on his shoulders.

"Stop Dwell. Let's take him with us. He can guide us to Civantes and his Lair. Maybe with this guy's help, we can convince Civantes to call off the search for our families before they find the canopy," yelled Callow in desperation.

Dwell ignored her and continued staring at the little man. So, she continued to plead.

"Come on, Dwell. He can help us; if he doesn't, you can do whatever you want for him. Please, we need to find the Lair. We can't turn around and head back home now; we don't have time. We must find them in Province II. We are so close. We're almost there!" He didn't respond.

She was screaming now, "Killing him won't help us."

Dwell backed away from the little man and left them, talking to himself. Minutes later, he returned calmer and more focused.

"Okay, Callow, we'll do it your way. Snag tied him up and put a muzzle on him. I don't want to hear him until I have to."

Snag bound the nasty-looking little man's hands and shoved a cloth into his mouth.

"Let's go," Callow told the group.

Rep said his goodbyes and reassured them that friends would soon come to pick up the children and bring them to the safe house. Dwell lead the group back through the tunnel to the truck. They cleared the debris concealing the truck while Snag half dragged, half kicked, the prisoner towards the vehicle. Callow drove with Dwell upfront while Snag sat in the back, tending to the prisoner. He tightly secured the rope attached to the little man to the holes in the truck box frame, then closed his eyes. Dwell did the same, but first, he cracked open the sliding window to vent the cab, but, more importantly, he listened to the men in the truck bed, who made him uneasy. Only silence could be heard for hours until Dwell's sharp hearing picked up someone whispering.

"You won't live once he finds out you're not one of them."

"And who will tell him I'm not one of them?"

"Ha-ha, look at you, you fool. All scarred up and worn out. You may have been pretty once, but that time is long gone."

"Shut up, you bastard."

Dwell heard someone get punched and fall, then the back of the truck went silent. He wondered what Snag was thinking about as they headed deeper and deeper into enemy territory.

Heading west, Brill and Dao walked lost in their thoughts, unsure of what the future had in store for each of them. Oblivious to the time, food, or rest, they did not stop. Their thoughts consumed them while the silence enveloped them.

They sat on the side of the ditch at dusk, concerned with finding Civantes and his Lair and what to do once they found it. Mama had discussed scenarios to employ once they got there to ease their minds, but the uncertainty of the situation weighed heavily on them.

"We're not too far from the Lair according to the map," Brill said.

"Ya, we should be there in about five or six hours," Dao responded.

"Ya, it won't be long now," Brill said apprehensively as he looked at the fields. "Boy, it must have been beautiful years ago when green grasses framed these fields, and the different colors of crops exploded from the land. It must have been something to see."

Dao stood and looked around, nodding in agreement at Brill, whose eyes were closed. He was fast asleep.

CHAPTER 48

Young Apprentice

While Brill slept on the bank of the ditch, Dao kept watch. Tired and sore, he continued to scan the tree line for danger when he heard engines, lots of engines, and they were coming closer.

"Brill. Wake up. Wake up. Listen."

Brill sat up, groggy from the abrupt awakening. He sat still, listening to the distinct sound of approaching vehicles coming from the east and heading their way. Crouching lower, they ran farther down the ditch where the banks were higher. With their backs against the dirt, they hid.

As the large convoy of trucks and men marched down the road, Dao and Brill watched.

Dao turned to Brill and mouthed, "Rooks!" Brill nodded in agreement.

An ample supply truck was the last vehicle in the convoy procession. They watched that vehicle's rear lights fade away in the early evening light. When the trucks were far in the distance and incapable of seeing them, they climbed out of the ditch. They stood on the road watching the vehicles' silhouettes become smaller as they drove away. Then without warning, bright red lights suddenly appeared at the back of the convoy, indicating they had stopped. Dao and Brill turned to look at each other simultaneously and said, "They've stopped."

Jumping back into the dry ditch, they ran towards the trucks. As they got closer, they saw men milling about outside the vehicles. Some were sitting and talking in groups; others were exercising, a few practiced hand-to-hand combat skills, and the remaining were sleeping against the vehicles' wheels.

Staying back to avoid detection, they strained to see what was happening. Brill watched the men and gasped as he pointed towards one truck; Dao looked to where Brill was pointing. Suddenly he saw what had startled Brill. In the middle of hand-in-hand training stood Jup. Instructing an incredibly young, inexperienced guard on fighting, but the young man spent most of his time protecting himself from Jup's blows. Even at such a distance, Dao could see the young guard fighting for his life.

More than once, Jup struck Aden so hard that he was knocked to the ground. Much to Jup's annoyance, the young man continued to get up. With each blow, Jup seemed to strike him harder until blood flowed from every orifice in his face and multiple lacerations on his body, but he would not quit. Jup's growing frustration was evident, and everyone watching became concerned for the young man's life. As Jup's survival skills kicked in, he raised his fist as if to crush the young man when Captain Mullins unexpectedly appeared from around the truck.

"Well, well, well. How's our training coming?" he asked inquisitively. Jup slowly lowered his clenched fist and turned towards the Captain. Mullins tried to intimidate Jup by circling him, but Jup didn't bite. He stood calmly and relaxed while Aden picked himself off the ground and wiped his face with the back of his arm, spreading blood from his mouth to his ear.

"Great," answered Aden cheerfully.

Mullins spun around and looked at the young man. He had not expected him to answer. Jup snickered when he heard the young man's response and thought this kid was not so bad. Mullins looked at Aden's battered and bleeding face, turned to Jup, and said, "Try not to kill him, Big Man; I need all the manpower I can get."

Then Mullins turned and walked away.

"Why didn't you stay down, little man?" Jup asked.

"Why? Because you are supposed to teach me how to fight, and I can't do that if I'm lying on the ground now, can I? I'm here to learn whatever you're willing to teach me, even how to die if that is what you choose."

"More men should have your spirit, little man," was Jup's only response. When training resumed, Jup began to teach the young man the fundamentals of hand-to-hand combat. The strikes were gentler, and the mood lighter. Jup decided to give Aden more instructions than injuries.

Dao and Brill watched them until they retired and sat across from one another in a group of men. Aden wiped the blood from his face as Jup laughed, prompting Aden to throw his blood-soaked rag at Jup's head, which he dodged. Both men laughed. Exhausted, they leaned up against the tires and closed their eyes.

Within the hour, Rooks appeared, yelling orders at the men.

"Pack up. We leave in 15 minutes. We need to set up camp outside of Civantes' Lair before nightfall. Get your asses up and move!" The Rooks kicked the stools from under the men, sending them toppling to the ground. When they noticed how jovial the conversation between Jup and Aden was, they just shot the two of them a dirty look. They dared not kick their stools.

Within minutes, the caravan was loaded and ready to depart. Until now, the men had ridden in trucks, but no longer. The majority decided to march in formation behind the vehicles to instill confidence in each other as their objective drew nearer. Aden watched the men march in unison, so professional and disciplined that he wanted to join them. After some coaxing, he convinced Jup to join the ranks, and Jup marched alongside him.

Mullins was happy to see the men take the initiative to parade into battle. He instructed the drivers to slow down so the men could keep pace with the vehicles. When Jup and Aden assumed their position in line with the men, they overlooked Jaes just feet behind them, watching their every move.

The trucks' gears grated against one another as the vehicles pulled ahead slowly, at a constant speed fast enough to stay ahead of the men walking in strict formation. Running within the ditch, Brill and Dao kept pace, waiting for someone in line to make a costly mistake. They waited patiently, and it did not take long.

A guard on the far side stopped in the middle of the road to tie his bootlace as the battalion continued marching. Brill watched the man kneel, thinking how costly a mistake he was making. Dao ducked out of the ditch, ran across the road, and crashed into the man from behind. The momentum catapulted the man headfirst into the ditch. Dao followed and cupped the guard's nose and mouth, extinguishing his breath. Brill helped Dao strip the man of his clothes, which Dao then put on. They stuffed the Rook's rucksack with Dao's clothes before placing it back on his back. Quickly, they used their strong tree legs and caught back up with Mullins' army.

CHAPTER 49

Home at Last

Speeding down the steep incline, Nutay skillfully navigated the bus toward the bottom of the hill while glancing at the children surrounding him. During the drive, he told the children funny stories and kept them abreast of where they were going and how soon they would arrive. Many held the seatbacks as they stood in the aisle, looking out the front window. In the distance, a few miles ahead, a vast mountainous wall could be seen directly in the middle of the road. The bus did not slow down. The children watched as the rock wall came closer and closer. A large black mound and the mountain's base were at the end of the road. Everyone's eyes were fixed on it, and neither the children nor Nutay spoke as the impending collision with the mound approached. The children held one another as the mountain's shadow engulfed the bus.

Flippy held the hands of the two youngest children while another sat on his lap asleep. He and the other children watched, trusting Nutay with their lives as the bus continued speeding towards the wall. Every child needs someone to trust, to be their hero or guardian; Nutay was theirs. Flippy gathered the children tight to himself. He looked at their small, worried faces staring back at him and remembered the words he had spoken to them about Nutay. "We can trust Nutay. He is good, and he will take care of us." They believed him, and Flippy hoped and prayed that he had made the right decision.

As they approached the wall, the bus tires sprayed more rock from under the wheels. Some of the children were too frightened and hid behind the seats as others burrowed their faces in the comforting chests of the older children. A little boy got up and walked to the front of the bus holding onto both aisle posts next to Nutay. Without wavering, he stared straight ahead, mesmerized by the size of the mound. Fifty feet from the impact, he did not flinch. One of the older children led the children in quiet prayer, holding hands and looking upward.

Nutay glanced in the angled mirror at the children but did not say a word. He hated to scare the children, but it was a necessity when living in such a lawless and frightening world. Everyone kept secrets to stay alive. Spies and collaborators were everyone, so one could never be too careful. It was the only way to maintain a semblance of normalcy and freedom. Yards away from the bedrock, an opened door suddenly appeared directly in their path. Nutay expertly guided the bus through the opening, stopped shortly beyond the closing door, and looked in the mirror to see the change of expression on the children's faces, from fear to complete joy. Their eyes opened wide, and a look of astonishment appeared.

Nutay turned around in his seat and said only one word, "Sorrie."

The children were now all standing and looking out of the windows.

"Dis is yur homes, fron dis day to forever, or til you wanna leav."

The children didn't speak; they were overwhelmed by the beautiful images in front of their eyes. Nutay opened the door, but no one moved. He looked at Flippy seated behind him and nodded towards the open door. Flippy smiled back at his friend, stood up with a toddler in his arms, and walked off the bus with the two young children and Dog following behind. The other children watched them go. The remaining children held hands, kissed Nutay, and did the same.

———◆———

Gotl assembled everyone in the circle square for an emergency meeting. Silent eyes watched the elders take their seats. The elders seemed to have aged in just a few short weeks since the couriers had left on their grain mission. As if in mourning, some held their heads low, not making eye contact with anyone in the crowd. Gotl helped Jith to Ilse's now-vacant seat and ushered Mama to her chair. Once the last seat in the circle had been occupied, Gotl stood and spoke.

"We have not heard from the children, not by a person or patch. We don't know where they are, if they are safe, or if they are even alive," he said.

Gasps and the intake of breaths could be heard throughout the crowd, but no one spoke.

"We cannot wait for our sons' and daughters' fate to save or spur us to action. We need to start our preparations for self-preservation today. Effective today, all portals will have around-the-clock surveillance. We must know if anyone is trying to access the canopy or our woods. We cannot wait for the wolves to be at our door before we act. We must confront them before they confront us. Long before they get to the canopy," he continued. He looked out at the room full of vacant stares and scared faces. He paused and waited for other elders to address the crowd, but they didn't. Many were deep in prayer, asking for the safe return of their children. He turned towards Mama, and she nodded, and seeing the spark in her eyes, he continued.

"We must prepare ourselves for when the Snatchers come and believe me when I say they are coming. We must defend, protect, and save ourselves."

"How are we supposed to do that against these monsters?" a woman pleaded while clutching her young son.

"Remember, they were once men like us, but now they are sick. We are not; we are healthy and strong. They are barbaric and brutal. We are not; we are good people full of hope and will defend ourselves with honor and integrity. We will prevail."

He approached a woman clutching her young son and looked into her eyes. Then, in a quiet voice, he said, "We are not sheep. We will not lie down and wait for them to come to annihilate us. We will not let them hurt our women or take our children. You must believe this because, without this belief, our fate is lost. We have lived for decades in peace because of our love for one another, and our willingness to support and help each other is unwavering. I will not let them destroy the goodness we have within ourselves and our Clan."

Jith got up from the table and joined her husband. She placed her hand in his, stared into his eyes, and kissed him. Squeezing his hand, she released it and stood directly in front of the crowd. Her determination was evident in her voice. "We will fight until we can fight no longer—all of us.

We will battle until we can battle no longer, -- all of us. If we die trying to live, we will die for our right to live for freedom, faith, and our families. This is precisely *why* we live. And when this is over, once again, we will live in peace without fear of these monsters and evil men. Remember, and never forget, that goodness always prevails even when all seems lost. It is this hope that sustains us."

The people throughout the canopy stood and cheered when Jith finished her inspirational speech. Everyone's voice rose in rousing support of her cry to battle just as a large dark shadow descended amongst the group onto the center square from above, captivating everyone's attention. All eyes turned upward as the leaves in the trees flapped and fluttered when the rest of the flock of Howls settled in the branches directly above the families. The strength of the birds brought a measure of confidence to everyone attending. As they quieted, a man climbed down from the giant bird, SheShe, and approached the crowd.

CHAPTER 50

Uneasy Uncertainty

Away from the prying eyes of Mullins and the Rooks, Jaes marched at the back of the parade of men. The Captain's truck kept pace in the middle of the caravan. Mullins sat in the back of his convertible, watching his troops from the shoulder of the road, looking for 'irregularities' he could address. Jaes kept his head down, but his eyes were on Jup, who was closer to the front alongside Aden. The men marched in silence, maintaining their strict formation much to the satisfaction of the Captain. A skittish young man stole a glance at the Captain as he drove by and accidentally stumbled into Aden, much to Jup's chagrin. Instinctively, the big man turned around and punched the man in the chest, causing him to fall to the ground. Aden and the other guards watched the injured man writhing in pain, but they did not break stride. Laughing to himself, Aden realized at that moment how beneficial his relationship with Jup would be.

Civantes emerged from his office and strode down the hall towards the labs. He didn't enter but merely stared through one of the large glass panels that lined the hallway. The medical staff didn't acknowledge his presence and continued working. They could ignore him, but not the growing stains of perspiration under their arms or the sweat dripping off their faces. Their discomfort was palatable, and he loved it. What he did not love was his reflection. The white coats did not realize his focus was no longer on them but on his image in the glass and his declining health, which was brutally apparent in his reflection. His thoughts returned to

Mullins. This re-ignited his anger, and he rushed down the hall and out of the building, yelling into his patch as he went.

"Tell all the men to assemble in the foyer of the courtyard NOW and tell them to prepare for battle."

The doors flew open as guards ran into the courtyard at a dizzying speed because the order to assemble could be heard reverberating throughout the compound. More men appeared in battle gear, ready and standing at attention alongside Snatchers, who lumbered slowly into position in the vast courtyard. Loud grunts and moans emanated from the huge, grossly deformed men as they pushed and pulled weapons and armaments into position. The fumes from the vehicles cast an eerie glow over the area as larger gunnery, missile launchers, rocket propellers, and ammunition were moved into striking distance. While the artillery was being moved, trucks loaded with bound children arrived. The Snatchers unloaded them, and they, like the artillery, were placed in prominent positions along the wall to deter Mullins from striking the Lair.

Dao and Brill kept pace with the troops while running alongside them in the ditch. Running was easy due to their great physical conditioning. The struggle came from the oversized pants that Dao fought to keep up while running. They needed a uniform for Brill. They waited patiently for their next unsuspecting victim, and their wait finally paid off. A middle-aged man near the front of the line proceeded to drop farther and farther back until he was at the very last row of men. He looked at the man marching to his right and grabbed his zipper, indicating that he had to relieve himself. His comrade acknowledged him with a nod. The man fell out of formation, stopped marching, and watched the caravan proceed.

The boys stopped running and watched him from the ditch. They waited for the man to take care of his business, but he didn't. He abruptly turned around and started frantically running down the road. A surprised Dao turned to Brill, unsure what to do next when Brill got up and started chasing the man. Dao, shocked by the man's decision, remained still. He watched Brill sprint after and caught up to the deserter. The man heard noises from behind and turned to see Brill gaining on him. Fumbling with his revolver, he opened the chamber to check for ammo; it was empty. His attempt to load his gun while fleeing resulted in most bullets falling to the ground; only two made it into the cylinder. Brill watched the distressed man struggling with his weapon while dodging the falling casings. Brill realized that the distance from Dao grew larger every second; he did not want to stop and return empty-handed, so he lunged at the man, catching his ankle and causing him to crash. He climbed up the man's legs, knocked the gun out of his hand, and straddled his back until he stopped moving.

"What are you doing? You're supposed to be pissing along the side of the road back there," Brill said while pointing behind them.

"What? You tackled me because I didn't take a piss? Is this a new rule? I didn't know." the man stated, Shocked at Brill's question.

Brill looked quizzically at the man, not understanding his question. Then he stammered,

"I want your uniform."

The man's body went limp before he spoke. "Well, why didn't you just ask for it?"

Brill didn't know what to say, so he got up, dusted himself off, and gave the man some space; the man did the same and stood before Brill.

"Now, ask me nicely," the man said.

"What? Are you serious? Brill asked incredulously.

"Yes, ask me nicely," he said again.

"Okay. Could I please have your uniform?" Brill said while rolling his eyes.

Without another word and within seconds, the man stripped down his ragged socks, and hole-strewn underwear, turned, and continued running down the road free of his regiment and dignity. Brill briefly watched the man sprinting away but didn't waste any time. He picked up the clothes and ran back up the road. Half a mile from the troops, he re-entered the ditch and returned to Dao as fast as possible.

"I think that we may have to stay in the ditch until the battle starts or at least until they enter the Lair, whichever comes first," Dao said.

Brill nodded as they hurried through the ditch in pursuit of Mullins' men when suddenly they heard Civantes' last transmission.

Hours away from the Lair, Mullins was alone getting some much-needed rest before they would have to stop to set up camp. Leaning his head against the headrest, he closed his eyes, trying not to dream, when the patch on his wrist lit up with Civantes' voice. Bolting upright in his seat, adrenaline washed over his body, and he discarded any notion of sleep. His nemesis spoke with a voice consumed with rage that crackled over the airwaves. To Mullins, it was music to his ears. Snickering at his enemy's distress, he pulled out his map and reviewed his strategy to annihilate his old friend.

In silence, Callow drove with Dwell at her side. Soon they would be crossing into Province II. Holding the wheel firmly with both hands, she straddled the road's faint center line with her tires. Dwell had spoken very little to her since the events at the last Snatcher location, but she did hear Snag. Her astute hearing and the open window allowed her to listen to the conversations in the back of the truck. Snag informed the prisoner that if he didn't provide directions to Civantes' Lair via the shortest route possible, he would personally deliver him to Civantes to reveal his betrayal. Snag's threat elicited the desired response from the man who cowered in the corner of the truck bed, shivering while pleading for mercy.

Civantes' reputation was filled with horror stories and circulated amongst the provinces for decades. No man alive was more hated or considered more evil-minded than Civantes. He treated friend and foe alike and was as apt to kill you if you did something right or wrong; it depended as much on the direction of the wind as it did on any rhyme or reason.

Looking visibly petrified at his impending doom at Civantes' hand, Snag assured the man that no harm would come to him if he would help them. He gladly agreed.

It took the little man only minutes to outline the detours on the map into Province II. Snag quickly passed the information to Dwell, who reviewed the routes with Callow. Soon they passed the border marker sign for Province II. The provincial sign welcoming visitors to the area was illegible due to the faded lettering and graffiti. A bold handwritten message in bright red painted letters stated, 'ONLY INVITED GUESTS WELCOME - UNINVITED GUESTS NOT WELCOME - LEAVE

AND LIVE!' was visible. Below that sign was another municipal sign of a silhouette of children playing with the caption, ' Watch for Children at Play' had been changed to read, 'Snatchers out for children.' Dwell was still staring at the sign when his patch came alive.

⸻◆⸺◆⸺⸻

Dao and Brill jumped when they heard Civantes' voice. Brill instinctively whipped his hand up, scratching his ear with his thumb, loudly exclaiming, "Ouch." Instantly, an exhale was heard over the patch. Suddenly a second minor green blip appeared on Brill's patch screen.

Brill touched the scrape on his ear and found blood. Alarmed at what had just happened, Dao looked over at Brill, who had taken off his patch and was looking at it. Dao grabbed it and threw it behind them as far as he could. "Brill, we need to get away from the road."

"Why did you…," Brill asked just as a small incendiary mortar hit the dirt beside them and exploded. Embracing the side of the ditch, Brill didn't understand what was happening.

"Your patch; when you put it to your ear, you must have pressed on it, and when you spoke, you gave up our position. Let's go; they know we are here."

Dao didn't have time to listen to Brill's explanation or excuses.

He bent deeper into the ditch and ran toward the motorcade; Brill did the same.

CHAPTER 51

Preliminary Battle

Mullins saw a second green light on his patch. Someone other than himself or his men with a patch was very close, as the patch's GPS indicated. He yelled for his driver to stop. This caused Mullins to fall forward in his seat. Gathering himself, he stood on his seat faced the trucks behind him, and with both hands lifted, he yelled, "Stop."

The brakes on the vehicles swiftly locked up and screamed at the abrupt engagement, causing dust from the dirt road to surround the vehicles and temporarily conceal them. Unable to see, Mullins bent down, felt for the trap door under his feet, withdrew a small missile launcher, loaded it, and fired it where he had seen the green dot on his patch. He watched the stream of fire etch a line in the dust on its way to impact. The Captain didn't wait to hear the impact and subsequent explosion; another shell was quickly loaded and fired. He didn't stop until he ran out of ammunition.

Dao and Brill dove to the bottom of the ditch when the second shell exploded yards from them. Brill dug in the guard's pack, removed the uniform, and put it on. While in there, he grabbed his red elixir, which was still half full. He took a large swig of the liquid. Unaware of what Brill was doing, Dao carefully poked his head over the bank when the explosions stopped. All he could see was a cloud of smoke ahead, so he prepared to run.

"Let's go, Brill."

Dao didn't see or hear Brill coming up from the rear, and he also didn't expect to be thrown onto his friend's back, but that is what happened. Brill raced through the ditch towards the convoy with Dao aboard, avoiding the missiles. By the time the smoke had cleared, the friends were safely under a large truck hiding inside the empty ammunition sideboards that ran the length of the truck below the doors. The back of the sideboards were open, unlike the front, which had a panel door.

The Rooks and guards fanned out in every direction, creating a large perimeter around the convoy, listening and looking for movement. Only the familiar sound of black military boots on the pavement could be heard. Brill recognized the boots from the lab in the compound. One of the Rooks stopped by Mullins' truck and shouted,

"Captain, we have searched the perimeter but found no intruders. Would you like us to continue, Sir?"

"No. No, we don't have time. Call it off. For some reason, they are not firing on us, just stalking us. Tell the men that just because they haven't found anyone doesn't mean someone isn't there. Someone is out there! They are so close that we should be able to smell them. Damn, we should have brought the dogs; they would find them. Until we reach the Lair, all troops will be on high alert. Double-check the security details. Tell the men that if Civantes' men are following us, they will not announce themselves. They will slice all our throats and cut out our tongues before our screams form on our lips. Move."

The Rook turned and left, but Mullins did not move.

"Tell them to sleep lightly," he whispered.

Angered at the search results, he turned and kicked the side of the truck, bouncing Dao out of the sideboard and causing him to catch the vehicle's underbelly and hang precariously by his arms and legs. Struggling to keep himself tight to the bottom of the truck was tough, and his energy began to wane. Afraid they would be discovered if Dao fell, Brill swung his leg under Dao, lifting him upwards against the truck. Dao gripped the frame, but his fingers couldn't maintain the grip, so Brill gave him another mighty shove up against the truck's belly, allowing more time for his hands to latch onto the vehicle's frame and work his way back into the sideboard. Once inside, he looked at Brill, who was effortlessly suspended across from him and smiling weakly.

The troops and trucks continued, rounding the mountainous range of Piking Pass when the engines slowed as the convoy pulled off the road onto a large area overlooking the valley that held Civantes' Lair. The men were told to disembark and set up camp. Brill and Dao removed themselves from their perches and hid behind the dual wheels at the back of the vehicle. They watched the men's movement as they set up temporary barracks, prepared, loaded their weapons, and set up the munition stations at the site. Each rocket launcher was set up, loaded with ammunition, and armed with around-the-clock guards. Every man knew their role, and they wasted no time performing their duties under the Captain's watchful eyes.

Footsteps approached alongside the truck. Dao peered around the tire to see men jumping down from the truck bed to unload the weapons stored above them. Missile launchers, submachine guns, incendiary explosive devices, assault rifles, and countless rounds of ammunition the guards unpacked and stacked. All the trucks unloaded their weaponry except the last five vehicles in the caravan. These trucks were backed up against the wall side by side. Their covered beds faced down into the valley. Dao watched the drivers exit the trucks and simultaneously pull back the tarps, exposing five massive twelve-inch guns.

"He's going to annihilate them," Dao said to no one.

Brill watched the men ready the big guns and aim them directly down the valley towards a large, smooth concave cement wall. The base descended into the valley and melted into the sides of the mountain. Brill could see a flurry of activity on the top of the wall.

"What do we do now?" Dao asked quietly.

Far behind the trucks on the camp's outskirts and away from the ammunition stockpiles, the men were putting up barracks, but Mullins sat in his personalized gazebo smack in the center of the camp. He could see clearly down the valley and all his men from his location. He would also have a clear view across the gorge of Civantes and his men, which he felt was a clear advantage in this battle.

CHAPTER 52

A Hero from the Past

The man approached the center square amid the sounds of shock and dismay. Gotl and the other elders stood mesmerized by the sight as the man neared them. Mama got up from her seat, walked directly to the man, and openly embraced him, which he warmly welcomed and reciprocated. They released each other and continued to hold hands. He looked deeply into her captivating green eyes, smiled, and whispered,

"Thank you, Mama."

She smiled back at him, released one of his hands, turned towards the crowd, and said, "Pley."

His shocked parents fumbled through the crowd towards their son, whose death they had been mourning for days. Pley turned and ran to his sobbing mother, engulfed her in his arms, and held her tightly. His father and siblings soon joined their emotional celebration. Mama turned towards the elders, who were shaking their heads in disbelief.

"How?" was all they said in unison.

Mama reclaimed her seat, and the people moved closer to hear her speak. Veme, an elder, sat Pley's Mother next to Mama, who focused on her as she spoke.

"Lida, it was a cold night when The Farm exploded. When SheShe carried Pley away from the explosion, he looked dead to the naked eye. His body was so beaten and broken when SheShe brought him to me in the forest that I began to prepare him for his ceremonial burial back at the canopy. As I was preparing him, SheShe continued to interrupt and nudge me so much that I swatted him away, but he was relentless. I was getting quite frustrated. When I told him to stop, he lowered his head next to Pley's with his beak touching Pley's open mouth and held it there, and that is when I saw the faint moisture on his beak. Pley was still breathing, albeit just barely. I had already checked his breathing and pulse, but his vitals were so weak; they were undetectable.

As I bent over him again, my hand brushed his pocket, and I felt his elixirs, which I immediately gave him. Because of the severity of his injuries and the massive blood loss, I wasn't sure if the medicines would work. Rejuvenation took much longer than usual, but slight improvements did occur, allowing me time to get him back to the infirmary and my remedies. On the way home, I thought he had succumbed, so I flew up to the top of the canopy to examine his condition. Thankfully, he was still alive. I was torn as to whether I should allow you to see him in that perilous state or wait until I had tried everything in my power to nurse him back to health without you knowing. I chose the latter. I am sorry.

The news of Jules' death devastated us all, and I didn't want you and your family and everyone else to hold onto false hope if I couldn't help him. When the couriers returned home, they assumed Pley had died at The Farm and dealt with his death in that madness. I didn't want to distract them from their mission by worrying about Pley, so I told them nothing.

Those kids had been through so much and were so physically exhausted from their mission that I decided that a much-needed rest was imperative for their health and survival, so I kept quiet. During the first few days, there were many times that I thought that I had lost him, but that boy of yours had such a desire to live that death could not defeat him.

As you can see, he returned to health, but his body has not returned to its 'normal' state for some unknown reason. It has remained heightened, as you can see by his current size, which could be due to the new therapies that I used on him while he was artificially suspended. Or it could be due to the copious amounts of remedies given to him by Dwell and myself. This enhancement isn't detrimental mentally or physically to his body other than you will have to feed him more. I will continue to investigate the results and his recovery. Lida, I am so sorry for causing you and your family any grief."

Mama glanced over at Pley; the young man was now twice the size of when he had left on the quest to find Wirl. He sat with his arms around his father, smiling from ear to ear while wiping tears of joy from his face. His siblings stood behind them while his mother softly sobbed, holding Mama's hand.

"Thank you, Mama, thank you so much," whispered Lida as she stood and hugged Mama. Pley joined them, followed by the rest of the family, and then they left for their nest. Standing, Mama addressed the crowd again.

"I have been thinking a lot about the precarious situation that our youngsters are in. I was originally unwilling to send support to help them and leave them to their own devices until now. Pley and I, with the help of SheShe and the other Howls, are going to try to find the children and help them, if possible. If we cannot locate the kids, we might be able to gather some intelligence on the Snatchers, their whereabouts, and what they are up to."

Mama turned to face Jith, "I make no promises." Then she left the circle square.

Jith watched Mama as she left and smiled; her prayers were finally coming true.

After many hours of sleep or unconsciousness, the little Snatcher began to stir. He struggled to pull himself off the truck bed. Holding his head, the creepy man found the large bump above his right eye and cringed when touching it. He tried to sit up again, and finally, after multiple tries, he sat on the wheel well and caught sight of Dwell staring at him.

"Where's that fiend?" he snarled.

"Driving so that you and I can review the maps. We are getting close to Civantes' Lair. If you know of a shortcut or a secret passageway there, you had better tell me, or I will send Snag back here," Dwell threatened.

"I hope the commander cuts the throats out of all of ya. Well, not the girl. I'd like to keep her for myself," the creepy little man said.

Dwell got up with a raised fist, ready to strike.

"All right, all right, all right! Show me the maps, and I'll show you the way," he stuttered.

Dwell hooked up at the solar panel, then removed and opened the maps from his pack for the Snatcher to see. Dwell watched him tip himself onto his knees to get a better look. Completely bent over, he scrutinized the routes with his face inches from the map.

"Well?" Dwell asked.

"Well, what?" he snarled.

"Well, is there a shortcut?"

"This way," and he showed Dwell the back way into the Civantes' Lair area. Dwell traced the lines with his finger, memorizing the path. He was very spatial and tapped on the window when he was sure he had learned the route. Callow opened the sliding window and peered out.

"Everything okay?" she asked.

"Ya, tell Snag to pull over. We need to review our new route courtesy of Sunshine here," Brill nodded towards the prisoner.

Dwell got out of the back carrying an armload of supplies that he dropped on the ground in front of the truck at Callow and Snag's feet. Both looked at the items on the ground, wondering what Dwell was doing.

"What, did you think we were just going to drive up to the front of his house and announce our arrival?" Dwell asked, laughing.

Brill watched Mullins meander about his tent ordering the guards here and there, exhausting them with his constant demands and instructions. Eventually, he sent them away and went to the barrier wall separating his camp across the chasm from the Lair. Mullins stared at the enormous cement wall that protected Civantes and his army and hoped he had enough firepower to obliterate everything inside.

CHAPTER 53

The Calm Before the Storm

Civantes watched the flurry of activity down in the courtyard as he stood on the floor which housed the labs, sleeping quarters, and his office. He watched from high above as the guards set up the defenses and the lab staff ran through the courtyard to escape from the mountain. He did not care if they fled; they would all be recaptured after Mullins was defeated.

The guards set up a barricade of terrified children directly behind the stone wall to deter Mullins from attacking the Lair. Behind the sacrificial children stood hundreds of fighters who were lifelong prisoners of Civantes. Encircling those men were the Snatchers, who tried desperately to stand quietly, but their large overweight heads refused to be still, much to the amusement of Civantes' guards who stood behind them trying to stifle their laughs. Civantes surveyed the ranks and wondered how successful his band of misfits would be, then turned to Vile.

"Make sure all the children and the first row of fighters are as close to the wall as possible. Mullins needs to see their terrorized faces before he gives the order to attack. Tell everyone else to hurry into the tunnels. We will exit at The Knob and attack him from behind, unbeknownst to him. Go!" he yelled. "Oh, and have the Snatchers put logs up against the wall for the children to stand on before they leave. I want to make sure that the youngest kids can be seen. That sight alone might pull at his heartstrings long enough to delay his attack. Hurry up," he barked.

Within minutes, Snatchers and men carried wood into the courtyard and placed it against the front wall. The thin and dirty children were then herded forward and told to stand on the wood; some were too small to get up on their own. The older children climbed up and assisted the smaller ones onto the wood until the whole wall was lined with a row of petrified children. Across the ravine at Mullins camp, their little heads could be seen in front of the row of fighters. A few guards lingered behind them to ensure they maintained their positions. At the same time, the rest left the courtyard and entered the mountainous caves and tunnels directly under the ravine and Mullins' forces. Silently they marched for three miles underground and resurfaced out of sight more than two miles behind Mullins' men. Civantes led his men and watched them mobilize and spread out in the valley, outflanking the Captains' troops on all sides, oblivious to Mullins and his men.

Satisfied with their formation, Civantes climbed onto the back of Vile, who headed up the hill to the highest vantage point in the valley, directly behind Mullins' camp. His men quietly assumed their battle positions. Even the Snatchers took their positions with little noise. The plan was to surprise and decimate Mullins' forces by ambush before he could fire off a shot. Looking through his spyglass, Civantes caught sight of the children at the wall; their placement was perfect, and their appearance pathetic, just the way he planned it. They dared not move. He surmised that fear must have paralyzed the children as they watched Mullins prepare his weapons which the children could see. Their tiny eyes couldn't avoid the big guns pointed directly at them, he thought, as he chuckled to himself.

Mullins watched the children assemble in front of Civantes wall, and he was disgusted that the coward would use kids to deter his attack. He cursed the man under his breath.

"All troops are to assemble at their battle stations now," came his loud and sudden command over the bullhorn.

Dao heard the orders and watched the flurry of activity before him. Men ran while struggling to get their boots on. Some had half-eaten food protruding from their mouths while getting dressed. Men ran with their pants around their ankles, trying to get to their stations before being noticed. And even some were half asleep and dragged by their friends to avoid the Captain's wrath. Mullins watched and was pleased with their quick response.

"All ranked men are to assemble immediately in the Captain's quarters," was the next order issued.

Thirteen Rooks, all dressed in black, entered the Captain's tent. While standing at attention, a fourteenth man slipped in behind them. He wasn't wearing a uniform, nor did he have a rank. He slouched behind the unsuspecting men near the flap door shrouded in shadows. He stood utterly motionless and invisible as he listened to the Captain's words. Jaes kept his head down and wondered where everyone else was.

The Captain sat motionless in his oversized ornate chair in front of the men until they arrived. Once they had stopped moving and he had their attention, he stood on a raised platform and addressed them.

"Well, men, we're here. We made it! Across that chasm out there is the Devil's Lair. My goal is to destroy my enemy and his band of murderers. I want every one of them gone except Civantes. I am going to kill him myself. But right now, I have a slight problem. No, I have a lot of minor issues, and they are currently lining his wall. Children! That bastard has lined his fortress wall with small children. What inhuman piece of garbage does that?

I do not have any affection for children, but it does make the situation a little more complicated. I propose using the twelve-inch guns to attack the wall from the bottom on the western side to weaken the structure. I don't know the depth of the concrete in that wall, but it looks formidable. I think we can pummel it and do enough damage to distract them. Then we launch rip ropes across the ravine and attack them above their troops. The Rooks will repel multiple men to the fortress while discharging the multi-launcher munitions. I plan to destabilize the structure's base before attacking the top. Once the top has been secured, we will enter the belly of the beast and destroy everything. Remember, I want Civantes alive. Now go, man, your stations and await my orders."

The men shuffled out of the tent and back to the posts. No one noticed Jaes. He had left seconds earlier and returned to Aden and Jup's troop. Standing beside Jup, he quietly called his name, but Jup didn't respond. He was too busy watching the mobilization of the guns as they were loaded, and the gun barrels positioned at their targets. Mullins stood in the back of his truck and watched with heightened excitement. He loved a good battle.

"Let's go, Brill; we have to get out of here," Dao told Brill.

They were still hiding behind the truck's wheels near the front line, too close to the action. Stand-alone multi-launchers sat on hollow steel platforms located directly behind the twelve-inch guns. Dao saw the opening at the end of the weapons' base and crawled from under the truck and underneath the platform. They followed the continuous line of multi-launchers until they reached the empty vehicles parked before the barracks. Running in the shadows, Brill still felt the elixir's effects in his body and was itching to use his strength and speed against the Captain. Dao convinced him to stand down and watch. They watched the guards move toward the front wall. The air was electric with anticipation, waiting to see who would strike first. Dao convinced Brill to follow him from the encampment to an area behind the tree line, where they watched the men from a distance and decided their next move.

CHAPTER 54

The First Strike

The Captain walked amongst the troops observing their preparations and their battle readiness. He was pleased that everyone was at their stations awaiting further orders. He ran his hand down the length of the missiles stacked in pyramids beside the large guns savoring the clean, silky feel of the metal beneath his fingertips. He loved war. He loved the raw aggression, the challenges, and the crushing defeats he had inflicted on his foes throughout the years. He loved the bravado feeling of superiority due to his leadership and expertly trained troops. He was born to lead and conquer. It was in his blood. Victory would be his. Of that, he was sure. He was going to crush Civantes.

A guard in charge of one of the twelve-inch guns watched Mullins as he caressed the missile. He was even more excited than the Captain for the upcoming battle. He idolized the commander and wanted to be just like him. Struggling to contain his excitement, he searched for an opportunity to impress Mullins.

Aden watched Jup separate himself from the others. He moved away from the light to a quiet secluded corner, settled down, closed his eyes, and placed his clasped hands upon his chest. Aden got up and moved in the shadows towards Jup. He watched the big man control his inhalations with slow, steady exhalations to regulate his breathing. He was so skilled at doing this that it was hard to discern whether he was breathing. His respirations became so shallow that the rising and falling of his chest was indecipherable. Aden was frightened for his big friend. He wondered how long it took Jup to train himself to detach entirely from imminent dangers to become calm and focused. His admiration for Jup continued to swell, inspiring Aden to be more like his big friend.

Jup slowed his breathing to concentrate on what was to come. His greatest asset when fighting in the arenas was his ability to remain calm and focused regardless of the dire situation. Staying composed under pressure allowed him time to recall similar experiences he used to inflict fatal damage on his adversaries. It was all part of his winning strategy. Relaxing with his eyes closed, his mind didn't wander back to his previous battles. Instead, he saw frightful images of his little brother involved in horrific experiments conducted on him at the lab. While his vitals remained calm and stable with no outward heightened physical response, anger rushed through his body.

He opened his eyes and saw the Rooks preparing for the looming battle against Civantes. Jup turned his energies towards the Captain and how he would kill him if the opportunity presented itself. Since his encounter with him at The Farm, most of his waking thoughts were involuntarily consumed with plotting the man's death. He knew it would be dangerous and a certain death sentence for himself, but he didn't care. He had already pledged to avenge his little brother's and his family's suffering. He wanted to make Mullins suffer a terrible fate like many of his young victims. Memories of his little brother were the only family memories he had. He wondered what had become of him.

Aden stopped spying on Jup, turned, and walked right into Jaes, who was standing nearby watching them.

"Whoa, sorry, man," Aden said.

"No problems Aden. What's going on," Jaes asked.

"I was just watching Jup ready himself for battle."

"Which battle?" Jaes said.

"What do you mean which battle? There is only one battle," he laughed and continued. "The one we're preparing for!"

"Aden, you are so young and so naïve. There is never just one battle. Remember that, and it will serve you well," Jaes responded.

Aden gave Jaes a bewildered look, and then the two turned and walked toward the wall where the weapons were positioned. Jup saw the two of them walk away together and wondered who the hooded man was, then resumed his mental attack on the Captain.

Mullins stood at the wall contemplating the first strike. He didn't want to hit the children, but there is always collateral damage with war.

"Lock and load gun one," he barked.

"Lock and load gun one," echoed throughout the hilltop.

The men loaded the missiles into the barrel and stood by, ready to fire.

"Gun one, loaded and ready for fire," came a response.

Mullins strained to see across the chasm.

"Aim for the lower west side of the concrete wall just above the waterline," he barked. "Fire."

The men detonated the blast, sending the projectile skyward toward the intended target. The children on the wall watched in horror as the missile approached and exploded into the wall below them, pulverizing the concrete and sending huge chunks into the water. The explosion rocked the mountain, sending vibrations throughout the fortress, causing the children to panic and scream. Many fell while others jumped from their woodpile and ran toward the back of the courtyard into the shadows and out the doorway. The fighters turned away from the wall, carrying the smallest children in their arms, and ran, shielding others, to safety and out of the courtyard. Mullins watched; within seconds, the courtyard was empty. He wondered why no one stopped them from fleeing, something wasn't right. Where were the guards?

Minutes passed. "Launch the rip ropes," the Captain yelled.

Three nylon ropes ripped across the chasm and embedded their hooks into the rock above the courtyard. His men could now safely cross the gorge and access the Lair.

"Gun number two, fire at the lower east end of the wall just above the waterline."

The missile blasted into the concrete, sending massive chunks of cement into the water, shaking the ground and the men marching below in the tunnels. Mullins and his men felt the vibrations and the ground shaking under their feet, but they had little concern stationed above ground. Below in the tunnel, the walls shook, causing rocks to fall on top of the frightened men who feared the tunnel collapsing and burying them alive. The hasty decision was made to exit the tunnels directly behind the Captain's encampment.

Gun number three was controlled by the guard, who was infatuated with the Captain. When he heard the command "Fire gun number three," he immediately sprang into action and sent the third missile towards the center of the wall causing a massive hole. Excited by his success, he whooped and hollered when the rocket found its mark. Confident that the Captain would also be pleased with his performance, he turned to look for acknowledgment or praise from his commander, but Mullins didn't even look his way. The Captain walked past the fourth gun to better view the damaged wall. Utterly disappointed, the guard stopped celebrating and wondered what it would take to capture the Captain's attention.

Mullins watched the destruction of his nemesis' hideaway crumble and fall away into the gorge. He had expected little resistance from his adversary, but this was too little. He thought of Civantes as a coward, confirmed at The Farm and reinforced now with the children on the wall, but he didn't expect him to retreat. Across the ravine, he watched the Lair grow eerily quiet; not a single shot was fired to defend her survival. Nor could any person be seen or heard. Suddenly he knew that something was not right.

"Fire guns four and five. Now!" The enormous dual explosions caused widespread damage to the wall. Massive vibrations flowed throughout the valley and mountain range. The vibrations caused large rocks and debris to fall into the chambers and tunnels below. Many of the Snatchers in the tunnels were trapped below or crushed to death. Dust and debris escaped from the portals at the ends of the tunnels, sending large, billowing clouds into the sky. Mullins didn't notice the clouds of debris behind him, he was too intent on watching Civantes' Lair fall into the ravine, but Dao did.

The smoke rose at three distinct locations behind Brill and Dao. Brill could see movement on the ground but couldn't determine who was moving. The boys moved farther up the mountain, putting distance between them, the Captain, and whoever was convening in the valley.

The detonations woke Jup, prompting him to get to his feet. He could see the men laughing near the wall beside the big guns. They were too relaxed and distracted for active battle. Making his way over to the wall, he saw that Mullins ordered the missiles to be fired, destroying the lower sections of the wall as a continuous flow of concrete crumbled into the water. Jup surveyed the compound of the Lair and saw nothing, no men, no weapons, and no action. From experience, he knew distracted fighters like Mullins' troops meant dead fighters. It was time to leave.

CHAPTER 55

The Ambush

As the wall continued to crumble and no counterattack ensued, the Rooks and guards lost their focus and left their posts. The lack of resistance from across the river gave the men a false sense of security that victory was theirs. The Captain was unnerved. He watched the wall disintegrate and fall into the gorge without resistance from Civantes. He retired to his tent to think about his premature victory.

Behind Mullins' defensive lines, Brill and Dao climbed higher to better view the valley and its activity. Brill's energy from the elixir had diminished, so they sat quietly, conserving their strength and watching the Rooks fire missile after missile into the ravine without any resistance. Brill thought about the implications of a one-sided battle. Mullins' success without casualties would mean a larger force would be looking for them along with the Takers, whom Civantes had already dispatched to find them. With so many searching for them, it would only be a matter of time before they would be found. The Clan's fate weighed heavily on his mind as he watched the missile bombardment and wondered where Dwell, Callow, and Snag were.

Dwell followed the prisoner's directions and drove the truck halfway up the mountainside before pulling into an obscure opening excavated into the rock. Easing the truck down into the tunnel, he turned off the headlights. The mountain's interior had been mined out except for a massive column in the middle, and the perimeter was littered with trails winding up and down the length of the mountain. Dwell crept along the narrow pathways guided only by shafts of light emanating from boreholes in the mountainside.

Callow whispered, "Is this the way to his front door?"

"I'm sure it is not, but it's all we've got to go on right now," Dwell responded.

The vehicle continued to crawl upward until they came upon a barely visible narrow runaway ramp. Dwell pulled over and parked. Quietly, they exited the vehicle, went to the back of the truck, and pulled back the tarp. Snag grabbed the legs of the little man and flung him out of the truck bed. He stood on quivering limbs and looked around while Dwell cut the ropes binding his ankles. He performed a simple stretching routine until the realization of where he was, struck him like a hammer igniting his panic. With bound hands and a gagged mouth, he began to convulse. It was a wretched scene to witness. Fearing that the man would die of fright, Snag slapped him hard across the face, causing his oversized head to bobble back and forth. Once his head settled down, so did the man.

Dwell whispered, "Show us the way into his Lair."

The little man was hesitant to move, so Snag helped him with a swift kick to his backside, causing his feet to leave the ground and propelling him forward. He stumbled but didn't fall and reluctantly started walking, but not before he shot an angry look back at his capturers. Snag playfully lunged toward him with a raised fist pretending to strike, which caused the man to scramble up the pathway spewing rocks at those following behind.

The group proceeded with Cat leading up the quiet tunnel until an explosion rocked the mountain, causing debris to rain down on their heads. Hugging the wall, they remained there until the vibrations stopped. Then they resumed their ascent.

"Hurry, we don't have much time," Dwell whispered as the dust settled about them.

Everyone ran, including the little man helped forward by Snag's strong fist clamped to his shoulder.

"Shh, what's that noise?" Callow stopped and whispered to Dwell. Dwell focused on the sound and grabbed Snag by the shoulder to slow him and the little man down until they stopped. He pointed ahead towards an opening. Snag pushed the Snatcher behind him and walked to the edge of the wall. Kneeling, he peeked around the corner to see men, a few women, and many children frantically running toward them, desperate to escape from something he could not see. People were colliding with one another, but that didn't slow them down. Adults helped the confused and frightened children. When they reached the opening at the end of their hall, everyone blindly followed the leader, who turned right and headed directly toward them.

Dwell and the others tucked themselves into the rock, hoping for obscurity as the stampede ran by. When the last person could no longer be seen down the trail, they cautiously continued upwards in the dim light. They continued for what seemed like an eternity before they came upon a tall, thick door that had been left open. Dwell looked back at the little man, who nodded that they were on the right path; then, he spit a giant ball of phlegm in Snag's direction, laughing as it sailed past his head. Snag raised his fist, but Dwell grabbed and pulled it down before Snag could do any damage.

"We need him," he said before waving them through the door.

High up on the escarpment, Brill and Dao heard and felt the vibrations under them as the missiles hit the wall. Quiet returned as the guns died down, so they laid back on the rocks relaxing. Brill closed his eyes while Dao struggled to find a comfortable position. Finally, he settled, stopped moving, and listened. Brill watched his friend fuss with his eyes open and again when Dao closed his eyes. It didn't look like he was relaxing, so Brill made his way over to him.

"Dao, what's up?"

Dao's eyes flashed open. "They're here," he said and scrambled to his feet.

Dao grabbed Brill by the collar and pulled him up higher on the mountain. Caught off guard, Brill looked terrified as Dao pulled him back up the rock face while precariously hanging him over the sheer cliffs. When he determined the height was safe, Dao gently placed his friend onto a ledge overlooking the valley. In the valley, Captain Mullins' camp was visible beyond Civantes' men, emerging from under the earth nearby and spreading out across the width of the valley floor towards Mullins.

Hideous mutant men were pulling large guns across the terrain, and they acknowledged Civantes positioned high up on the ridge overlooking the planned battleground.

"Let's go," Dao said as he returned towards the Lair with Brill in pursuit.

———◆———

Realizing that his troops needed more time to move and position themselves behind the enemy, Civantes sought out Vile.

"Fire a missile at the lower left side of our wall," he commanded.

"Sir, that will destroy the Lair," a shocked Vile replied.

"Are you questioning me?" Civantes turned and asked.

"No Sir, no Sir, right away Sir," stammered his assistant.

Within seconds, the missile was redirected from its original target and was launched to give the impression that it was fired from Mullins' camp. This missile caused more destruction against the Lair's wall than the combined efforts of Mullins' rockets. The loud shell sunk deep into the mountain, destroying any remaining cement structures on the wall and penetrating deep into the supporting rock face. When they heard the explosion, Mullins men jumped up from their naps and ran to the wall to get a better look at the damage. The men looked around at each other, wondering who fired the missile because their guns had been retired earlier in the day. The Captain also heard the explosion and hurried to the wall to investigate. As he watched what remained of the wall fall into the gorge, a smile appeared on his face. The Captain was pleased, incredibly pleased that the wall had been destroyed. The problem was that he had not ordered the strike. Swiftly he turned and faced his gunnery crew.

"Who fired that missile?" he commanded.

No one spoke. No one looked up as Mullins passed each man.

"Tell me who fired that perfect strike!" he asked again.

But again, his question was met with silence. Mullins approached each gun, jumped onto the decks, and ran his hand along each barrel. The first four guns were cold. On the last gun's platform, he turned quickly, smashing his injured arm on the barrel, causing blood to appear on his shirt.

"Damn," he said as he grabbed his injured arm and squeezed, trying to stem the blood flow.

Seconds later, he re-focused and felt the last barrel; it was also stone cold. Suddenly it dawned on him. Ever so slowly, he turned around, and with his good eye, he looked enraged behind his camp.

"Man, the stations, load the guns, and turn those barrels around," he yelled.

CHAPTER 56

The Battle

Dao heard the whistle and saw the missile heading *over* Mullins' camp. Brill stood watching the projectile fly over the men and explode on impact, destroying what remained of Civantes' concrete wall. He turned to see who owned the missile and saw that Civantes' men had flanked the Captain's forces and trapped them against the wall. They could see guns and men scurrying in Mullins' camp. From his vantage, Civantes also saw Mullins' forces scrambling. This brought a smile to his face.

"Ready, aim, fire," Civantes yelled.

The weapons unloaded their projectiles onto Mullins' camp, destroying trucks, guns, and men. By the time the Rooks had reversed the barrel positions of the big guns, only three were still functional.

"Fire the damn guns! Now," yelled Mullins.

An onslaught of missiles flew in all directions, destroying everything in sight. The battle raged until the ammunition supplies on both sides were depleted, forcing the armies to march. Mullins' forces moved in unison down the mountain en route to the inevitable hand-to-hand combat with Civantes' forces, moving up the valley.

As the Rooks marched down the mountainside, Jup grabbed Aden and pushed him behind. The Captain's sharpshooters assumed their perches high on the rock face setting their sights on the oversized heads of the Snatchers, which made for easy and amusing target practice. While the Snatchers proved easy to neutralize, the mutant creatures proved to be much more formidable foes.

It wasn't long before the two groups converged, and hand-to-hand combat ensued, reducing the field to a slaughterhouse full of dismembered and bleeding bodies. Brill and Dao watched as Mullins' men fought desperately to survive, but their survival was short-lived against such savage creatures.

Forward motion on the congested battlefield was impossible for either side. Mullins watched his men fight valiantly only to die; few were left standing. Civantes stood on his ridge watching the carnage, wondering where his nemesis was.

Jup ran down the hill destroying everything in his path. His career as an arena fighter had served him well. Aden quickly fell behind Jup's frantic pace and was left to fend for himself with his newly acquired fighting skills. While he survived the initial onslaught, he was soon overcome by the chaos of battle. Exhausted, he fell to the ground as his attackers pummeled him, poised to strike the fatal blow when Jup arrived and destroyed the combatants. He helped his young protégé to his feet. From that moment, Aden resigned himself to the idea that if he wanted to survive, he needed to stay in Jup's shadow. From that point on, he fought less and ran more. As Jup won battle after battle, Aden's confidence soared.

Watching the creatures advance toward them, Jup hid with Aden behind some carcasses to allow them to pass before he fell in step behind them toward his goal, Mullins.

Jaes watched the battle rage on from far behind the front line. He no more wanted to fight for Mullins than he wanted to fight for Civantes. He hoped that they would all die this day. He scoured the hillside behind the parked vehicles when the sunlight caught something moving on the ridge above the battle site. Curious, he ran in the direction to see who was up there.

Brill watched the battle rage below and the carcass pile grow as the fighting became increasingly desperate and barbaric. He watched in dismay as the evil leaders commanded their respective armies to conduct their futile orders to fight to the death while hiding far from the carnage. His eyes followed the creatures' advance up the mountain towards Mullins' precarious position. The lead creature slowly and deliberately moved forward, scrapping its claws on the hard rock. Its head lulled back and forth just inches from the ground as the hair on its body stood up straight, amplifying its incredible size. A menagerie of wildly deformed creatures followed in its wake. They climbed higher and higher towards Mullins' last defense, his Rooks. Their challenge only served to delay their inevitable demise. Understanding the direness of the situation, Mullins headed for higher ground, back towards the wall as the enemy advanced.

Jup zeroed in on Mullins, who was trying to escape the battle. With Aden alongside, they sprinted towards the Rooks, but the distance was too great. They slowed and watched the Captain climb the wall and stand on the cap overlooking the ravine. Turning one last time, he surveyed the carnage behind him and yelled for his men to throw him a rip clip; the throw was wide. The hook brushed his fingers before floating down the chasm into the bowels of the ravine as Mullins watched. He yelled for another clip; it was thrown, and he caught it and attached it to the line. He held on with both hands and ziplined across the cable onto the portico of the Lair. His remaining men followed. When the last man touched down and unclipped his line, Mullins took out his gun and shot the two zip cables that had supported them across the canyon. The loose ends of the wires swung and fell into the gorge. Satisfied that he had destroyed access to the Lair from across the valley, he turned and headed into the mountain. Jup and Aden watched the broken cables fall. Aden saw a third cable higher on the mountain wall, which was still intact. With great excitement, he pointed it out to Jup, whose hope returned as they headed for the wall.

CHAPTER 57

A Close Call

The boys made their way to the wall. Dao told Brill that he had seen someone repel across the ravine from Mullins' camp. Brill jumped onto the wall cap and grabbed the zipline handlebar when a shot rang out, hitting Brill in the arm. Dao quickly jumped, ducked down, unsure where the shooter was positioned and stayed near the wall.

Hanging precariously in the air, Brill tried to regain his grip on the zipline bar with his injured arm, but the damage was too extensive. Certain that he could not support his weight on one good arm, Brill stretched his leg, trying to catch the wall with his big toe to steady himself. Focusing all his attention on his toe, it grazed the wall close enough that he could walk his toe onto the cap, giving himself a slight reprieve. Unable to help his friend, Dao dug into his pocket, felt his last yellow ball, and pulled it out. With Brill's life in his hands, he needed to find the shooter. Time was of the essence as Brill's toe slid off the wall, and he was left dangling by one arm.

Dao looked under the vehicles for legs, but there were none. He stood and scoured the area but did not see anyone. The creatures had left Mullins' vehicle graveyard to feast on the massive heap of carcasses in the valley. Mullins' men were dead or had escaped over the ravine. Most of Civantes' troops had died in the valley, so who shot Brill, Dao thought.

Sweating profusely, Brill lowered his head and closed his eyes. Still hidden, Dao saw the weight and strain of Brills' body on his one arm, triggering a hand cramp, forcing him to relax his grip and causing his palm to slide off the cable. Hanging dangerously by four fingers, Brill hung on and stared silently down the canyon. He began to sway his body slowly, hoping to regain a foothold on the wall.

Dao focused on the sounds around him and heard the faint insertion of a load into a stun gun. Without hesitation, he moved toward the sound, searching under the vehicles. Glancing back at his friend, who was no longer moving but was hanging on for his life, Dao searched at the back of the destroyed trucks. Suddenly, he saw a young Rook advancing towards the wall with his weapon raised and sights set directly on Brill. Dao got behind him, stood up to his height, towering over the young man, and grabbed his gun. With little resistance, he elbowed the young man in the head. He fell, smashing his head on the truck and knocking him unconscious.

Dao dropped the weapon and ran towards Brill, reaching him just as his fingers slipped off the cable and his body descended into the canyon. He dove and grabbed Brill's belt. The jolt startled Brill, causing him to open his eyes while Dao hauled him over the wall. In severe pain, Brill remained quiet. Dao handed Brill his blue elixir vial, with just a few drops remaining. Brill held the bottle upside down until every drop had drained from the bottle into his mouth. They sat, waiting for the healing process to begin.

Finally, Dao held his hand to Brill and said, "Let's go."

Dao climbed the wall, attached himself to the last remaining cable, repelled to the other side, and dropped onto the courtyard. Brill slowly climbed the wall and attached himself to the line. He started to shake as he stood on the wall gripping the bar. Dao became concerned.

"Come on, Brill, you can do this," he yelled.

Brill turned and looked at Dao with sadness in his eyes. Even across the chasm, Dao could see his friends' pain. Slowly, Brill inched himself towards the edge. Placing one foot in the air, he closed his eyes and stepped off the edge. His body moved slowly at first, then picked up speed across the canyon, nearing the Lair. Relief washed over Dao as he watched Brill careen towards him until the blast of a weapon broke the silence. Dao saw the revived young guard aiming at Brill's cable, shattering it in two.

Brill didn't see the young man or realize that the zipline cable had been shot out until he felt weightless. As his body's momentum careened toward the Lair, Dao jumped onto the wall and grabbed the line pulling

Brill upwards. Brill hit the wall with great force knocking the air out of his body. Feeling the weight on the rope get heavier, Dao felt for his red elixir; it was gone. With sheer determination, he pulled Brill up. With Dao's help, Brill climbed up and over the wall. Injured from the impact of the wall, Brill struggled to catch his breath. He consumed half of his remaining red elixir, hoping it would work with the blue potion he had taken minutes ago. It did; he felt stronger. Then sealed the bottle and tucked it away.

"Ready?" asked Dao.

Brill nodded and got up with Dao's help. On the other side of the canyon, the young guard continued firing in vain until all his ammunition was gone. Completely frustrated, he walked away, knowing he had failed.

Civantes watched all this from his peak in the valley. He had seen Mullins and his men repel into the mountain, but he was much more intrigued by the last two men who made it across the gorge. His excitement grew as he wondered where they had come from. Looking over the valley at the carnage of broken bodies, he turned to Vile and said, "It's been a good day, Vile, and it looks like it might get even better. Let's go find out," and they left.

CHAPTER 58

Mountainous Revelations

Cat jumped into Callow's bag, happy to be away from all the excitement. Callow followed the boys down a long corridor lined with large wooden doors. Each closed door had a symbol carved into the middle of it.

"What are these?" Callow asked the little man.

"Experiments sites," he hissed.

She gently ran her hand along the innately carved wood and turned to look at him.

"Testing sites for what?" she asked again as her hand gripped the doorknob, softly pushing the door open.

"Testing sites for children and the infamous tree dwellers," he said. "Ya ever heard of the tree dwellers? They are pretty and have no scars on their bodies. Look a lot like you," he said as he nodded toward Callow. Then he laughed and said, "They're all lookin' for you, Girlie, they all lookin' for you, and you walked right into their trap. You might be as pretty as hell but aren't too smart." The Snatcher then turned away and silently laughed to himself. Snag smacked him on the back of his head, quieting him down.

Callow turned away from the little man; she opened the door to a hallway lined with doors. Snag lifted the little man, forcing him into the first room. Callow entered the next, and Dwell turned into another farther down the hall. In each room, they found various diagnostic medical machines and monitors. A sizeable surgical light hung from the ceiling over a surgical table, and beside each table were fully stocked surgical trays with instruments and more monitors. Gurneys of various sizes with restraints lined the back walls. Most gurneys were tiny and haphazardly constructed, as though insufficient supplies could satisfy the demand. Snag gripped his prisoner a little tighter as they walked around the equipment. When he reached the gurney, he understood what the tables were for.

Running his hands along the side of the table, he felt and saw the drainage ports cut into the steel at multiple sites along the bottom and edges. Snag bent and looked under the table, following the clear tubes that were now permanently stained black and brown. One end of the line was attached to the drainage holes under the table, and the other ran into a translucent hole covering the middle of the floor. He moved toward the hole, bent down, and peered inside. A sickening pain gripped his stomach when he saw hundreds of similar tubes coming from other areas along the ceiling and converging into an enormous, enclosed steel apparatus on the floor below.

Pulling himself back from the hole and falling onto the floor, he covered his mouth with his hand while the little man pulled away, backing himself into a corner as far away from Snag as he could. Dwell and Callow was also peering down the holes in the floor in their rooms.

Their disgust was not as intense as the massive wave of anger in them all. Snag grabbed the little man and began to walk him out of the room when his eyes caught sight of writings on the wall. He had difficulty reading the juvenile script, but it didn't take him long to figure it out.

'Help me, they hurt me please,' was written in a smudged black material.

Snag felt the now familiar pang of guilt in his stomach and an overwhelming sense of sadness because of the events that must have taken place at the Lair.

"What did they do here?' Snag yelled at the little man.

"Everything," was all he said.

Snag shoved him away hard and went into the corridor to breathe. Leaning up against the wall, his friends joined him.

"We have to destroy these rooms," Dwell said.

With eyes clouded with tears, both Callow and Snag agreed.

"Let's see what we can find to help us blow this place up," Dwell said. "I wish we could also destroy the memories made here," he muttered as they walked down the hall towards other rooms, forgetting about the little man.

The Captain followed his Rooks down the dimly lit stairway with his firearm aimed straight ahead. At the end of the descending stairwell, they came to a corridor. Waiting for further instructions, the Rooks looked back at the Captain. He indicated for them to turn right. They proceeded cautiously down the hallway until it turned into a large round empty room wrapped in mirrors. Scanning the walls around them, they were amazed at the mirror images. Not only could they see their pictures, but they could also see the images of others who had previously been in the room; all images projected onto the glass lingered for a time before disappearing. They could see fighters, women, and children fleeing through the room, along with the faint images of Civantes and his Snatchers. The more recently a person had been in the room, the more vivid the image.

The Captain moved close to the mirror, focusing on the fainter images. He could barely make out a large group of horrified people in white coats streaming out of the room. He didn't spend any time looking at Civantes. Instead, he turned his attention to the center of the room where his men were standing. He joined them and scanned the panoramic mirror encircling his men. Without warning, he fired his gun into each mirror, demolishing the glass and ensuring no intact panels remained. The men covered their heads to avoid the flying shards, but not Mullins, who was so happy to watch the images before him, pass away into obscurity.

If only I could make them all disappear so quickly, he thought.

Once the glass settled, they left and headed down the stairwell.

Dwell and the others stopped moving when they heard the explosion of gunfire. The sound was amplified in the cavernous surroundings causing Callow to cover her sensitive ears; Dwell also winced. When silence returned, Dwell whispered, "They must be above us. Let's go."

They re-entered the hall when Callow noticed that their prisoner was missing.

"Hey, where's our prisoner?" she asked, looking around for the little man.

Snag ran down the hall, and within minutes he returned dragging the little man beside him. He held a small jar and was eating the sludgy contents with his fingers. Disgusted, Dwell knocked it out of his hands, much to the little man's disappointment. They went to another room down the hall with rows and rows of cabinets along each wall.

Dwell tossed the Snatcher into the corner and barked, "Stay there." The man curled into a ball, snarling at his captor.

Each friend opened a separate cabinet and flipped through the files. Dwell thumbed through the papers reading names aloud, "Braidy, Missy; Darlin, Park; Bonnell, Lyr; Thomps, Huds." The names went on and on. Snag thrust his cabinet closed and opened another, reading those names, "Vokam, Pal; Belang, Bryce; Caruth, Gregor. He shut that drawer and opened another; they were all the same. Callow read the names and ages, "Waddo, Kel – 7; Beck, Patt – 9; Cabal, Joen– 11."

She stopped reading, to upset to continue as her tears soaked the pages. They checked every file drawer, and the result was the same: more names and young ages. Dwell and Callow slowly closed their drawers, looking at each other, fearing the worst.

"They're all the same," they heard Snag say to himself. He shut his drawer and walked back towards them.

"What are these?" he asked the little man while pointing at the cabinets. The little man placed his hands in front of his face. He didn't utter a word and finally peeked through his fingers and saw they had not advanced on him, so he lowered his hands.

"Them's the kids they worked on to try to make Civantes well," he said.

"What does that mean 'worked on,' and where are they?" Callow pleaded.

"You don't want to know, and most of 'em gone," he said as Callow moved closer.

"Gone where?" she asked.

He looked at her suspiciously until he saw the genuine concern on her face. He drew his legs up and placed his elbows on his knees and his hands under his chin to balance his head. Finally, he began to speak.

CHAPTER 59

Reap What We Sow

"You care, but people here stopped caring about kids long ago. It makes no sense to me at all because every single adult started as a kid, but they don't want 'em. They don't have any patience, time, or love for 'em. They only have and want time for themselves, consumed with greed. It began a long time ago; adults just up and decided to eliminate the kids. Took 'em before they had a chance. Didn't want 'em or need' em, can you imagine? Not need'en kids and they made laws to do this. But no one was thinking in the long run what was goin to happen. They really thought that they could stop having kids and everythin was goin to be all right. Well, they was wrong.

Back then, when people still used money, fewer kids paid for the old people who couldn't work anymore, so there were fewer people to work everywhere, not just on the land. So, they tried to make the ground give them more than she could, and they made her sick, really sick. First, the farmers and people like me who drank the damn water got ill. We didn't know it would make us sick, just like the farmers didn't know all the garbage they put on the land would make them sick – but it did! They were told that it was safe – bullshit! Then everyone got sick, even the men with power. They were the ones who made everyone sick. Then they started looking for ways to improve themselves because medicines no longer worked. The treatments were just as poisonous as the disease! So, they turned to the kids. They thought 'cause the kids spent very little time outside that they were healthy, and they used 'em as lab rats. There weren't many of them around, so we were sent out looking for 'em, and when we found 'em, we snatched 'em. That's why they call us Snatchers. We took as many of 'em as possible and kept 'em, and you're looking at them now.

They did experiments on 'em here 'cause some weren't as sick as the adults, and some weren't sick at all 'cause they was so small. They weren't around long enough to get sick. They weren't strong enough for all the tests, but Civantes took 'em anyway and tried to get better using 'em. He drained them to make himself stronger, but it didn't work, but he just kept trying," he said as he looked around at the cabinets.

"But where are they now?" Callow pleaded impatiently.

"Most of'ems gone. They got sick from the experiments and died, and I don't know what they did with the bodies, so don't ask me." The prisoner continued, "He won't stop looking until he finds healthy samples to make himself well again, and right now, he's look'in for you," he said as he pointed at Dwell and Callow.

Dwell moved over to Callow and placed his arms around her to console her. She kept crying quietly and moved closer to his embrace. Snag regretted not moving quicker to Callow's aid and vowed never to repeat that mistake.

<hr />

Jup and Aden were in the stairwell when the gunfire started. Jup continued while Aden stopped and sat on the stairs. When the gunfire stopped, Jup descended just in time to see Mullins and his crew leave the mirrored room. The overhead lights illuminated the broken shards that lay on the floor. Taking a closer look, Jup picked up a piece of mirror with the vivid imprint of a guard's uniform. He discarded it quickly. He picked up another with the imprint of the Captain's face on it, which he threw against the wall shattering it into a hundred pieces. Walking around the glass-strewn room, he stared intently at the images below his feet when another image caught his eye. Reaching down, he looked at the picture on a larger shard and recognized the person in the white lab coat; childhood memories flashed into his consciousness. He remembered this woman conducting experiments on him and his brother. He smashed the edges to make the shard smaller, wrapped it in a torn piece of his shirt, and put it into his pocket as he looked around the room.

Aden remained on the stairs trying to gather himself; he was exhausted.

What a day, he thought to himself. Relying on, Jup had dulled his senses, and he didn't see the shadow approaching him from above. Dao saw the young man on the stairs and was on him before he could react. Aden tried to fight, but Dao was much stronger and more experienced and had him subdued quickly. Brill moved gingerly due to his injured left side and sore arm but did catch up with them. Leaning against the wall, he wiped the sweat from his brow.

"That's the fellow that Jup was training," Brill said in almost a whisper.

When Brill spoke Jup's name, Aden's eyes lit up, and he turned towards Brill. The slight young man seemed harmless, so Dao relaxed the grip on his neck.

"Where is Jup?" Dao asked him.

Aden didn't speak, so Dao tightened his grip until Aden's face turned red and his eyes started to squint, but still, he didn't utter a sound.

"What do you have left in your pocket?" Dao asked Brill.

Brill put both hands in his pockets and pulled the contents out. A few yellow balls, herb stems, and a small green bottle lay in his hands. He put the bottle up to his eyes and read the label.

'Roll this lotion onto the temporal region of anyone's head, and you will hear 'truth' but only for a time. Don't be fooled by your victim's passive behavior; like the truth, it will not last long.'

"I may have something here, Dao," he said as he opened the lid on the bottle. "Keep him still for a second," he told Dao.

Dao held Aden while Brill rolled the sticky green lotion onto the temporal regions of Aden's head.

"What's your name, and where's Jup?" Dao asked.

"My name's Aden. Jup continued down the stairs when the explosion went off. It rattled me, so I stopped and sat down," he said.

"How long ago," Brill asked.

"About twelve minutes ago," he replied.

"Where is he going?"

"To kill Captain Mullins," he said flatly.

Dao looked at Brill with a raised eyebrow.

"Let's go," Dao said.

"Wait," Brill said. "I want to ask him a few more questions." And he bent down in front of Aden's face and asked,

"Do you like Jup?"

"Yeah."

"Why?"

Aden explained, "Because he's huge and so strong but also because he's such a great fighter. Everyone's afraid of him, including Mullins, but he likes me, and we get along fine. Oh, and most importantly, he protects me."

"And why does he protect you?" Brill asked.

"Because he said that I'm like him. I never give up, and he admires that. I'm his only friend. He told me they took his brother away or maybe even killed him when they did experiments on them when they were young, so he doesn't have anyone, just me. I'm his best friend."

"And what is he going to protect you from?" Brill asked.

"From the other soldiers when I take over from the Captain after Jup kills him, of course. Then Jup will be my assistant when we are in charge," he said with a kind smile.

Surprised by the young man's ambition, Brill spoke to Dao.

"We won't be able to stop Jup; he's too big and too strong; besides, we don't have any elixir left. Instead, we're going to use Aden here as a bargaining chip. He can have Aden back if he doesn't harm us. We call a truce, and all of us live."

"But how can we trust him? He turned on us before?" Dao said.

"We don't, but we don't have many options. There are too many enemies about," Brill replied. "Come with us, Aden. Let's go find Jup."

Aden nodded, stood up, and moved forward as they made their way down the stairwell to the room of mirrors. Jup had shattered the glass into smaller pieces before he left the room, leaving little for the boys to look at. They left the room with Aden in tow, creeping further into the mountain in search of a skilled killer.

CHAPTER 60

The Assaults

Civantes notified his remaining troops to head toward the Lair. The collapsed passage under the mountain was no longer an option. Instead, they would head up the valley crossing at the Meandering Bridge at the pass. The overland trek would take longer, but Civantes would put the extra time to good use devising a plan to ambush and destroy Mullins. Mullins didn't know that there was only one way in and out of the valley. He planned to have his Snatchers lie in wait to ambush Mullins on the way out of the Lair. Destroying Mullins would be easy; capturing and keeping the tree dwellers alive would be much more challenging.

* * *

Dwell and Callow walked away from the little man, sickened by what he had told them. In the hall, they waited for Snag. When he didn't follow, they returned to the room, and that is when they realized he was gone. Dwell grabbed their prisoner and headed for the stairs, where they heard a commotion from above. They stopped and listened. The noise grew louder, something fell, and someone was coming towards them. Hiding around the corner, they watched Jup tumble down the bottom stairs onto the floor, and Snag appeared behind him on the stairs. Jup slowly staggered to his feet with blood from a large gash on his forehead that clouded his vision by dripping into his eyes. Using the back of his hands, he wiped his eyes, straining to see.

"You again," he said, staring straight ahead, trying to focus on Dwell.

"Jup, we don't have any quarrel with you," Dwell said as he moved farther away from the big man.

Snag continued down the stairs and stood in front of Jup. "Sorry, Man, I reacted too quickly. Instinct, you know, and it was dark. I didn't even know it was you. I thought you were one of those nasty Snatchers cause you're so damn big. Hey Buddy, no hard feelings? I'm sorry," Snag said as he extended a hand to his friend.

Using his sleeve to wipe his face, Jup stared at Snag as the creepy little man piped up.

"Don't listen to 'em, big man. They've been talkin' about kill'in you all along. Don't you be fooled by 'em. They're killers; they are. Get 'em while you can," he screamed.

Jup rapidly blinked, trying to clear his vision to see how many people were near him. Snag cautiously moved away and raised his fist towards the little man, silencing him. Jup charged toward them. Snag turned his raised fists towards the big man who plowed into the prisoner with such force that he was sent flying down the corridor about fifty feet, fell, and didn't get up again. Jup straightened himself out, turned to Snag with a big smile, and said, "Okay, I accept your apology. Where do we go from here?"

Snag approached his big buddy and embraced him.

"You remember Dwell and Callow, don't you, Jup?

Jup acknowledged both and waited for further instructions. Callow was not as welcoming and subtly smiled at the fighter.

Dwell said, "Jup, we are here to find that monster Civantes."

Jup stopped, and everyone else did, also.

"Civantes? You aren't going to find Civantes here. He's gone. Let's find Mullins," Jup said enthusiastically.

"Gone, gone where?" Callow asked.

"He's on the other side of the canyon," Jup said.

"Well, who's here?" Dwell asked.

"Probably Snatchers, maybe some kids and the Captain and some of his men," he said.

"Mullins?" asked Snag.

"Yeah, that's why I'm here. He's mine. I'm going to kill him," Jup said with no emotion.

"Okay. That sounds like a great idea. Let's go," laughed Snag as Dwell headed down the stairs on route back to their truck.

"Whoa, Dwell. Where are you going? We need to go up, not down," Snag said.

"No, we've already been up; no one is there. We must go down if we want to find Mullins," Jup interjected.

Snag conceded and followed the group down the stairs further into the mountain.

Brill, Dao, and Aden continued downward until they came upon the prisoner Jup had crushed in the hallway. Brill inspected the body, which was still warm with a faint heartbeat.

"Let's go; we're close," he told Dao.

"Where are we going?" Aden asked in a calm and compliant manner due to the lingering effects of the green lotion.

"We have to go farther into the mountain to find Jup," Dao explained.

Brill thought to himself that he wasn't so sure he wanted to find Jup, but he knew if they wanted to leave the mountain, they had better find Jup before he found them. Down the stairwell they went.

Jup stepped off the stairs and approached the first door he saw. The nameplate read 'Genetic Diagnostics and Testing Solutions.' Opening the door, they entered a large white room. The room reminded Callow of Dr. Swallow's lab at the compound. It was also filled with microscopes, flasks and funnels, computers, and other laboratory equipment, but the lab didn't have scientists. It was empty. They walked around checking out the facility. Callow read the reports on the bulletin board. She pulled off one that was dated earlier in the week. It read,

'Continued target probe experimentation with minimally contaminated tissue samples for DNA stem cell rejuvenation and replication have proven ineffective for the transposing of essential cellular RNA levels required for healthy long-term success of toxic compromised cell structures and mitochondria in vectors. Any future restoration of damaged tissue to long-term health will rely on the crossover of samples to host tissues that are uncontaminated by any manufactured synthetic or non-synthetic toxins and are of only the purest form that only DNA testing will confirm. To date, the transfer of DNA material from any host agent to reverse the toxicity of agricultural pollutants in the affected host person has been unsuccessful. Only agents free of any foreign agents with zero contamination will be considered for further testing.'

Callow opened her pack and checked on Cat. It was content to be away from all the activity and safe in her pack. She closed her sack and read the bulletin with some relief. To date, no cure has been found to reverse the damaging and deadly effects of the soil and water contamination widely present in humans. But she was also heartbroken that so many children had been tortured in vain to further Civantes' ruthless campaign to improve his health. This information confirmed her belief that they had to destroy the Snatchers, the labs, and anyone associated with them.

Dwell, Snag, and Jup split up and looked around. They searched the lab for any information that might help them locate Civantes. Mutated body parts were growing in glass containers everywhere, and compounds were still reacting in solutions throughout the deserted lab. Jup was looking at ear tissue samples that were twitching when he remembered Aden and ran for the door.

"Jup, where are you going?" Snag yelled.

"I forgot someone," he yelled back.

Snag and Dwell looked confused, so Snag took off after Jup, who ran back to the top of the stairs where he had last seen Aden. His young friend was gone. He checked the mirrors' room, but he wasn't there. Jup proceeded to the examination floor. Walking purposefully, he checked out all the rooms but didn't find Aden. When he opened the door to the last room, he saw Aden next to the examination table. Relieved that he found his friend, he casually entered the room, unaware Brill was behind the door and Dao behind the table. Brill squeezed a yellow ball and threw it at the big man when he entered. The room was instantly consumed with thick yellow smoke, causing Jup to gag. Brill and Dao had covered their mouths with the white cloth. They quickly grabbed Aden and pulled him out of the room and down the dark stairwell, taking two steps at a time until someone on the stairs met them.

Immediately Dao went into attacked mode. Unable to identify the person, he pummeled the person into submission. Brill bent down, grabbed the man's upper body, and Dao grabbed his legs, and together they carried him to the next floor.

"Turn him over," Brill said.

"It's Snag," exclaimed Dao.

Brill felt a weak pulse. They both realized simultaneously that if Snag was here, Dwell and Callow must also be.

"Help me get him up; the others must be nearby," Brill pleaded.

Aden and Dao lifted Snag and carried him down the stairs to the next level. Aden followed.

"Hurry, we've got to find them if Snag's going to live," Brill said.

CHAPTER 61

Perilous Reunion

Dwell, and Callow cautiously spread out throughout the lab, searching amongst the refrigerators, imaging gear, tissue grinders, and other sophisticated equipment looking for clues to the whereabouts of their friends, Mullins or Civantes. Dwell heard the lab door blast open. He instantly guided Callow towards a small office off the main floor of the lab. The top half of the office wall was clear glass allowing the person in the office to work while observing activity on the floor. The bottom half of the wall was opaque and blacked out. Crouching down, they hid in the office, listening as the intruders ventured deeper into the lab.

Aden watched Brill and Dao half-carry, half-drag Snag. They searched the sterile environment for medical supplies; Snag's dead weight slowed them down. Dwell listened, fearing the worse. The slow dragging movements of the intruders confirmed that the Snatchers had found them. Quietly he took the gun out of his pack and removed the barrel. It was the gun Callow used to kill the Humonster. He checked the chamber and saw it was loaded, so he crept toward the door and waited.

Brill's pain from his injuries made it impossible for him to carry Snag. His hands kept slipping off his friend's legs, causing his feet to drag on the floor, creating strange noises. Callow placed her hands over her mouth to stop herself from screaming while Dwell steadied his nerves and readied the gun.

Brill stumbled and stopped in front of the office to better grasp Snag's legs. He knew they were making too much noise and could alert their enemies, so he froze and listened. Dao watched Brill struggling to lift Snag when Dwell flew out of the office door, raised the gun, and fired. The bullet hit Dao square in the chest, catapulting him back against a cabinet and onto the floor. Immediately, Dwell dropped the gun, horrified at what he had just done.

"Noooooooooooo," was all Brill could say.

Callow heard the familiar voice and ran out of the office in time to see the horror on Dao's face before he closed his eyes and slumped to the floor. She ran to his side as Dwell threw her his blue elixir, and she poured some into his mouth and waited. Nothing happened. Dwell was overcome by his actions and looked down at his nonresponsive friend. Infuriated by his actions, he hauled off and punched the cabinet directly behind Dao, causing his body to jump and inhale. Callow's grief overwhelmed her as she dropped to the floor and began to sob uncontrollably.

Holding her brother's hand, she cried, "Please, Dao, please don't leave me. Please don't go."

Brill was still holding Snag's legs as Aden watched from a distance. Snag was still breathing, just barely. Brill didn't want to let go of Snag for fear that he would forget about him and he, too, would die, so he held on. Dwell dropped to his knees and felt for a pulse on Dao's neck when he saw the miraculous repairs in his chest. The healing started slowly and more rapidly as Callow sobbed in her anguished state while mumbling incomprehensible words. Dwell wiped away his tears and gently touched Callow's shoulder to get her attention. She raised her head.

"Callow, Callow. Look," Dwell said as he pointed at her brothers' chest.

Callow slowly lifted her head up, and through her reddened eyes and tear-streaked face, she looked up at Dwell.

"He's gone, Dwell, he's gone. I don't know what I'm going to do without him," she sobbed.

"No, Callow, he's not gone. Look."

She wiped her face and looked towards her brother and his chest, which was repairing itself before her eyes. She laughed through her tears as Dao began to respond to the elixir. Brill was grateful that his best friend was returning to health, but now he needed Dwell and Callow to turn their attention to Snag.

"Hey, Snag is dying over here. He needs elixir now," he yelled.

Dwell grabbed the bottle from Callow and moved over to Brill.

"Open his mouth," Dwell yelled.

Brill placed Snag's legs on the floor, moved to his head, and opened his mouth as Dwell slid beside him.

"Pour it now,' Brill pleaded.

Dwell fumbled with the lid, which dropped to the floor. He immediately began sweeping the area with his hand.

"Forget the damn lid. Dwell, pour," Brill exclaimed.

Dwell steadied his hand and poured most of the liquid into Snag's mouth. Brill grabbed the remainder and drained the rest into his mouth. Still suffering from his recent injuries, he needed help if he was going to get them out of the mountain and return home. Snag's body responded within minutes to the powerful potion repairing and replacing his damaged tissues. Soon he was sitting up and asking Brill what had happened. Brill sat beside his friend to allow his body to regenerate while explaining where they were and how Dao had mistakenly attacked him in the stairwell. Snag laughed weakly and gave Dao a thumbs-up.

Within minutes both Dao and Snag were up and walking about slowly. Dao's pain was much more intense than Snag's, as evidenced by his slow gait and gentle movements. After embracing the others and engaging in small talk, Brill stressed to the others their need to get out of the lab and the mountain as soon as possible. Heading out of the lab, Brill stopped Dwell and asked if he had any red elixir left. Dwell gave his full vial to Brill, who took a drink and waited for the enhancement to occur while looking for Aden.

"Hey, has anyone seen Aden?" he asked.

Callow said, "He ran by me earlier and took off out the lab door."

She helped her brother up, and with her arm wrapped around him, they left the lab to find Civantes or Mullins. As they headed out the back of the lab, they saw that the area was in complete disarray, and papers were strewn everywhere, indicating that the staff had left quickly. They exited the back of the room and descended the stairs descending deeper into the belly of the mountain.

Cautiously, they returned to their vehicle without any sign of Jup. When they took a quick inventory of their remaining supplies, they realized that everyone was out of the blue elixir for tissue regeneration.

Callow had all her red, and Dwell had half of his. Everyone understood that they could not afford any more injuries. Without the lifesaving blue elixir, their lives were now truly on the line as they headed downward. Suddenly loud sounds began resonating from below them.

"What's that?" Callow asked.

"There's someone below us," Dwell whispered.

"Stay close to the wall," replied Brill.

The sound from below rose into the mountain's interior, reverberating off the rock walls as it went. Uncertain of what was causing the noise, they hurried to their truck. Dwell unlocked the doors, and they got in when another engine fired up.

'Time to go," he said.

CHAPTER 62

Rollercoaster Ride

Brill, Dwell, and Dao jumped into the front of the cab while Callow and Snag climbed into the back, pulled the flaps down, and held on. Dwell gunned the engine, steering the vehicle onto the pathway, causing the truck to race down the mountain at breakneck speeds. It took all of Dwell's concentration to keep the truck wheels on the road and avoid plunging them off the precariously narrow ledge into the abyss. His overconfidence and lack of driving experience made everyone in the cab nervous as the tires skirted dangerously close to the precipice edge.

More than once, Dao closed his eyes, afraid to yell at Dwell to slow down, fearing it might distract him and send them all to their deaths. Brill kept his eyes wide open while his mind was deep in thought, trying to figure out how to get everyone back to the canopy safely after they killed Mullins. Loud sounds coming from below jolted him out of his trance. Dao opened his window to hear engines firing and men yelling, but no one could determine what was being said. They needed to get out of the mountain not only to avoid detection but also to avoid detention. Dwell circled the mountain's interior, slamming the wall as they headed downward and sending large chunks of rock that had broken away from the wall, sailing past their windshield before falling into the chasm and onto the road below. Again, Dao closed his eyes to focus on the sounds below but also to slow his heartbeat.

Dwell glanced at his brother, who saw the danger ahead and was now looking at him. "Stop!" Brill yelled. Dwell turned his attention back to the road as Dao opened his eyes. The alarming look on Dwell's face told him everything he needed to know. There was debris on the path. Dwell slammed on the brakes, fishtailing the truck before the tires locked up. He could no longer steer the vehicle as it slid sideways straight for the open air and, ultimately, the chasm. Instinctively, Dao closed his eyes again to avoid their inevitable demise while Brill and Dwell prepared for impact. The front tires left the road, spinning effortlessly in the air as the back tires prepared for liftoff from the pathway. The truck and all its contents were launched across the vast opening in the heart of the mountain and headed for the opposite wall.

Snag whipped the flap off the back of the truck just in time for Callow to launch a projectile high above the truck into the mountain. Just as the projectile embedded itself, Snag fired a second round, and both barbs anchored themselves deep within the stone. The ends of each rod had a thick metal rope descending from it attached to the truck bed. While sitting in the back earlier in the day, Snag, concerned with Dwell's reckless driving, had attached ropes through the holes in the truck bed, creating a web; the other ends were attached to the projectiles. He was so grateful that Puppa had given them the weapons. In their web lay Callow, Snag, and Cat, who was out of the bag, secure and snug because of their handiwork.

Unaware of their friends' lifesaving efforts, Brill and Dwell continued to brace themselves for the crash as the truck rose in the air with only seconds to impact. Brill looked over at his younger brother and, with a choking voice, said, "I'm very proud of you, Dwell."

Dwell didn't look at his brother but, with tears streaming down his face, said, "Brill, I have wanted to be like you my whole life. I am so sorry."

Dao heard the two brothers and rolled his eyes just as the ropes grew taunt, jerking the truck back towards the pathway. The steel fibers were a Mama Kileee concoction; the more pressure on the cord, the stronger it became.

The truck's back tires left the ground just as the slack in the ropes vanished, bouncing it off the rocks below the pathway where it settled. No one dared move until the truck stopped, and when it did, the front was pointing downward at a ninety-degree angle. Brill could see the men and machines moving toward the exits on the mountain floor. He planted his feet on the floorboards, pushing himself against the seat.

"I'll climb out and secure the vehicle to the wall," he said.

"No, you're still hurt. I'll go," said Dwell.

"No, you can't go. You don't have any experience," Brill said. He knew as soon as he said it, he was in for a tongue-lashing from his little brother.

"What? You're shitting me, right. Experience? How many upside-down trucks have you crawled out of? What, you don't think I can manage this after all we have been through? Is that what you're saying?" he yelled.

"No, that's not it, Dwell. It's just that this is serious," he replied. Again, as soon as he spoke, he wished he could take his words back.

Dao closed his eyes again and covered his ears anticipating Dwell's explosion.

"Unbelievable," an exasperated Dwell said as he lifted himself towards his window.

"I didn't mean that, Dwell." He said as he struggled to keep himself off the dash while Dao slid onto the floor."

"Brill, you and I," he said, as he tried to wave his hand around but fell into the steering wheel, "have done a great job keeping us all safe. You alone cannot keep us safe. 'We' can. 'We' are in this together, and the sooner you realize that 'we' as a group are much more capable than just you alone, we will get home," Dwell yelled.

Brill cringed from the pain in his bruised side and his brother's whipping and apologized.

"I'm sorry, Dwell, you're right. I can't carry this load by myself. I need your help, and everybody else's too. Please forgive me."

"Finally," Dwell said as he smirked back at his brother.

"Now, get your ass out of the truck and secure us to the wall?" Brill laughed.

"No, I think Callow should go," he said, as he turned to Brill and flashed a big smile before climbing out his window onto the back of the cab where he could see Callow and Dwell tightly cocooned under the web of ropes in the truck bed. Grabbing the metal ropes, he pulled himself towards the tailgate, but the extra pressure on the strings caused the metal to expand, creating friction and causing the truck to slip further down the wall. They didn't have much time; the ropes would hold, but the vehicle's weight would continue to stretch the metal.

"Don't put any pressure on the rope Dwell," Dao yelled.

While walking amongst the metal webbing, his weight and force on the ropes increased the rope slack, again causing the truck to lurch forward. Dwell lost his footing and dangled over the side of the truck. Waiting until the truck settled again, he scurried to the gate and jumped onto the path.

Callow and Cat watched Dwell while Snag watched Callow. Dwell rummaged in his pocket, pulled out his red elixir, and drank some. Exhilarated, he bent down, grabbed the tailgate and one of the ropes, and pulled. Slowly the tires met the rock. He pulled until the vehicle stopped fighting his efforts and dropped back onto the pathway. As the truck settled on the dirt, Dwell opened the driver's side door, got in, and without saying a word started the truck.

Brill stretched his hand to his brother, which he took and held tightly. Cat crawled into the cab and jumped onto Brill's lap.

"Great job, little brother," Brill said with admiration.

"Thanks, Brill. Now let's get the hell out of here while we can."

He popped the brake and started driving slowly down the pathway until they reached the bottom of the mountain and skidded to a stop in the vast, deserted cavern; it was empty.

This must be the control center of the mountain, Dwell thought. There were buildings, vehicles, huge cisterns with running water, machines, and elevated areas with cubicles that looked like rooms. Unlike earlier, there was no activity or noise. Whoever had started the vehicles had left. Brill and Dao exited the truck, marveling at the equipment. Dwell got out of the vehicle, returned to see his friends, and found them under the webbing in each other's arms. He was shocked. Snag had his eyes closed and his arms around Callow, who also had her eyes closed and her head resting on his chest.

Furious, Dwell punched the tailgate and waited for Snag to look at him before he shot him a dirty look. Then, he cut the ropes and helped them out of the truck.

CHAPTER 63

The Belly of the Beast

"What is this place?" an amazed Dao asked Brill.

"I think this is the heartbeat of Civantes' Lair. I think unbelievably bad things happened in this place," Brill responded.

"Well, what do we do now?" Snag asked as he approached the others.

"We need to find Mullins and destroy him and his goons," Brill said as he turned to face them. "But first, we need to blow this place to smithereens." He then enthusiastically slapped Dao on the shoulder, triggering huge smiles on everyone's faces.

"Well, just don't stand there. Go get supplies. Let's send this place to hell."

Everyone scattered; back and forth, they came and went with supplies until Brill decided they had accumulated enough ammunition to bring down the mountain. When Brill called Dao over, Dwell felt that all too familiar twinge of anger at being excluded from the conversation and turned away. Brill turned just in time to see his little brother leaving.

"Hey, Dwell, I need to talk to you," he called after his brother.

Dwell continued walking without acknowledging his brother's request, so Brill ran, caught up, and placed his hand on his shoulder to stop him.

"Dwell, I need to talk to you.

Dwell turned around with a look of rage on his face.

"What?"

"I need to ask you something?" Brill explained as he grabbed his brother's arm.

Dwell looked down at Brill's hand on his arm and then at Brill. His eyes told Brill to remove his hand immediately, which he did, and returned his hands to his pockets as Dwell turned to walk away.

Brill wouldn't be deterred. "Hey, I said I need your advice."

Dwell stopped in his tracks and turned to look at his brother, who was now behind him. When he saw the genuine interest and concern in his brother's eyes, his anger dissipated, and the tension left his body. Ashamed of himself for jumping to conclusions too quickly, he wrapped his arm around his brother's neck and steered him back toward the group.

They discussed their plan to get out of the mountain safely. Some suggested staying and blowing it up, while others felt they should leave immediately and get as far away as possible and out of harm's way. Snag and Dao were selected and agreed to coordinate the detonation of the Lair after the others had left. The detonators would only have about five minutes from the fuse's lighting until the blast's time to join them. With everyone's help, they constructed a large pyre of materials to demolish the mountain.

"All right, you guys, get out of here, and we'll meet you in five," Dao said.

"Ya, okay. We'll see ya out there," said Brill as he moved towards Callow to help her to the truck. Dwell was already in the truck, loaded with guns and ammo. The others refused to say goodbye to one another. Callow and Snag looked at one another, but not a word was spoken, so Brill grabbed her hand, headed to the truck, and left. Snag, and Dao finalized the arrangements of the detonators, accelerants, and the long fuses that they trailed towards the exit.

Dwell drove down the ramp that served as the main entrance to the fortress and continued outside. They parked far away from the mountain to avoid any falling debris and stood on the far side of the truck. Looking around in the distance down in the valley, they could see the tail of a small convoy driving away. Brill used the spyglass on the dash to see and counted five trucks, a few missile launchers, and a small battalion of soldiers walking in loose formation. Concentrating on the missile launchers, he could make out someone standing very erect on the first launcher. The man extended his right arm, pointing at the road in front of them. Brill enhanced the magnification; it was Mullins.

"Let's go; Mullins is just down the road. We can catch up to him if we hurry," he said.

Callow turned her head towards him and, with her hands on her hips, asked, "Great, and what are the three of us supposed to do when we catch him?"

Brill stood before her, grabbed her around the waist, and spun her around.

"I don't know, but I'll think of something," he laughed.

Dwell grabbed the spyglass from Brill's hand and looked towards the mountain. He saw Dao and Snag exit the ramp and start running toward them.

"Give me a minute, Brill, and I'll be right back," he said before he jumped in the truck and took off.

"Ya, okay. Don't be too long."

He shouted after his brother but didn't take his eyes off Callow.

Dwell mumbled something under his breath as he raced after Snag and Dao.

Callow glanced down at the ground when she caught Brill staring intensely into her eyes, so she lifted her chin, and her eyes met his. Looking into her stunning blue eyes, he pulled her closer and tightened his grip on her hips. Oblivious to their surroundings, she raised her arms and gently placed them around his neck. Her warm soft caress of her gentle touch caused his body to heighten and hers to shiver. They moved closer in unison until their chests touched and their lips met. Their first intimate connection sent electric charges from their mouths to every facet of their bodies while they held one another. Nothing else mattered for those few precious private moments in each other's arms. Not the battle, mission, Snatchers, or safety, just them in their first embrace. Detached from the danger of the situation, they continued to kiss until a projectile screeched by, just missing Brill's head. Ducking down, they separated and looked in the direction the missile had come from and saw Snag walking quickly toward them with a weapon in his hands.

"Sorry, the damn thing misfired," apologized Snag as he banged the butt of a large gun on the ground.

"Hey man, you just missed my head," shouted Brill.

"Ya, I know. I said I was sorry," Snag replied.

"Damn, you could have killed me."

"Ya, I know," was all Snag said before he picked up the gun and advanced toward them.

Dao arrived along with Dwell.

"We need to get away from here, Brill, because it's gonna blow any second," Dao said as he put his weapon into the back of the truck.

"Now," Snag said.

"Let's move," Dwell said. They sprinted towards the truck when a missile exploded nearby, propelling them into a ditch. They looked around, confused as to who was firing at them. Then, an explosion closer than the first sent debris showering down atop them.

Shaking the rocks from their clothing, they ran towards the truck and entered when a gigantic explosion detonated behind them, sending the top of the mountain into the sky while simultaneously blowing the base out on all sides. They raced away from the mountain through the dust and debris with the windows up and the flaps down. Dodging left and right, they avoided the massive boulders ascending from the sky as the ground shook. Dao accelerated while everyone braced themselves for his defensive driving while the remnants of the mountain threatened to swallow them. They headed towards the valley and Mullins' convoy. The engine screamed as it made its way toward the pass.

Civantes' excitement grew as he watched an unsuspecting Mullins approach with his men toward the narrowest part of the pass. His soldiers and archers were stationed on both sides of the top of the canyon with weapons aimed directly at Mullins. His men were ordered to shoot to kill, leaving no survivors, including the Captain.

As Mullins' force drew near, the Captain stood defiantly atop the missile launcher as they descended the dirt road toward the canyon. He was on high alert, as were his men, scouring the walls looking for any sign of trouble when archers were spotted high up on the ledge. Mullins stepped off the gun barrel without breaking the convoy's stride and keeping his eyes looking forward. Quietly, he instructed the Rook staffing the missile launcher to turn the gun around quietly and slowly towards the left and fire once they were within striking distance.

The sudden missile launch caught the archers off-guard, disintegrating the rock beneath their feet, destroying the ledge, and plunging them to their death. Mullins' eyes lingered too long at their demise, so he didn't see the archers on the right side fire, striking the gas tank on one of the vehicles and turning it into an inferno. Another lance struck the barrel of Mullins' gun, causing him to slip and reopen the laceration on his arm. He stood looking for Civantes, barking at his gunner to draw the barrel to the starboard side and fire. That missile struck the rock below those men causing many to fall into the canyon below.

Mullins waited for a counterattack from his nemesis, but there wasn't one. An uneasy smugness crept into Mullins' psyche. As quiet returned to the valley, the Captain thought falsely for a second time that he had won the battle. Onward they continued towards the narrow pass when the mountain behind them erupted in a massive explosion causing the earth to shake. He watched as the remaining archers fell off the ledge. He didn't see the lack of obstructions to his advancement through the pass. With eyes wide open, he blindly went forward.

CHAPTER 64

Escape from The Mount

Dao sped toward the two enemies, hoping they were too distracted trying to kill each other to notice their advancing vehicle. While Dao drove, Snag clambered into the back of the truck, where Dwell and Brill readied their weapons. Grabbing a gun, Snag looked back through the flaps at the inferno that was once a mountain and wondered where his friend Jup was.

"Remember to fire sure and often," Brill instructed the others. "Make your shots count. So, shoot to kill. Our lives depend on it."

They roared forward in the truck without any regard to concealing their advancement. Dao steered the vehicle with reckless abandonment, as fast as the engine would allow. The men readied and aimed their weapons at Mullins, who was back atop the missile launcher yelling at his men. In minutes, they were within striking distance. Callow removed the tarp and tossed it haphazardly onto the truck bed.

"Get ready to fire. On my call," Dwell yelled.

Brill glanced at his younger brother, standing stoically and unwaveringly behind his weapon, anxious to put a bullet into the back of Mullins' skull. Dwell peered through his scope at the Captain as his finger danced on the trigger. He opened his mouth to yell "fire" when the Captain abruptly turned around and looked directly at him.

"Fire," he said as he squeezed his trigger.

The bullet spiraled out of the barrel, locking onto the Captain's skull. Seconds from the impact, he abruptly turned sideways, avoiding the projectile as it continued forward unimpeded. When Brill and Snag fired,

Dwell continued staring through his scope; they also missed. In unison, they lowered their rifles and looked at one another, amazed.

"What the hell just happened?" exclaimed Snag.

"Forget it. Let's all fire at him together at the same time." Dwell yelled. "He can't dodge us all. I'll aim for his head. Brill, you aim for his neck, and Snag, you shoot for his heart."

"Three, two, one, fire," he yelled, and the three guns fired simultaneously: sounding like one discharge. Waiting, they watched with anticipation for the bullets to find their target when suddenly the Captain turned again, allowing all the shots to sail right past him. The men watched in horror as the Captain threw his head back and started to laugh. Convulsing in laughter, his body moved back and forth, relishing the situation. Then he stopped and stared directly at them, prompting Dwell to drop his rifle as the others lowered theirs. It was then that they realized why the Captain was smiling. The barrel of the gun he was standing on was now aimed directly at them!

"Jump," Brill screamed as the missile rocketed out of the barrel.

Callow and Cat jumped out of the box, hit the ground, and rolled away. Dao jumped out of the cab while the vehicle continued moving and rolled. Brill leaped over the side, and hit the ground running, as did Dwell. Snag jumped, but his foot got entangled in the tarp. Struggling to free himself, he panicked, but his foot would not break loose. Frantic, he looked to the others and saw Callow watching him at a distance as the vehicle continued to drive away. She stepped towards him, but Brill grabbed her hand, pulling her farther away from the vehicle as she struggled to keep him in her sight. Snag's survival instincts overtook him, and he drew the tarp toward his body. Brill stopped running and turned back towards Snag. He saw that he was still entangled and saw Dao and Dwell on the other side of the truck running away, unaware of Snag's dilemma.

Brill released his grip on Callow's hand and ran back toward the truck when the missile struck the front of the vehicle, propelling Brill into the air and away from the blast. The shockwave also thrust Dwell and Dao into the air, depositing them farther away from the explosion.

Callow dropped to her knees as she watched the vehicle burn. Thoughts of her friend flooded her mind. Tears clouded her vision and flowed down her face; she collapsed and was overwhelmed.

The heat of the burning motor vehicle was too intense, so Brill searched for their friend at a distance circling the perimeter. He remembered that the back of the truck bed was full of incendiary explosives, and it was just a matter of time before that ammo would start lighting up the sky. He ran back to Callow as the flames grew and the ammunition began to fire in every direction, forcing them to abandon their search for Snag. When they were far enough away, they turned back to see a massive fireball that used to be their truck spewing small-caliber rounds into the sky. Realizing Snag was gone, Dao grabbed Brill and Dwell, saying, "Let's go. He's gone."

Dwell continued watching until Dao put his arm around his shoulder and guided him away from the truck towards Callow. Brill reached, pulled her up, and held her while she sobbed in his arms. For a brief time, Dao and Dwell joined their embrace before they had to run again.

Mullins laughed as he watched the vehicle jump into the air when the fuel tank exploded. As those flames roared, he returned to the road and his problem at hand: Civantes. He and his small brigade grew anxious as they entered the narrow canyon. They scanned the walls and ridges for trouble as they continued cautiously on their way. It was quiet, and there was no sign of anyone or anything on the rise or the ground before them. The men relaxed with a sigh of relief as they entered the narrowest part of the canyon without confrontation.

Feeling confident, Mullins barked, "full throttle ahead," he yelled. The drivers gunned the engines to the max speed to get through the most vulnerable section of the narrow passage as quickly as possible. As they made their way through, Mullins' concern grew. This canyon section was so thin that it wouldn't allow his launchers to fire with any accuracy, nor could they pivot the guns in any direction except forward. The first two vehicles made it out of the canyon into the mouth of the large open valley unscathed. Mullins held his breath; he was in the middle of the caravan. He knew a good commander never let down his guard and constantly expect the unexpected.

As his vehicle drove beyond the mouth of the canyon wall, a barrage of munitions struck and destroyed the lead vehicles sending the men and the machines flying into the air. Straining to see through the smoke, Mullins tried to determine where the shots had come from. Unable to see, he frantically wiped at his eyes to clear his vision. Disoriented, he jumped down from the launcher and ran up the side of the hill as more and more shots rained down on his convoy. The canyon walls intensified the devastation's sounds and turned black from the fires. Mullins hid behind a boulder, mortified as he watched the annihilation of his forces.

It only took minutes for his men and weaponry to be destroyed by Civantes. Heavy smoke lingered in the air obscuring his vision. He didn't know where the enemy was, so he climbed higher like the smoke. He went up the mountain, scrambling over the rugged terrain in search of clean air and a hiding place. With limited vision, he went higher and higher up to the top.

He ignored his injured blood-soaked arm and focused on his breathing. He was so focused that he didn't see the Snatchers following behind and encircling him. Determined to get to the top, he continued upwards. Finally, he leaned against a rock at the top, inhaling deeply. Straightening up, he peered into the canyon below at the carnage of his men and his power. His goal to destroy Civantes had failed miserably. His men were dead, his weaponry destroyed, and his victory snatched. The battle was over. Wondering how everything could have gone so wrong when he was so close, he turned away from his defeat. Standing up straight, he took in the view above the mountain and the vast expanse beyond. Then he heard.

CHAPTER 65

The End to an Evil

"**W**ell, how does it feel to have success stolen from your grasp?" Mullins spun around to see Civantes and a group of his Snatchers with drawn weapons surrounding him. Before he could react, he felt his guns being removed from their holsters.

"Devil," the Captain hissed.

Civantes laughed. "You look more like a devil with that hideous face of yours. Besides Mullins, I prefer to be known as a scientist. As you know, we are all just following the science. Isn't that what you did, Mullins? Didn't you snatch the children? Didn't you conduct horrific experiments, all in the name of science? You hypocrite. I know what you did. Greed and power are the truth, not scienc!" He laughed again.

Mullins didn't respond.

"I have dreamt of this day, as you have. I wanted to end your miserable life more ceremoniously, such as in a battle with one of my creatures or fighters in the ring. No matter.

Unfortunately, we can't always get what we want. Isn't that right, Captain?" Civantes continued.

"Like your health?" Mullins interjected.

Civantes' smile slowly disappeared as he stepped forward towards the Captain.

"I am closer now than ever to getting my life back, you bastard. Furthermore, long after your corpse has rotted and become food for the Howls, I will have found the tree dwellers, and with my lab, I will have my health. On the other hand, you will have nothing," he said as he removed a flask from his pocket.

Mullins focused on the bottle as the men grabbed his arms and subdued him. Stiffening his body, he realized that retaliation was futile, so he relaxed as Civantes advanced on him while removing the stopper from the flask. Mullins seized the opportunity by kicking Civantes' arm, causing the flask to fly back, spilling its liquid which oxidized with the air. It landed on the head and face of the Snatcher standing behind him. The illuminating liquid quickly and thoroughly covered the man's head, then moved down his body, reaching out and touching all exposed flesh and disintegrating all tissue as it went. It didn't take long for the man's body to melt, leaving nothing more than a puddle amongst a pile of personal effects on the ground. Enraged, Civantes turned to Mullins, who was forced to his knees with his hands tied behind his back.

Civantes stood inches from Mullins' face, ranting while spewing spittle onto his nemesis.

"This is for all the lies, the cheating at The Farm, the stealing of children that you have done to me over the years. I have waited too long to rid myself of you. Now is the moment," he said as he held the flask above Mullins' head.

"Wait, wait,' the Captain pleaded.

"For what, Dead Man?"

"If you kill me, you'll never know where the tree dwellers live," the Captain said.

Civantes lowered his arm.

"You think you know where the tree dwellers live?" he asked sarcastically.

"Yes, and if you kill me, you'll never know," Mullins rebutted.

Civantes put the stopper back in the flask and strolled around Mullins.

"Okay, Mullins, I'll play along. Let's see how much you know?"

Mullins remained silent.

"Tell me, what provinces do the tree dwellers live in?"

Without missing a beat, the Captain responded, "Province IV."

"That's right. Perfect, my dead friend. Now, tell me. Did you locate their home in Province IV?"

"Yes, yes, I have," he stammered.

"Really? When was that?" Civantes questioned as he continued his interrogation.

"Just recently," replied the Captain as he scrambled for an answer.

Civantes eyes filled with rage as he shouted, "You liar! You would have taken them to the Compound if you had found them. I am not an idiot, you fool. I have people working at your compound that would have told me. You have not located their home, nor have you ever captured one," he said as he poked at the damaged side of Mullins' face.

"If you had, you wouldn't be here. You would be back at your compound extracting every ounce of health out of them, as would I. See, we are not all that different. We both want to live, but unfortunately, your time has expired," Civantes said as he quickly removed the stopper from the flask and poured the contents over the Captain's head.

Horrified, the Captain screamed, "I did, I did...I d." The Captain was no match for the quickness of the liquid as his body dissolved before their eyes.

"You were never a match for me," Civantes said as he threw the flask onto the ground where Mullins had stood, turned, and walked a short distance before stopping. He turned back, staring at the remnants of what was once the notorious Captain and muttering to himself, saying, "Maybe you did find them, you crazy bastard. Even to the end you…." Disgusted with himself for being too hasty and missing an opportunity with the Captain, he kicked dirt at his remains and walked away.

Turning to his closet guard, he shouted, "Get the truck ready. We are going to Province IV."

"To find the tree dwellers?" he asked.

"We sure are, you mutant freak and your life depends on it," he yelled as he descended the mountain.

Brill struggled as he half carried Callow up the mountain while Dwell, Cat, and Dao followed. They watched Mullins climb the rock and stand on the mountaintop surrounded by the Snatchers, and they stopped advancing when Civantes appeared. Hiding under a jutting ridge of rock directly beneath the men, they listened to their heated exchange. When Mullins told Civantes that the ree dwellers lived in Province IV, which was true, terror gripped them. Everyone realized that time was running out and that they needed to stop the Snatchers, or they would never be able to return home to their families. The canopy would never be safe until all Snatchers and Civantes were dead. When the talking above stopped, they froze as they watched Civantes and his men descend the mountain without the Captain.

Waiting until they were certain no one had remained at the peak, Dao climbed over the ridge to the top. It was quiet, and he couldn't see anyone. Pulling himself up to a standing position, he peeked from around a boulder to see Civantes and his men descending halfway down the mountain. He didn't see Mullins, so he dropped low to the ground. He waited and watched, but no one appeared. Cautiously he walked around the perimeter of rocks glimpsing in all directions looking for Mullins. He wasn't there. Convinced that Mullins was gone, he walked to the center of the mount towards something he couldn't identify and where the men had just been standing minutes ago. Moving closer, he saw that the object was composed of a pile of black cloth. Looking down directly above the material, he could make out a small shiny rectangular item sitting atop the pile. Using his boot, he nudged the thing moving it around and exposing the words "Captain Mullins."

Realizing that this empty black cloth was the uniform of the Captain and all that remained of him got him excited. He ran back toward his friends, yelling over the side.

"You won't believe this! Hurry, get up here. Mullins is dead!" he said.

Dwell quickly scrambled up the rock face and joined Dao while Brill took his time helping Callow to her feet. She seemed to be in a state of shock, struggling with her balance and footing on the jagged rocks. As they made their way to the top of the ridge, she leaned heavily on Brill and buried her head in his shoulder as he lifted her over the edge. Once atop, they made their way over to Dao, Cat, and Dwell, standing around the pile of empty clothing.

The group stood in a circle, looking down at the empty uniform, staring at all that remained of Mullins. His thick-soled black shoes lay under his pants and shirt in the dirt. His wrist patch lay off to the side, and guns haphazardly set upon his holsters. Brill picked up the wrist patch and put it into his pocket while Dao bent down and grabbed the guns and holster.

"One evil monster down and one more to go," Dao said as he stood up quickly. "And there goes the other." He said as he pointed downward at Civantes and his men who had reached the valley floor. They were walking towards a group of strange-looking vehicles extremely low to the ground. A row of large tires protruded through the tops of the vehicles. The vehicle disappeared right before their eyes when the light shone on the white patches in the silver paint. The men approached the vehicles and opened the gullwing doors.

"We need to get down there," said Brill. "Callow, I need you to help me get you down the mountain." Callow looked at him and nodded. He hugged her tightly, then grabbed her hand and led her down, never once letting go of her hand. Carefully they descended, concealing themselves behind boulders as they went.

CHAPTER 66

Justice for Some

The Snatchers tried to follow ten paces behind Civantes due to his unpredictability of randomly killing those around him. Civantes paid no notice. However, on this day, he was too busy with his thoughts to pay attention to anyone around him. He opened the door to the vehicle and was about to step in when he was surprised by a young man who appeared from nowhere.

Civantes stopped abruptly in his tracks as he warily spied the man.

"And who the hell might you be?" he asked condescendingly.

"Does it matter, Civantes? A man like you wouldn't be particularly interested in the lives or identities of lesser men like me. Besides, anybody of any importance to me already knows my name."

"Suit yourself," he snarled. "What do you want?"

"Justice," was all Jaes said.

An exacerbated and tired Civantes rolled his eyes while the nasty Snatchers rolled their large heads.

"Okay, I'll play. Justice for who? I don't know you, and I have no quarrel with you. " So, get on your way," he said snidely as he returned to the vehicle door. When he heard a gun cocked, he stopped, turned, and faced Jaes.

"Justice for everyone. Every single person, and especially the children that you experimented on, hurt, killed and threw away. That's who." Jaes yelled.

Civantes started to laugh his evil, sinister laugh, trying to distract Jaes, but Jaes didn't flinch. Then he decided to walk towards the young man.

Again, Jaes didn't flinch. Civantes didn't recognize him, but he could tell by his battle scars that he must be an excellent fighter because his body was riddled with large, raised welts, indicating that he had received much punishment, but he had probably given out even more. He decided to keep his distance from the young man.

Jaes was no fool. He aimed his weapon squarely at the middle of Civantes' head for all to see, especially the Snatchers who had now caught up to their master and were standing directly behind him. The ammo launcher Jaes was holding could shoot multiple rounds of various projectiles, all with heat-seeking capabilities for short- and long-range kills. The shots varied from small ammunitions to large explosives, torchbearers, tasers, and even a laser cutter that could slice a man in half, like a hot knife in butter.

Civantes didn't fear the weapon. He feared his lack of knowledge about the firearm. He couldn't tell which attachment was on the launcher. If he attacked the man without knowing the gun's capabilities, he could set himself up to be barbequed or sliced in half. If he retreated, the heat-guided sensors could destroy him from a long distance, so he decided to stall for time and learn more about the man. He needed to get closer to the weapon to check out the ammo chamber, which would tell him what type of ammo was loaded.

"Why should you, a fighter, care about justice for others? You have spent your whole life in the ring amongst people who cared nothing for you. Being a little on the small side, most of the spectators probably cheered for your death," he said as he moved slightly closer to him.

"*Someone* must care, Civantes. We, the people, were not given life to serve a few, like you, who serve only yourselves. We have the right to be happy, to live in peace, and to care for our families and ourselves. Someone must do the right thing," he cried as he pounded his chest. He yelled, "Our fate, regardless of whether it is good, bad, or indifferent, should be our fate; and not yours to determine. All men are born free."

Civantes stopped and strained his eyes without indicating to Jaes what he was looking at. He knew he needed to change his strategy because the young man was getting increasingly agitated.

"Well, you're right. I should stop 'victimizing' those around me." He waved his arm around at the Snatchers standing nearby, who looked utterly clueless about what Civantes was talking about. "Okay, I'll do that. I will allow the people around me to have some dignity and ownership over their lives, and those men will do what's right, and we will all live in peace, working and helping each other. We can start a commune and spend our days hugging one another." He wrapped his arms around himself as he advanced slowly towards Jaes with his head down and his right hand on his chin. When he pulled his hand away, a large piece of skin tore away and was attached to his hand. Civantes didn't notice, but Jaes did, and he lost focus for a second as his eyes followed the piece of floating skin.

The break in his concentration was all that Civantes needed to pull out his gun and fire at Jaes, who instinctively raised his launcher to shield himself from the bullet which ricocheted off his weapon. The Snatchers retreated away from Civantes when he fired his gun. He then fired again in rapid succession; at the same time, Jaes pulled his trigger, releasing a massive stream of fire that most of the mutant men avoided except one. He was looking up the mountain, watching Brill and his crew descend. When his body caught fire, he tried to warn Civantes by waving his engulfed arms toward the intruders and then back toward Civantes, Civantes didn't understand the warning, so he backed farther and farther away from the guard. The burning man frantically tried to warn them with his spastic actions as everyone stopped to watch him, but no one could understand his message; they thought he was upset that he was on fire. The burning man, desperate to warn Civantes, advanced towards him, but Civantes had run out of patience and shot him dead.

Jaes immediately gathered himself and fired the flame launcher in all directions, causing a wall of flames to rise high and wide. He continued firing until his gun ran out of fuel. When the fire and smoke cleared, Jaes was standing alone, and in the distance, he could see Civantes and his men escaping in their vehicles.

CHAPTER 67

The Chase Continues

Jaes dropped his weapon and slumped to the ground. Defeated, he drew his legs up to his chin, closed his eyes, and dropped his head. Brill and the others ran from the mountain towards him. Dao, being the fastest, reached him first. He placed his hand on Jaes' shoulder. Jaes' leg shot out, tripping Dao, and had him mounted within seconds.

"Well, it's about time," Jaes told Dao, who was momentarily stunned. With Dwell's help, they got Dao to his feet. Everyone embraced Jaes and shook his hand. All were happy to see Jaes but especially Brill.

"Where did you go?" Brill asked.

"I didn't go anywhere! You took off and left me. Thanks a lot," he said with a big smile. Jaes looked around, "Hey, where's the Big Man, Mr. Wonderful, and the kid?"

Dwell stepped towards Jaes as Brill placed his arm around Callow's shoulder.

"We think Jup and Aden were both in the mountain when we blew it up. And our buddy Snag, he couldn't get out of the truck before Mullins hit it with a missile turning it into a fireball, along with everything in it," he said.

"So, this is it?" Jaes asked as he encircled everyone in his arms.

"Yup, it's just us, Jaes," Brill replied.

"All right then, let's get going. Civantes isn't going to rest until he finds your friends and family. And he's already got a head start on us, so let's go," Jaes continued.

"Yes, and he knows we live in Province IV, so we need to hurry," Brill said.

"Well, we can't walk faster than they can ride Jaes, even if we do know the way," Dao said.

"Oh, I don't intend to walk, my friend. Follow me, and I'll show you the way," he said, walking back towards the mountain.

Callow turned and placed her head on Brill's shoulder, then started to weep, saying, "I don't think I can go on Brill."

Brill stopped and took her face into his hands, "You have to Callow because every person in the canopy depends on us. Your Mom, my parents, Mama Kilee, and Callow, the kids. We can't let them down and subject them to his horrific experiments. They will kill many of us and take the rest to their labs. Callow, they will take our babies! We can't let that happen after all this," as he waved his hands around. "We can't, Callow! I will take care of you, and we'll be fine together."

He was pleading with her now. "We must stop them or die trying. There is no other way."

Cat rubbed itself on Callow's shin, purring while looking at her. Brill wiped her tears as they laughed, watching Cat run between Dao's legs while poking him with its barb.

"Where is Dog, Brill?" she asked.

"He's safe with our friend Nutay and the children. Hopefully, we will see them again," he said as he thought of Dog. Callow called Cat and affectionately rubbed its head, then opened her sack into which Cat jumped. With her spirits lifted, she took Brill's hand. He, in turn, stole a kiss from her before they followed Jaes. Dwell glanced back and smiled at his brother, who returned the gesture.

Jaes passed a row of large boulders, and on the other side was a sleek, black, circular vehicle that did not have any wheels and was levitating above the ground. Jaes and Dao were already inside, and Dwell held the hatch for Callow and Brill to enter.

"Whoa, what is this, and where did you get it?" Dwell asked in awe.

Jaes poked his head around, "I don't know what it is, but I found it at the end of the tunnel Civantes and his goons came out of. It must have been too far away for them to return to get it, so I took it. It took me a while to figure out how to start the darn thing, but I've got it now. While you were playing in the mountain, I took it for a drive. I don't think 'drive' is the right word. More like I took it for a float. Get in; we're going hunting."

A soft glow in the chamber emanated from under the seating platform surrounding the perimeter. The seating had deep grooves that 'captured' those sitting in the seats because they were challenging to get in and out of. The circular control panel was filled with lights and switches and wasn't attached to any structure. It floated in the middle of the vehicle. The outside was not visible from the inside of the craft through any window or opening. Instead, a computer-generated panoramic image of the exterior was projected onto the interior walls of the vehicle.

"How could you know how to drive this thing? "Dwell asked.

"I don't! The damn things are too complicated for my small brain. That's why I just tell it to go," he said.

"Tell it to go? "Dao asked with a confused look on his face.

"Yup. Just watch," he said with a huge smile. "Start. Follow the last 'hot' vehicle."

Immediately, the craft's engines fired up, causing the vehicle to levitate off the ground while all the diagnostic systems calibrated and displayed that information on the gauges. Within seconds the engines settled into a rhythmic hum and accelerated at a breakneck speed, pressing the occupants deep into their seats until Jaes yelled, "Whoa, slow down."

The craft instantly responded and slowed as it banked around the mountain's base, whipping around boulders and zigzagging back toward Civantes' Lair. Jaes didn't understand why the craft was heading back toward the mountain entrance because the only vehicle in the valley were the ones Civantes and his men drove away in. Confused, he saw the smoke rising above his friends' burning vehicle.

"Stop," Jaes yelled, and immediately the vehicle slowed and came to a smooth stop. Brill, Dao, and Jaes got out.

"Your craft has our burning truck as the last 'hot' vehicle in the area, but it's not the last 'moving' hot vehicle, as you can see." Brill laughed.

"The craft's sensors were right. "This is a 'hot' vehicle," said Dao, who joined Brill in laughter.

Jaes smiled at his friends and then stared at the charred shell of the vehicle; everyone got quiet. Brill slowly wandered around the debris field, looking for any sign of Snag, while Dao stood motionless. Finding no reason to linger, Jaes headed back to the craft.

"Awful tragedy. Nothing we can do here. Hey, when you're ready, we'll head out," Jaes said as he entered the vehicle.

When Jaes lifted the door, he didn't notice Cat escape. Cat was so amped up being with the family it rolled around in the dirt, trying to expel some energy, when it saw the bars attached to the back of the vehicle move slightly. It latched on and started to swing. The depth of crossbar was deep enough for Cat to swing completely unimpeded around the bar without stopping. The increased momentum and g-force caused the crossbar to break away from the bracket and send it flying with Cat still attached, landing a great distance from the vehicle. Crashing to the ground and dazed from the impact, Cat was slow to get up. Suddenly it jumped onto its hind legs scanning the area and sniffing at the air, then snarled and took off for the hills.

Following its nose, Cat climbed the hill, hunting for the prey whose scent was getting stronger. The smell was so intense that Cat ran directly to a large boulder and abruptly stopped when Dao called out. Hey Cat, come on, buddy, get back here. Let's go."

Cat hesitated, rapidly sniffing the air, then took a few more steps around the boulder, finding his target when Dao called out again. Cat reluctantly headed back to the vehicle.

Dao joined Brill, and they walked together around the large ring of fire caused by the explosion. Without speaking, they were both searching for the same thing, their friend. Little evidence of the truck remained after the massive explosion and the intense heat from the fire. Both agreed to find any remains from Snag seemed hopeless. Saddened and discouraged, Brill turned back to enter the vehicle but stopped, reached for his pack, and took out his spyglass. He scanned the area because he had an eerie feeling that someone was watching them from afar. Unable to find the reason for his discomfort, he continued looking at the hillside while his ears focused on the surroundings.

'What's up?' Dao asked.

"Something just doesn't feel right, Dao," he told his friend.

"Did you see something?" he asked.

"No, nothing. That's the problem," he said.

Brill entered the door of the craft and stopped again. The hair on the back of his neck stood straight up, so he looked again toward the hills. " We are not alone," he thought as he took his seat.

Brill got into the vehicle just ahead of Cat and took his seat.

"Okay, let's try this again. Follow the last *moving* vehicles," Jaes instructed the craft, and the engines started.

CHAPTER 68

On the March

Their footsteps could be heard long before their bodies appeared, so when Flug and Dreg approached the famous peak at Highpoint, sixteen other Takers were already on their feet to greet them. Highpoint was the highest point in the mountainous range that housed Civantes' Lair and was located near the borders of Provinces II and III. The location's namesake was given for the long jutting rock that stuck out of the center of the mountaintop and pointed directly skyward. The site had been used for centuries as a rendezvous point and a lookout tower because of its sheer height and spectacular unobstructed view of the valleys and regions below.

Civantes commanded the most talented of the Takers from all Provinces rendezvous at Highpoint to organize and strategize their mission to find the tree dwellers. It was not only an opportunity for them to meet one another but also for the group to get a good look at the landscape below to map their route. Two Takers sat in worn holes grooved into the rock, and a few had bedded down for the night.

Like all Snatchers, the Takers were massive in both stature and weight. The difference between a Taker and a Snatcher was the difference in their size. The Takers' build was larger and stronger than any other mutant group, and the strongest of all was Flug. He entered the clearing, followed by Dreg, who was carrying most of their supplies. The two latecomers surveyed the gang of misfits who had beaten them up the mountain. All the men were grotesquely mutated with large heads and bodies with very prominent features that were all very distinctive. Flug didn't greet his fellow Takers. Instead, he just stared at each of them, trying to recall whether he had met them before or to see if any of them would be foolish enough to challenge him.

Like the Howls, Demonis, and Shivers, the Takers had the size but not the numbers. No one knew why their bodies had developed so differently than other Snatchers. Many had speculated that years ago when the bonfires burned day and night, some infected men had partaken in the charred remains in the fires. It was unknown whether they had eaten the carcasses of the livestock or humans; no one was brave enough to ask. So instead of dying from the chemical exposures, they grew larger and stronger than those around them, and with their excessive size came their insatiable desire to destroy and control others.

After a thorough inspection of the others without anyone challenging him, Flug walked over to a Taker lying on the ground asleep. He turned back to smirk at Dreg, then bent down and grasped the man in his oversized, disfigured hands, effortlessly lifted him into the air, walked over to the edge, and threw him into the valley and rocks below. He did this so quickly that not a single Taker moved or spoke. In fact, most were still standing in the same spots they were in when Flug and Dreg arrived.

Flug walked towards the silent group with his fists clenched and a smile on his face. No one moved! The cords in his muscles ripped through his skin, exuding incredible strength just as his wild eyes exuded unspeakable evil.

"Let that be a lesson to all of you. Stay awake, stay alert, and maybe you'll stay alive. My success does not depend on you, but your lives do depend on me," Flug barked. "Now get your gear. We are going hunting."

They left the clearing as the others scrambled to get their belongings together. The band of miscreants descended the peak, following Flug, their self-appointed leader at a distance. As the Takers trekked down the mountain, the glow of the half-moon revealed other shadows also on the move. Hunting season had indeed opened, for everyone.

The End.

Printed in the United States
by Baker & Taylor Publisher Services